SHOOT ME IN THE FACE
ON A BEAUTIFUL DAY

SHOOT ME IN THE FACE ON A BEAUTIFUL DAY

a novel by

EMMA E. MURRAY

Apocalypse Party

Cover Design by Matthew Revert
Typesetting by Mike Corrao

Paperback: 978-1-954899-21-6

For Martin,
who taught me I am deserving of love
and a healthy relationship.

F

R

E

S

H

BODY

Veins of leaves lay rough against my tongue, dried blood sticking them together in a gluey, immovable clot, so thick that I wouldn't be able to breathe, if I still could. No, not a breath of life is left inside me, and yet I remain.

It's been hours since he left me here. I'm not quite sure how long, but the first rays of dawn creep into the darkness, diluting it to watercolor gray as the sun awaits its debut. My eyes, left open and already shriveling into themselves, can still perceive the world, and yet, I'm dead.

There's no pain, but I can feel the way my muscles have begun to stiffen, my organs to consume themselves as their cells desperately try to live on, doomed to decompose inside me. I can even feel the way my skull lies shattered, open to the air, icy fingers of wind raking through my mashed brain matter with each gust, leaves blowing in and penetrating the most sacred, secret of places. I don't understand it, but already, I've accepted it. There's no other option. And there's strangely no panic, not even a trace of fear. I suppose that left me alongside the pain in my final breath.

It was dark for a while. I don't know how long, but when I came back, I wasn't myself anymore. I don't remember anything before the man. I would love to mourn the life I surely had, something nebulous beyond my unexplainable consciousness. The family and friends I might've had that loved me and I loved in return. The career, accomplishments, maybe pets, maybe children. But there is no pain of any kind, so I stay calm. Only the tingle of absence nags at my brainstem, reminding me that I once had a life. Something beyond these woods, these leaves, this dirt that lodged in my ears and crammed into every crevice I fought to protect as he ripped off my pants and tore me open.

The farthest back I can remember is a blurry struggle on the path. I'd been walking through the woods. I don't remember anything about my life before the man appeared, lurking ominous in the foliage when I noticed him. Before he attacked. There was pain. So much pain. Though I cannot feel, there's an ache that lingers in the air around me, so profound was the suffering. I screamed, dragged my nails across his flesh, dug my teeth into his shoulder and listened to him yelp like a wounded dog. He pinned my legs, shredded me to pieces with his hands, his body. The branch was too much, and I would've expired no matter what as the blood poured out, puddling around me, but he couldn't leave me to die in peace. He removed it, struck me again and again, bashing my head until it broke open and every trace of life had been snuffed out.

I was gone, the darkness swallowing me, but then I came back. I hope this isn't what eternity is, laying broken and gathering flies with the sickly-sweet smell already emanating from deep within. There must be a reason. I'll be patient. What else can I do but wait?

The warmth has all but left me. It's a strange sensation, your own body cooling to an ambient temperature. The tickle of grass against your cheek gone, no need to brush it away. Your ear welcomes a stray ant. Absurd to be conscious. Surreal to watch the smearing of pink and orange beyond the piney crowns, branches scratching at the air the way my nails wrenched through his skin. I'm thankful that his poor attempt at hiding me didn't obscure my vision. I couldn't stand it if I couldn't see. It is the sole thing I hold onto now.

The blood has settled, coagulated in dark spots against the ground. I can't see it, but I can feel the heaviness, the thick clotting inside, bacteria already proliferating and taking me over.

A glimmer of memory stirs in my mind. This isn't how I imagined it would be to die. I thought there'd be a bright light, maybe an afterlife, or maybe nothingness. The faint memory of relaxing in savasana, and to quiet the humming in my brain, I'd imagine I was a real corpse. Breathe as shallow as possible. Feel the insects running over my legs, across my open eyes. Scavenger birds circled overhead. It was relaxing in a morbid way, but this is not.

There is no panic, only a deep, aching sadness. A hollow mourning and a longing to be found. I miss a life I can't remember, but I know there were people I loved and that they're missing me already. Wondering why I haven't come back.

Find me, I whisper in my broken mind, scattered across the leaves.

Find me.

THE BEGINNING OF SPRING

Nearly a Year Earlier

Luz

Luz was on the couch, her torso contorted so she could half lay on her stomach as she mindlessly scrolled on her phone. A movie played forgotten on the tv across the room, more background noise than entertainment. The curtains were parted enough that a slit of the dark, humid spring night beyond revealed itself, but it didn't bother her like it used to when she lived in the city. A house with an alarm system in a good neighborhood, snuggled deep in the suburbs of winding sidewalks and parks with playgrounds, made her feel safe. The window faced the fenced backyard. There was never a feeling of unease, never a sense of being watched from the outside.

Her husband snored in the bedroom down the hall and the twins were nestled away, slumbering in their rooms. A lazy golden retriever snoozed on her feet at the end of the couch, his warm fur and weight comforting against her skin. Luz glanced at the time on her phone: almost one in the morning. She groaned, stretched and considered going to bed, but then something in the movie caught her attention and she abandoned her fleeting plan.

The man outside panted quietly, inhaled sharply as he finished, leaving a pool of sticky white slime just inches from the window. He watched her for a little longer, soaking in every detail of her private nighttime hours when she assumed she was safely hidden away behind closed doors. His eyes roved her body, her face and its sleepy, late-night stupor. She didn't try to sit or pose in any particular way, didn't try to hide her double chin or care about the smeared makeup on her right eye. She thought nobody would see her like this, not even her husband or children. There's an intimacy in his voyeurism unlike anything that could be produced through consent, and he reveled in it.

He watched her at her most private, most vulnerable, and then, just before he left, he pounded the window with his gloved hand and watched as unfathomable fear shot across her face. She scrambled to cover herself with a blanket, as if it offered some sort of magical protection, but he wasn't there to hurt her. Only in his fantasies did the gloved hands entwine themselves around her neck and wring out every drop of life.

He was gone before she could stumble into her bedroom and wake her husband with soft cries, demanding he search the perimeter of the house. As the voyeur rushed through the night, he laughed imagining the fruitless search of the grumpy husband, the many plausible explanations the family would tell themselves, and how the woman wouldn't sleep easy for at least a week, maybe a few months. How he'd wait until he was sure she had finally let down her guard, then he'd be back.

Birdie

I get home at seven and Russ has the nerve to ask me why I'm home so early. It's already dark out, for God's sake. I don't take it too personally though. I can tell by the jumpy way he's acting that he was up to no good, probably looking at porn again and nervous that I almost caught him. Wouldn't matter so much to me if he'd be like he used to be. Now it's mostly a drought between us with a few downpours now and again, sprung on me the same as a surprise shower. Sometimes leaving me bruised more like a sudden hailstorm than anything pleasant.

First thing I do is open the fridge and see that nagging feeling in the back of my mind all day was right. I forgot to take the damn chicken out of the freezer. Even though my back's to him, I can feel Russ' eyes burning into me. He knows and he's just been waiting for me to realize.

"Guess it's gotta be sloppy joes again tonight, babe. Sorry 'bout that. I'll take the chicken out right—"

"Fucking pathetic." He's suddenly next to me, his whisper harsh and burning hot against my ear. "Do you even love me? You know how hard work has been, but do you care about me and my needs? Not at all. All I wanted was a proper dinner from my girl." His words are lower, softer, and yet bite into me with needle-sharp teeth. "Do I need to teach you another lesson? Show you what you really are?"

I've gone rigid, bracing for the inevitable fight, when he sighs and melts into something completely different. Sad, empty, pawing at me like a needy child. I hate these mercurial tendencies.

"I'm sorry. I don't even know what got into me." He's cooing at me, all syrup and sugar as he pulls me out and into his arms. He smells like cough drops and pomade. "I had such a hard shift, but that's no excuse. Fuck, I'm so sorry I snapped."

"No, no, baby. It's my fault. I know you're sick of all this garbage food and got that chicken special for tonight. You'd asked so nicely for your favorite, and here I've gone and fucked it up." I'm trying my best not to cower. I know he hates when I do that. Gotta stand up straight, don't shake, don't you dare show that he scared you. The man can be the most loving thing, but when he smells fear, there's a wild beast in him that can't be stopped. I push down the shudder that threatens to convulse me at the thought. "How can I make it up to you, babe?"

"I don't know. I'm so sorry, sweetcakes. I think I just need something to calm my nerves." He's already pouring a triple of bourbon before he's even finished his sentence. "That asshole Brian was up to his usual shit, and it took everything I have to not punch his stupid little face in."

"I'm sorry. I don't know why he's like that. Usually, everybody loves you." I'm frying up the meat, hoping the slight sour smell doesn't mean it's turned. Still looks good but my stomach flips, shrinking at the pungency. I've just gotta cook it real good, maybe dump some garlic on there, cover it up. Russ can't handle it if I let it go bad when meat is so expensive.

Thankfully, he doesn't notice. Already gone to the living room, turning on the tv but scrolling on his phone, not even looking up. Just noise to drown it all out. A flicker of empathy tickles my chest. Poor Russ. He can't help it. Things are tough right now. Money's tight. His boss is working him like a dog, driving all over without enough rest between jobs. I get it. I really do.

While the sauce simmers, trying its best to neutralize the slightly rancid sweet fragrance with vinegar and tomato, I watch Russ. He's slack jawed, staring at his phone, and I screw up my mouth to the side, thinking about how different he looks when he doesn't know someone's looking at him. Always a looker, chiseled jaw and mussed dark hair, shockingly blue eyes, he still loses a bit of the glamor when he's not trying. The sharp intellect and suave charm drain out, leaving him less than empty, like a human costume waiting to be filled again by that contagious personality. I notice I'm grinding my teeth and stop myself. There's just always something unnerving about him when I catch him in a candid moment. But maybe I look like that too when I'm doom-scrolling. It doesn't mean a thing.

"Dinner's ready," I call to him, filling a plastic cup with some water in the hope he'll drink something other than alcohol, if only so he doesn't get a headache in the morning.

Taking small tentative bites, I watch him across the table, trying to read his mood. It changes so fast sometimes,

I'm hopeful we can still have a good night, but the fragile hope breaks away, bit by bit, like the fragile skin off an onion. He's trying to mask it, but I can tell by the way he's breathing that rage is still burning within.

It's not a good night to bring up any of the things we need to talk about, like how we need to scrounge up some cash because the heater needs to be fixed before the cold sets in. Not even any of the things I want to talk about, like how Linda thinks Henry might propose soon, or that rude customer who sent her looking in the back for something she knew for a fact was out of stock, but even these trivial things might set him off. Russ always says he hates small talk, but sometimes he indulges me in my gossip or rants. Tonight's not the night for that though. Buckle down and smile, but not too big, not too timid either. Poor baby. He's had it rough lately. As I watch him finish his second sloppy joe, I pray that tomorrow's a better day, for both our sakes.

After scrubbing down those damned plastic plates, forever stained with spots of red from years of microwaved spaghetti leftovers and nights of saran-wrapped hamburger helper congealing onto them in the fridge, I join Russ on the couch, scrolling my own phone a few minutes before I try to engage again.

"So," My hand runs down his jeans, over his muscular thigh. "Wanna play around a little?"

He pulls away.

"Naw. I think I'm gonna go out for a bit."

"Oh, you're gonna be taking the car?"

"Yeah, what's wrong with that?" He shoots me a crocodile-eyed, snarled-lip look, but it slips away back to neutral so fast I almost didn't catch it.

"It's just that I was gonna see Juliana. I told you this morning–"

"She's got a car. Why doesn't she pick you up?"

There was no use in arguing. He's stuck in a mood so there'd be no swaying him. I could take the bus or call her up, cancel like the last two times. Maybe he was right, and I could bother her for a ride. I breathe out a long, quiet exhale through my nose, letting the frustration fade away.

"Okay, hon. I'll figure it out, don't worry." I try to smile that disarming one he likes so much, and I can tell he appreciates it. "Have fun with the guys."

"Heh," he just snorts and starts to head out, but then he stops at the door, hands clutching the doorframe. The oxygen seems to freeze in my lungs, pricking me like a thousand needles as I hold my breath. He turns around, but it's not anger in his eyes. Rushing forward, he grabs me like a hero from some cheesy romance book and dips me back, kissing me with such force that I feel woozy.

I love him. I love him. I love him more than ever. See? We can be just like we used to be. And then he's gone out the door, leaving me gasping for air as the car revs to life and headlights shine through the sheer curtains, lighting up the living room with gold. *He's a good man. The same man I fell for three years before.*

I take out my phone, scrunch up my mouth, and force myself to make the call.

"Hello?"

"Juliana, I'm sure you already know why I'm calling but—"

"You're canceling? Again? What the hell, Birdie?"

"Russ had another hard day, and he needed the car, so I'm just kind of stuck here. You know how last time I took the bus this late that guy tried to grope me, and I just can't get myself to do it again. I know, I shouldn't let fear control me like that, but it was so scary. So, I guess I've gotta cancel. Unless…"

"Unless what?" Juliana's voice is dipped in suspicion and my stomach gurgles from the guilt of asking for her help.

"Maybe you could come get me?"

"Aw come on, you're clear across town! And you know how much gas is nowadays."

"I've got a few bucks I can give you for the trouble, you know, to help cover it."

"Okay, fine, but only because I haven't been able to see you in so long. I miss you! But you know Angel's gonna bitch me out when he notices in the morning." She laughs her soft, rounded laugh and I relax a little. She isn't that mad, maybe a little perturbed, but mostly just playing around.

In her car, the radio serenades us with a slow, tragic country song. Juliana's hand is hanging out the window, fingers pinched around a Virginia Slim while we roll down a potholed, lonely stretch of highway.

"So, what set him off this time?" Her eyes are black diamonds, the blue lights of the dash reflecting in their sheen. She always sees through my lies, so there's no use trying.

"He just had a hard day at work is all. I fucked up dinner and it was a last-straw type of thing. But he's sorry. And it was just name-calling this time. Nothing big." She raises an eyebrow. "No, really. He meant it this time, and I believe him. He's just out cooling off a bit with the boys. Probably playing poker or something."

"Whatever." Juliana takes a long drag, letting the smoke spill out in a thin ribbon. "He's more likely over at the Yellow Rose than just playing some cards."

"Well, so what if he is? Looking ain't the same as cheating." Even though I say this in a casual tone, jealousy snaps through my gut. She's almost certainly right.

"He's got no place treating you like that. You should leave, but I know you're not gonna." She takes another slow drag. "So how 'bout we don't speak another word of him tonight? He doesn't exist when you're with me."

The way her mouth curls into a rosebud smile, lipstick always perfect and her hair smelling good like department store perfume, it breaks me down. I smile back. Things are okay, even good, when I'm with Juliana. I can worry about Russ later. He'll be back, we'll make up, and this evening will be something in the past. I nod and she gasses it, laughing and turning up the music.

Back at her place, we sit out front and are quiet together for a long time in the white noise of cicadas. She's chain smoking, but I don't mind. The smell of her cigs reminds me of back home with Mama and my brothers, not like the nasty ones Russ picks up when he's drunk. Somehow, I escaped the clutch of nicotine addiction, but still revel in the warm smell and the way it tickles my throat. It's comforting as it wraps around me like a hug.

"I'm gonna start those classes I was telling you about soon. Finally went through all the hoops and got it set up."

I hate how much pride shines through my voice, as if just signing up has made me some kind of professional or something. I try to stifle it back down, but Juliana's mouth is hanging open, wide-eyed and grinning.

"That's huge! Why didn't you tell me earlier?"

"I don't know. Guess my mind was elsewhere."

"Girl, we gotta celebrate!"

"Aw no. I haven't even started yet," I laugh, my face going hot and prickling red. "We can celebrate once I actually make it through. Who knows if I'm even cut out for nursing."

"What! You're the most nurturing person I've ever met, and I know you're obsessed with all that medical stuff, you'll have no problem memorizing it. You're gonna be a nurse in no time, just watch."

I love the way her words physically embrace me in a cloud of warm smoke, knowing her encouragement lingers around me, soaks into my clothes so I can smell them later and remember.

"But," Juliana's back goes stiff, her eyes narrowed, catlike, "Have you told him yet?"

For a moment, I consider lying. I don't feel like talking about Russ anymore, but I'm a terrible liar, so I know I might as well not even try.

"No." The word tumbles from my lips, trembling like a child awaiting a lash of the belt. I gather myself together, quickly launching into the usual excuses. "I'm going to tell him soon, but you know how work has been really rough lately, and I know he's gonna bitch and moan about the money even though I got most of it secured through those grants, so it really won't cost us all that much. I thought maybe I'd squirrel away a little bit of my paycheck, just enough he wouldn't notice, and that could pay for it. Then say I'm taking up extra shifts, and then he—"

She stops me with a hand on my knee. Her eyes are huge and so full of sorrow, it nearly breaks my heart.

"That's not how it's supposed to be. If he loves you, he should support you. I don't understand any of this. You're trying so hard to improve yourself, and he just seems to drag you down. And you know he'll catch you in that plan of yours, and I just can't imagine..." She trails off, a flash of fear shrinking her pupils.

"You're right. Fuck." I lean back in the chair, run my fingers through my hair, massaging my scalp. "No, you're right. I'll tell him. There's no reason for me to keep it a secret. He loves me." She casts me a look, but I double down. "He does! He just has a hard time showing it. He'll be okay with it. I'll tell him tomorrow. That'll give him plenty of time to adjust before classes start."

We sit in silence while she puffs away. I know she doesn't believe me, though I'm not sure whether she thinks I won't tell him or he won't be accepting. He's got a temper and a need to always be right, but she doesn't know him like I do. He'll support me if I just find the right way to explain it. The problem is I always get my words all mixed up in the moment, and when I'm flustered, I say things wrong. It's really my fault, but she'll never understand that. Nobody knows a relationship from the outside the way they think they do.

The tension fades the longer we sit in the quiet chorus of the night insects. I'm grateful when she finally speaks, changing the subject.

"Well, just like I'm proud of you, you ought to be proud of me because I have something pretty sweet up my sleeve too."

"Wait, did you get it?" The smile grows across my face, comically large, but I can't help it. "Tell me you got it."

"I got it," she says with a smirk and a wink.

"Ahh! A raise like that is gonna change you and Angel's lives," I say, my voice breathy with awe. "If you save up for a bit, you'll be able to build that ranch house you've been dreaming of, with a little chicken coop in the back and a dog run for Ginger. Oh my god, that's huge! I can't believe you didn't tell me right away."

"I didn't want to brag or anything." She's being coy, but I'm so excited I can't help but get up, pace on bouncy steps like a child. She giggles at me. "Girl, calm down.

It's not *that* much." But she's smiling through the veil of smoke. "It'll be a long time 'til we can ditch this dump of a prefab, but...you're right. Maybe it's out there, on the horizon. Things are looking up for us, girl."

I'm hugging her and she's laughing again. A deep, throaty laugh. A genuine laugh. It flutters in my ears like a song, and for a moment, I don't want to go home. But then I remember everything that needs to get done before Russ gets back. I like to make him happy. Nothing gives me more joy than when he's happy, and one little snort of his laugh is worth a thousand of Juliana's.

"Let's end on a high note. Mind taking me home?"

"Already? You're only two beers in. Come on, the night is young."

"I know, but I've got a lot to do tonight. And I'm opening tomorrow, so I wanna make sure I get enough sleep." I try to play it off nonchalantly, but I cringe at the sheepish sound of my voice in my own ears.

"Okay. You got it." Juliana drops the butt of her cigarette and snuffs it out with her toe before she stands up, walking toward her truck, but there's no visible disappointment on her face. That's what I love most about her. No matter how she feels, she doesn't guilt trip anybody. Not her prerogative to make anybody's life worse. She might give her opinion, try to dole out some advice now and again, but in the end, she respects that everybody's gotta find their own way, and I appreciate that kind of friendship more than anything in the world.

"Thank you for driving me. I've only got a couple bucks, but I'll get you some gas money next time I see you."

She waves me away as she climbs into the driver's seat, our seatbelts clicking into place.

"No, don't worry about it. Remember? I just got a raise. I'm good."

I glance at the red glow of the alarm clock when Russ crawls into bed, spooning me, moving up my shoulder to my neck with light kisses. Nearly six in the morning. But the time doesn't matter. What matters is the way his gentle whispers declare his everlasting love, the way he apologizes and tells me I'm a goddess, that he could never love another, that I'm all that he needs in the whole world. The way his hands make me melt, he kneads and molds me into the woman he sees me as, and I let him. I feel beautiful under his hands, and I love him. I'll always love him. No matter what.

Heather

The man walked through the house, dimly lit by the early morning sun through the half-drawn blinds, until he came to the living room and saw the woman. The light fell in stripes across her dark form, wrapped in blankets. Her mouth gaped open with the deep, quiet breathing of true exhaustion. An infant, limp with sleep, was pressed against her chest. The child cuddled against her exposed breast, a pale globe in the cool blues of the morning before dawn, a dribble of milk at the corner of its lip.

As he approached, the baby turned and looked at him with wide, clear eyes. A gummy smile bloomed across the tiny face. The innocent eyes, half-mooned from the grin, sparkled as a tiny giggle escaped, followed by a quiet cooing, beckoning to this stranger in his house.

When the stranger didn't return the smile, his shadow instead falling across the two warm snuggling figures and blocking out the light, the baby's smile changed to quizzical, though still devoid of any fear. The stranger looked into the trusting eyes, sighed and turned to leave, but as he neared the hallway from which he came, he heard a gasp and then a shrill scream for help from the couch.

He wheeled around. The woman clutched the infant tightly to her chest, which rose and fell with the speed and tremor of a cornered rabbit.

"Who are you? What are you doing here?" Her voice a soft whisper, like a feather ready to be blown away by the slightest gust. The man stared back, walking deliberately slowly back toward her. She trembled below him, collapsing into herself as she pressed back deeply into the cushions, trying to disappear. Her eyes darted with primal fear, more animal than human in the moment.

He loomed over her in silence. She waited, watching his lips, each sip of air fleeting and full of anticipation. Not knowing ate into her brain, drilling holes of panic through any reasonable thought or reaction she could've mustered. She needed to move, to get away, but her body refused to budge. The baby whimpered, a string of drool dripping onto his mother's shaking hand protectively clawed into his soft stomach.

"What do you want?" Her voice was even smaller, barely more than lips moved in silence. "Just leave us alone." Then the blue of her irises steeled over for just a moment, and she found her voice enough to add a threat, "Don't hurt my baby."

"Put him on the floor."

The man's voice gave no hint of feeling, cold and robotic in its restraint, hiding something pulled within. The woman's lip twitched, and her eyes grew wider as the realization hit her: he wasn't wearing any sort of mask. No disguise. There was a knife in his hand, the short blade just visible past his clenched fist. This was no burglary. He wasn't going to rob her and leave. She'd seen him. He wanted her to see him. A stream of heat flowed down her pajama pants leg, instantly cooling to shivering cold.

"Put him on the floor," the man repeated. "And I won't hurt him."

With the stilted movements of a newborn deer, she struggled to her feet. Slowly, she lowered the infant to the carpet, her eyes large, pinprick pupils despite the dark, never leaving her captor's face. She slipped her foot under the infant, feeling his weight against her, grounding her and bringing the slightest comfort. He didn't cry, didn't even mewl, but laid with his own wide eyes looking between his mother and the man.

"Lay back down." He gestured to the couch with the knife, its blade flashing in a stripe of subtle sunlight that peeked through the blinds. She whimpered and murmured nonsense syllables to herself as she forced her body to climb back on the couch, eyes as wide as her infant's, but full of terror. She kept one foot on the floor, still cradled under the baby, giving the slightest comfort that he was still there.

"Good girl, Heather. I've been watching you for a while. Think back. I'm sure you'll remember the feeling of my eyes on you through the window." He smiled, almost purred the words, and the woman gagged, swallowed down burning bile. "Think back. Two days ago. You were undressing, heard a tapping, but then it stopped. Couldn't see me past the reflection of yourself." He moved closer, pushed a lock of curls behind her ear, whispered in it. "It was hard not to laugh when you pushed your pigface against the glass. I was right there, but you didn't see me."

His hands moved snakelike up her neck and into her hair, breathing in her scent. His body was on top of her, and she could feel his hardness pressed against her thigh.

"You smell like lilies. And fear." His voice quavered; fingers of his free hand trembled as it ran down her side. Her stomach revolted, tried to empty itself, but she once again made herself swallow the acid down.

The baby cooed and smacked his lips in little kisses. Silent tears ran down his mother's face. Her whole body quaked with stifled sobs.

"You're so lovely. Do you know that, Heather?" Each word drew out in a lusty whine, his hands busy with something that she quickly realized was protection. She'd never hated anyone more in her entire life.

"Please, don't hurt me," she croaked through her parched throat, drained by an absolute fear unlike anything she'd ever experienced.

"Mmm, I love a girl who begs." He shifted against her, a moan smothered by closed lips. "Beg me again."

Her eyes darted to her baby who was trying to roll over to his stomach, off her foot. Gathering all her strength in a split second, she brought up her knees and planted her feet against his chest, screaming while she kicked him off. He stumbled backward, nearly falling off the couch as she wrested her way from beneath him, landing on her knees on the carpet. With shaking hands and a prayer on her lips, she scrambled to scoop up her son, but just as her hands slipped under his small body, trying to support his head, she felt something.

A hard pressure, like a punch against her back, and then a searing pain that ripped through her entire being.

She struggled to breathe, felt her left lung collapsing inside her, but that moment of panic was interrupted by the wrenching back of her head, yanked by her long, loose curls, exposed in absolute vulnerability.

The knife slid across her throat with little resistance from her taut skin, her muscle, even the chords and tendons gave way under his guiding pressure. A downpour of wet heat cascaded down her chest, across her belly, puddling between her legs as she fell heavily into a wide-kneed sit. Her son cried in bleating, gasping grief and confusion as the blood soaked into his onesie, cooling quickly against his skin.

The man ignored his cries, even as they crescendoed in blind panic, as he assaulted the dying woman, finishing long after the last spark of her had left. He let the child cry himself to an exhausted sleep while he took his time meticulously cleaning up anything he felt could link him to the scene but leaving the blood. The thought of neighbors or family members finding her, the shocked disgust of investigators when they too discovered his handiwork, he savored it like a treat.

The child sniffled and snorted in the troubled slumber he'd fought so hard as the man slipped through the front door and left it slightly ajar.

Birdie

I feel Sheena's eyes on me all the way from when she gets back from break to when I'm almost done stocking my last case on the shelves. She's new. Only her second or third shift, at least that I've seen. A deep sigh builds in my lungs and forces its way out, past my clenched jaw. Someone must've told her.

Doesn't matter how many times I say it's nobody's business but my own, they still talk about it. Everyone's a fucking gossip, and I'm the one who has to deal with the consequences. As if the memory wasn't heavy enough on its own, they've gotta bring it up any chance they get and pile it back on my shoulders. I think of that story Russ told me about Sisyphus and his rock, but it's worse than that. At least his boulder didn't burn him to touch, didn't make him want to shrivel up and leave his skin an empty sack just at the slightest brush against it. That's how I feel every time someone brings it up.

Shit, she's walking over to me. Her eyes are moist but hesitant to make eye contact, soft with pity yet hard with curiosity and judgment. It's inevitable that she's going to ask something wildly inappropriate without realizing it.

"Hey, uh, do you need any help with that?" she asks, pointing at the shelves as if I wouldn't understand what she was talking about. I know she's just nervous. They always act weird when they find out. I'm grateful she at least didn't start the conversation by jumping right in. Maybe there's still a chance for me to wriggle away before she asks too much.

"No thanks. See, all done here," I say, quickly shoving the last few boxes of vitamins into place and grabbing the cart handle, pulling it with me as I start to walk away. *Please don't stop me. Please don't make me explain.*

"Wait, it's Birdie, right?" Her hand reaches out, grasps the cart handle beside my own, and I'm stuck.

"Yeah. And you're Sheena, the new girl. Remember, we met a couple days ago. Anyway, I need to get going. My shift's ending." I take a step, but the cart fights me. She's holding it back.

"Um, I just wanted to talk to you about something."

And there it is. Another inquiry into the past that I've tried so desperately to leave behind. I guess no matter what I do, people will find out. It's a part of this life sentence I'd never anticipated.

"Listen, I know what you're going to ask, and I don't like to talk about it. He was my son." An unexpected sob creeps up, choking me, but I manage to push through. "Can't y'all understand that? I don't want to remember for your morbid curiosity. Now please just leave me alone."

"No, it's not like that," Sheena says, her hand moving from the cart to my shoulder, but I bristle under her touch. She's so young, maybe not even out of her teens, so she probably just doesn't get it, but I don't have the time or energy to educate anyone on social norms. I wrench the cart away, its wheels squealing with a blood-curdling shriek, and I've got my back to her. If I can just get to the backroom, I can breathe again. Push down the tears that just that single word brought up: *son*.

But it's no use, she catches up to me in just a couple quick strides. The breakdown is building inside me, a hurricane swirling and battering against my organs. I'm not sure how much longer I can last before it spills out. I need to be alone. Now.

"Birdie, stop. I don't want to pry. It's nothing like that."

"No, go away," I attempt to say, but the crying distorts the words into something barely intelligible.

"I lost my daughter last year."

I stop, frozen in shock.

"What?" I feel stupid as the one-word question floats in the air between us, and yet, I still don't believe the stark confession that she could utter with no tears, back straight and eyes hard. It can't be true. She's too young. This must be her angle for more information.

"She was only three months old. Her heart, it never worked right. But she lasted longer than they'd thought." As she talks, calmer than I could ever muster, there are tears in her eyes. Real tears. Guilt tightens around my chest, and I hate myself more than ever. "Her name was Gigi."

"I'm so sorry for your loss." The same hollow words that are thrown at me somehow slip out. She nods the way I always do, just acknowledge it and move on.

"Someone told me about what you went through, and I get it if you don't feel like talking about it yet, or ever, but if you change your mind, there's a group I go to every other Wednesday. It's helped a lot."

The cracks in her demeanor show through, and I know Gigi existed. She held her in her arms. She loved her more than the sun, the moon, and life itself. She understands exactly how it feels to gain the world and lose it again, and I feel myself soften toward her.

"Thank you. But I—"

"It's called The Child Loss Support Group, over at First Methodist. I'm going there tonight at seven, as soon as I get off. If you want to hang around and go together, it might be nice. But I understand either way."

I glance at the clock and see the hands closing in on six-thirty. I'd only have to wait a little longer.

"I don't know. I've gotta eat dinner and—"

"No, it's fine. I get it. But they do have food there, just little snack tray sandwiches and coffee, but it's not bad." She also looks at the clock and then back through the aisles at her own half-full cart she needs to finish putting out before she can leave. Anxiety dances across her eyes for a second, but then she's back with me, open and vulnerable. Offering something no one else has in years. "If you change your mind, just meet me out front. I can give you a ride if you want. Even back home if needed. I don't mind."

And then she's gone, scurried back to finish stocking so she can leave on time. I'm a ghost as I push the cart back, clock out, and exit into the crisp, night air. The pungent smell of rotten food lingers even though the dumpster was emptied earlier that day, and my stomach twists in knots of acidic bile. I imagine catching the bus, eating dinner alone in front of the television, warmed up three-day-old leftovers. Russ already texted me to say he wasn't coming home until late, so nothing waits for me there except the same empty rooms, vapid distractions, and my grief.

I can barely believe it when I find my legs taking me to the front of the store. Just a little while later, Sheena comes out, the same expressionless look on her face until she sees me. Then a rosy bloom spreads across her nose and cheeks, a tiny, crooked smile, and a raised hand.

The reception room of the church is exactly as I'd imagined. Navy blue Berber and gray walls, wooden tables straight out of the eighties and fold-out tan chairs. A quilt with a cross hangs at the front of the room behind an oak podium. The sandwiches are dry turkey and ham with sad slices of lettuce drooping over their sides, and there's no sugar for the coffee, only powdered creamer, but I'd never complain. I take a small plate and paper cup and join Sheena at one of the tables. There's less than a dozen of us, though that's still more than I'd imagined. But my predictions of their melancholy and awkward expressions were spot on.

"So, what happens next?" I lean toward Sheena and whisper.

"George kind of leads the group. I've only been a couple times, but it seems pretty usual to start late. He's over there." She nods in the direction of an elderly man sipping coffee and talking to a couple clothed all in black at another table. *Mourning clothes.* My stomach flips over onto itself, and I'm hit with a wave of nausea. How recent was their loss? My limbs ache with a longing to dash out of the room, but I force myself to stay. Somehow, I felt I owed it to Sheena.

The group leader's face is a map of vertical lines, all drawing downward to a puppet mouth, nearly lipless but honest. Glasses perch on the end of his nose, threatening to slip off but somehow keeping their grip on his head bobbing as he speaks. I wonder who he lost. Or is he just an old preacher trying his best to comfort the heartbroken? Tears slip down the couple's faces, but their mouths are shut in tight lines. I wish he'd walk away and leave them alone. When things are that fresh, they're impossible to handle. They're not ready for his words. There's nothing but denial at that point to save your sanity.

I've finished my sad sandwich by the time he's behind the podium, clearing his throat with that typical old man's cough and looking around the room so his small, watery eyes meet with every attendee's, probably unaware of how uncomfortable that makes us.

"Thank you everyone for joining. I see a couple new faces and let me be sure to welcome you to our support group. I promise this is a safe place, free of judgment, for you to share or not share as much as you're comfortable with. It's a place for healing, and we're all here for each other as we walk this path of grief. Now, before we begin, let us bow our heads in a silent prayer for our loved ones, the ones we've lost, and for our own mercy in the Lord's loving heart."

I lower my head and close my eyes like everyone else, but I don't let myself think about Noah. A black void slowly graying into a white one. That's my trick to keep my emotions at bay. I don't want to start bawling in front of all these strangers. What if some of them know about me? My face is burning hot, and I slither out of my jacket, draping it over the chair back behind me as the prayer interlude concludes.

"Alright, let's begin our group healing by inviting anyone who wants to share to come to the podium, or share from their seat, whichever feels more comfortable." He clears his throat again. "For our newcomers, please know that nothing is expected from any of you. This is a place for sharing and being there for each other. Please, no negative comments, and though you're free to share advice or things that have helped you personally, we try to not be too pushy or force people through their feelings. We're all hurting, and more than anything, this is just a place to share with others who are going through similar grief."

"Uh, I'd like to share today, if that's okay." Sheena raises her hand, her voice much softer and more childish than I'd heard it before. "I know I've only been a couple times, but I think it'd be helpful to talk about my Gigi."

"Of course, of course," George beckons her to the podium with open arms and she makes her way up, chin tucked down and arms close to her side as we all watch on.

"Um, hello everyone. I'm Sheena and I lost my little girl a little over a year ago. Actually, it'll be fourteen months without her on the fifth." She sniffles through the last part. "She was just a little baby. We didn't get much time together, but I miss her more than I've ever missed anyone." There's a pause as she looks around at us, and I can't help but look down at my hands on the table. The grief in her eyes is too palpable to bear. "She had a heart problem. Was born with it. They thought she wouldn't even make it earthside, but they were wrong. They didn't know how strong she could be. We had three beautiful months together, and she made it through her first surgery, but she never woke up from the second one." Her voice breaks, but she keeps going. "I got to hold her until the end. The nurses and doctors, everyone was so sweet. They even pitched in for the funeral costs. But what bothers me most is how angry I still feel at them. Why couldn't they save her? Sometimes I even feel angry with God. How dare he take her away like that?" The tears are streaming down her face now, running troughs through her foundation and matting her eyelashes together in sticky clumps.

"I feel angry like that too. All the time," a middle-aged woman near the front pipes up. "Doesn't matter how long it's been, seems like I'll never stop being pissed at the whole world for taking my Ernie."

Sheena's nodding at the woman, her face full of genuine gratitude. I guess it's nice to have someone acknowledge the truth we all try to mask. I put on what I imagine to be a supportive face, but she doesn't look my way.

"Anger is a normal part of the process. Even anger at God. Give yourself the space and time to work through it. Your wound is fresh. He'll understand." George is back next to the podium, one hand on Sheena's shoulder as he speaks. "How about you tell us a little more about Gigi."

Her lips quiver, but she shuts her eyes and shakes her head back and forth like a child. George dives into his fatherly role, shushing her gently and rubbing her shoulders a little too frantically to be pleasant.

"Oh, that's okay, I didn't mean to push you." He tries to hug her, but she's turning away, walking back to her seat, and he's alone again at the podium. After a beat, letting us all recover from the anguish, he gives his well-worn sympathetic smile. "Does anyone else want to share?"

Horror clutches my lungs, squeezing them breathless, as my hand raises against my will. I look at it, will it back down, but it's too late.

"Yes, feel free to come on up, or you can stay where you're at if you'd prefer."

The words come out before I know what I am asking.

"But what if you're angrier with yourself than God? What if it's your own fault?"

"Oh dearie. Oh no." George speaks slow and with a distinct warble of pity in his voice. I hate myself for saying something so stupid, but maybe this is yet another facet of my punishment. Another way to be humiliated and shamed for what I've done.

After a long pause, the room unsure how to break the awkward silence, he continued, "It wasn't your fault, my dear. You've got to forgive yourself before you can even begin to process your terrible loss."

Sheena was staring at me, but not with the uncomfortable gaze of the others. The anger stewing inside her was aimed straight at me. I could feel it as hot as an oven vent, ready to broil me alive.

"So, it's true? I thought it was just a rumor, but here you are admitting it." Her words, a hiss through her clenched teeth, send me shrinking into myself, trying to disappear. She can hate me all she wants, but she'll never understand that my own self-loathing is incomparable and infinitely worse.

George is saying something at the front of the room, trying to quiet the grumbling rabble growing around us, the undercurrent of resentment that had been there as soon as I'd entered the room finally revealing itself. I wasn't a stranger to them, not in a town so small and slow that they dig their claws into any rumor they can get their hands on. They knew all along.

It's no use. I stand up, withdrawn like a snail into its shell as I walk out into the dark parking lot. It's a half mile to the nearest bus stop, but I don't register the movement of my body or the time pass as I dive into a self-induced fugue state.

But as soon as I see the trailer lit up, warm light pouring out of every window through the cracks in the blinds, I snap out of it. Somebody's home. *No, no, no. Not tonight. Please not tonight.*

The idea to run away, abandoning everyone I know and all my belongings, flies into my mind but I swat it away immediately. I love him. This is my own fault. I never even texted him to tell him I was going somewhere other than straight home. He's probably been worried sick, wondering if I'm hurt somewhere, or worse, being unfaithful. I swallow hard, forcing the lump down my dry throat, and walk up the cinderblock steps.

There's no sound inside. Not a tv or a radio or the muffled sound of small phone speakers. He's waiting for me. Just waiting. In silence.

"Hon?" I ask, my voice dripping with sugary sweetness, hoping to dilute the bitterness palpable in the still air within. He doesn't answer.

Slipping out of my shoes, setting them on the shoe rack, padding catlike across the shag through the living room, I don't hear a thing. I let the hope bud in my heart that he's sleeping, passed out on top of the comforter, all the lights left on accidentally as exhaustion overtook his need to admonish me. I flip each switch and swathe the home in soft darkness. A sense of safety wraps around me in the quiet night, comforting like a security blanket. Still not a sound from the bedroom, the only room I haven't checked. The blanket tightens, caressing me with hope, as I realize that room has been dark all along. *He's sleeping. He must be.*

I want to call out gently to him, hear him groan and rustle against the bed, but I don't dare to test him. Instead, I slide off my clothes and make myself feather-light as I join him, curling against him, holding him.

"Where were you?" he asks, his voice powerful, not a hint of sleep in it. I startle, nearly falling off the bed, only stopping by clinging to his arm to steady myself. He wrenches himself free, sitting up, and in the silver slivers of moonlight, I swear his eyes glow iridescent like a wild animal.

"I'm sorry. I should've told you–" I begin, but he interrupts me with the crashing thunderous voice he saves for late night fights.

"Should've told me what? Where the fuck were you?"

"It's dumb, really. There's this new girl at work, and I just went out with her."

"Out where?"

I consider lying, but he always sees through even my mildest twist of the truth, so I brace myself for the onslaught.

"She heard about Noah, and she's lost someone too, so she asked me to go to a grief group with her. That's all."

"That's all? *That's* all?" Rage shakes his voice, dripping with bitter acid that burns holes into any shred of confidence I'd gathered to shield myself. "And why the fuck did you think that'd be okay?"

"It's not a big deal–"

"You have no business going there, spoiling their meeting with your sob story. You stink of guilt, you know that? I bet they smelled it on you the second you went in, just like that other group back three years ago."

"No," I say, but my voice has disintegrated to a scarcely audible whimper.

"What did I tell you about going places and forcing your pity party on everyone?" He's standing now, towering over me. Heavy steps in the dark, a click, and I'm exposed in the stark light of the bare bulb overhead.

Balling myself up, I've become a helpless insect, praying for the dark so I can scuttle away.

"Go on, tell me. Did they take you in with open fucking arms, or did they sniff out the rat you were right away? Huh?" He slams his palm against the wall, and I swear the whole world shakes. "You pretend you're a victim, but you're not, are you? Or did you finally convince yourself to believe your own lies?"

"No, you're right. You're right, okay?" My voice bursts free, full of salt and phlegm, my face drenched with a mixture of tears and sweat.

"And you didn't even think to text me. Who knows if you're telling me the truth right now. Maybe your new beau made this lie up for you. It's pretty convincing. Doesn't seem like you'd think up such a good lie on your own."

"No! There's nobody else, Russ. I swear." I'm pleading, on my hands and knees on the bed, crawling toward his stony presence. "I'd never do that to you."

"Who knows what you're capable of? And here I thought you loved me. After all I've given you, all I've done for you, I really thought you'd respect the few rules I have, but no. You don't care about me at all."

"But I do! I do! I just forgot to text you, and you said you'd be out, so I didn't think–"

"No, you didn't think, did you? You didn't care if I worried where you were. What if I'd gone out searching for you? You knew I was going out drinking with the guys, and you'd play me like this? Oh, I understand now. You were hoping I'd get hammered and find you gone, go out drunk driving in the dark searching for you. Maybe get arrested so you could have this place all to yourself, see whoever you want, fuck them on my bed. Or maybe you were hoping I'd fucking die out there. That's what you want, right? You want me to die?"

"No!" I scream, my throat painfully tight, my arms reaching out for him like a child.

"That's exactly what you want. Well, how 'bout I give it to you, right now?"

He storms out of the room, stomping into the kitchen while I scramble on unsteady legs after him. My heart pounds in the back of my throat, throbbing so hard that I'm choking on it. My shrieks have devolved from words into guttural animal sounds, begging him to stop. I'll do anything.

He's grabbed a knife from the block, the biggest butcher knife, its blade glinting with moonlight. I fall to his feet, wrap myself around his legs, clawing at him and trying to form the words to beg him to stop. He's holding it at his neck, ready to drive it into the tender flesh where his pulse throbs, his eyes cold as iron, lips pulled into a dog's snarl.

"Is this what you want?" he shouts, asking over and over again as I strain to get my pleas heard.

"No, stop! I'll do anything! Anything!"

Finally, I get through. He drops his arm to his side, the knife dangling in his loose grip. He's crying. I feel the drops falling into my hair and I cherish them.

He loves me. I know he does. I'm so sorry. Why am I like this?

He crumples around me, his arms embracing me uncomfortably tight. The knife clatters to the floor.

"I'm so sorry. I'd never hurt you on purpose," I choke through my sobs. "It was just a mistake. Please forgive me. I'll do anything. I promise."

He's hushing me, rocking me like a baby as he strokes his fingers against my scalp and down through my hair. We sit deflated and spent on the cold kitchen room, holding each other.

The quiet is finally broken by his voice, deep and calm. "I forgive you."

Lorelei

Lorelei thought she'd seen something outside the window, but when she'd turned out the light to see past the glare, there was nothing but the shadow of the oak tree, illuminated by a small light at its base, in her backyard. She shook her head at herself. It seemed old age had been lurking ever since her fiftieth birthday, ready to pounce and deem her incapable of independence, or maybe that was just her midlife crisis speaking. She never knew anymore. Still fit for her age, she looked at her arms roped with veins and legs stippled blue and purple with broken capillaries as she rubbed lotion into her skin, a part of the desperate anti-aging night routine she'd started a few months prior when she noticed the slightest sag at her neck and a spattering of sunspots across her forearms.

A sound somewhere in the depths of the dark, locked house, like the thud of something dropped or the shutting of a window, startled her, sending her shoulders to her ears and her heart pounding in her clenched jaw. She thought to call out, but then reconsidered. If someone was in the house, why would she let them know where she was? Maybe it was a burglar, thinking she wasn't home. Hadn't there been a news story earlier about a break-in that ended in murder in a neighborhood a few minutes away? Had she remembered to set the house alarm or forgotten like most days? A shudder traveled from the crown of her head down her spine, and she instinctively wrapped her arms around herself.

She looked around the room for anything that could be used as a makeshift weapon but found little that made sense. After settling on a geode bookend that she kept as decoration on her nightstand, she worked up her courage to turn on the hallway light. The rock felt solid in her hand, but it was foolish to assume she'd be able to strike anyone with it. Every inch of her trembled with fear, every breath was a prayer.

The banister cast bands of shadow across the stairs that she padded down as quietly as a cat, but as she reached the bottom, another sound, quick, quiet, but real, sent every muscle in her body into a tense paralysis. It had been a footstep. She was sure of it.

Raising the geode up to shoulder level, she moved toward the front door. It was only a couple feet away. Nearly within an arm's reach. The patter of her heart sped to a level that blurred her vision and turned her stomach with dizzying lightheadedness. Her free hand on the handle, she began to turn, fully focused on the door, she didn't notice the man had moved from the shadows of the living room to stand right behind her.

"Don't scream or I'll kill you."

The rumble of his voice, deep and throaty like a growl, shocked Lorelei with a mortal fear like nothing she'd ever experienced. The blood in her veins seemed to thicken and freeze, her heart not pounding faster but momentarily in stasis, waiting for her mind to compute. *Think of a plan. Do something. Anything.*

Instead of action, a screech of absolute terror rang out, forcing her mouth wider and wider, transforming into a human siren. She imagined it traveling through the door, out into the quiet, night air of her cul-de-sac, begging someone to notice. But it was less than a second before the man's hand was clamped over her face, muffling her alarm. The fear burned brighter, cutting bright white through her vision, and she edged her teeth over the top of his hand.

Lorelei bit down with a strength she didn't know she possessed. She was a rottweiler, a pit bull, a tiger, a crocodile locked in a death roll. She made herself fierce and animal, hearing the crunch through his glove, his sharp inhale of agony. She wanted to taste the blood she was sure she'd drawn, but the leather kept it from her.

"Stupid whore, you're dead," he said through gritted teeth. Instead of letting him intimidate her, she fought harder, a surge of hatred and desperation rushing through her. Twisting and jabbing with her elbows, she managed to wriggle free, accidentally dropping the rock to the ground as his swinging arms missed her. *Go. Go. Go.* She panted and groaned as she tried to crawl away on hands and knees. He tried to grab her, but she saw it coming and rolled out of reach. Staggering to her feet, she dashed to the door. Her hand on the handle, she turned it, struggling as it slipped in her sweaty grasp.

His arm wrapped around her neck, yanking her body backwards against him in a chokehold. Her fingers clawed at his arm, her eyes wildly sweeping the room.

A veil of darkness fell over her vision, growing dimmer with each second. Her throat ached as his arm pressed steadily into her. A heaviness began to fill her head, growing more intense with every moment. The pressure was unyielding as it pounded through her sinuses, bulged her eyes, broke the capillaries along her eyelids. As her panic peaked, her vision completely blacked out, and she was awake and terrified in the dark for a moment before being granted merciful unconsciousness.

The man released her as soon as he was sure she'd passed out. He brought her gently to the ground, sat cross legged next to her, and waited. Her chest moved with shallow breath, and he wondered if she dreamed. Did she dream of him? The idea excited him, but he waited the minute or two it took for the blood to circulate, bring a blush back to her cheeks and across her chest, cause a flutter to dance along her eyelids.

She rocked her head back and forth slowly against the hardwood floor, her hair sticking to her clammy forehead as she let out a faint groan. Groggy eyes opened and closed slowly. Confusion spread across her face as she stared at the ceiling. Then dread washed like a shadow over her features. She turned to him. Their eyes locked. Her lip trembled and her hands clenched into fists, but she didn't fight, didn't scream.

The man swung his leg over her torso, straddling her body between his knees and staring down into her pale, frightened face. She was begging, he could tell by her tone, but the words were jumbled together into unintelligible rambles. Then he brought his hands around her neck, felt her pulse rabbit-fast against his palms as he squeezed.

Her hands darted to pry his free, but it was no use. Excitement built in him, and he slid his body down, laying over her like a lover, the pressure on her neck even harder than before. She tried to kick at him but was too weak and scared to do much. The life drained away and he cursed to himself at the built-up tension, unsatisfied. There could be release, but it wasn't his preference. It was over too soon. He'd had more in mind, wanting to bring her back again and again, but she'd faded too quickly.

Birdie

I'm putting away the dishes, my hair thrown in a clipped-back mess, face clean and plain, when Russ busts in through the back door, rushes to me, and literally sweeps me off my feet with the biggest smooch I've gotten in months.

"What's all this for?" I say with a laugh, my feet dangling while he holds me up, kissing my neck. I feel him bury his face in my hair and take a deep whiff. I giggle uncomfortably, playfully pushing him away. "Stop it. That's weird."

"You smell like heaven, you know that?" He pulls away, showing me that toothy schoolboy grin. Always mischievous, always charming. "Like home baked cookies and whiskey and pussy, all mixed together. Fucking intoxicating."

"Ewww, get away!" I shout, but he's throwing me over his shoulder in a fireman's carry, and I can't stop laughing. When we get to the bedroom, he tosses me on the bed, and I nearly bounce off. Now we're both laughing.

"Don't you try to get away now, ya' hear?" His arms land on either side of me as he pins me down, one eyebrow cocked. "I'm the man of the house and I always get what I want."

"Oh, is that right?" I'm laughing so hard now there's tears running down my cheeks. "Get off me, you big goon. I've got chores to finish." I bat at his shoulder like a kitten. He smiles, growling as he kisses up my neck and inhales into my hair again. We make love the way we did when we first met, full of passion and breathless whispers.

When we're finished, lying naked on top of the comforter, staring at the ceiling fan and holding hands, I smile. In moments like these, I'm genuinely happy again, something I never thought would be possible. All because this man decided to take a chance on me.

"Whatcha thinking about?" I ask, flipping onto my side to face him. He laughs, brushes the sweat-stuck strands of hair off his forehead, and closes his eyes.

"Honestly? I wasn't thinking about anything at all."

"Aw, come on. Guys always say that, but it's not possible you're thinking about absolutely nothing. There's gotta be something. Tell me."

He opens his eyes again, but doesn't look at me, his gaze is far away, beyond the ceiling, somewhere in the void of space. I wait as the silence builds heavily over us like fresh fallen snow. Is he trying to think of a good lie? Why won't he answer me? Finally, I can't take it and break the layer of quiet settled over us.

"I'll go first." I cuddle against him, loving his slick skin against my own, the way the hairs down his stomach tickle me. "I was thinking about how happy you make me and how much fun we always have together."

He looks at me, rolls his eyes a little but smiles. Every time I look at him, he takes my breath away with those sky-blue eyes framed by long, dark lashes. I've never seen such a beautiful man in my life, and he's mine. *Mine.* The thought makes me giddy.

"Yeah, I suppose I was thinking the same sort of thing."

"No, you weren't!" I play-punch him. "Why can't you just tell me what you're thinking?"

"Because I wasn't thinking about anything." He shrugs and joins my laughter. "Sometimes it's nice to not have a single thought. Just lose yourself in the blank white slate. You should try it."

"God, I can't imagine. Even when I took yoga classes, I couldn't clear my head during the end meditation. Everything on my to-do list just popped up, or worse, some cringey memory that I couldn't stop from replaying over and over. The closest to nothingness I get are benign memories, or lazy but happy ones. Like the one we're making right now."

"Huh, well then I guess we should bask in this one as long as we can." He taps my nose with his finger. "Any girl of mine needs as many happy moments in her life as she can get." He leans closer, whispers in my ear, "And it's my job to give them to her."

We make love again, then Russ orders a pizza so I don't have to cook. Drinking beers on the front porch while we wait, he smokes a cigarette and I point out the fireflies as the dusk darkens enough for them to come out. Snuggles on the couch, feeding each other pizza and laughing at the stupid comedy playing on the TV, and everything is perfect. He dozes off first, his head nestled in the crook of my neck, against my shoulder, and at some point, I fall asleep too. In the early morning, we drag ourselves to bed, backs aching a little from the awkward angle and thin cushions, but in no time, we're curled up together under the blanket.

"I love you," he says, his voice muddled with sleep.

"Thank you," I say, and I mean it more than I've ever meant it, but he's already asleep before the words have left my lips.

Birdie

The moment Russ walks through the door, leaving it wide open behind him, I know something is up. His face looks uncannily drained of color, almost amphibian with its network of blue capillaries just visible beneath the skin, and his eyes nearly glow in their unearthly pale blue as he looks out, seeing yet somehow sightless.

"What happened? You look like you've seen a ghost," I mean it as a joke, but instead the words wisp out uncomfortably real. Russ doesn't acknowledge I spoke, or even that I'm in the room. He shuffles like a zombie into the bedroom, and I follow after, peeking around the doorframe while he rummages in the closet.

"Russ? You're acting weird. Are you feeling alright?"

I make my way into the room as he emerges from the closet, the pistol he'd bought years ago for "self-defense" in his hand.

"No! What are you doing?" I'm shouting before I even register what's happening, careening across the room and jumping on him. He tries to shrug me off, but I'm stronger than he remembers, and I wrestle his arm down, the gun pointed at the floor. The ghostly veneer cracks and life rages back into his eyes.

"Get off me," he hisses through clenched teeth, "I need to do this."

"Stop! I won't let you!" My hand slips down the butt of the gun, fingernails digging into the backs of his hands to pry the weapon from his grasp.

"I said, get off!" he roars, and my vision goes black for a second as his elbow slams into my cheek. Somehow, I manage to keep my grip on the gun, but the pain throbs through my head like an excruciating heartbeat.

With a wild pant, I execute the only idea that comes to mind in my frantic state. Twisting my body with every ounce of force I can scrounge, I pull myself away from him and feel the weapon come free.

It worked. I have it. I can't believe it, but I have it. Looking down, the gun is a void in the room, sucking the light to it like a black hole, swallowing any good, happy thought in and regurgitating only one sentiment forever: death.

My legs carry me feather-light through the house and out the door, more leaping than running, my whole form burning with the only solution, *get rid of the gun. Now.*

Russ doesn't follow. I only hear a long, low wheeze and the soft thud of knees falling to the carpet behind me. He's conceded. I won.

I run and run, not sure where I'm headed. The only thing I know is that I have to get rid of it, someplace he'll never find it. That's when I see the bridge.

The highway booms across a grass median, big rigs rushing off to their destinations, then there's the empty feeder road and then the bridge. Just a little creek that the highway needed to circumvent, the bridge is an ugly mass of concrete, tagged with a few amateur, faded initials, and overgrown with invasive vines and sturdy weeds that found the smallest anchor of soil among the cracked rock. Beneath, the creek creeps along slowly, not deep but the murky water and stirred up sand obscure the true depth. The shadow of a fish and even a turtle scuttling along can be seen if I look hard enough, but mostly all I see is litter. Any bit of refuse tossed or lost from travelers has accumulated here: styrofoam cups, disintegrating fast food bags, unmatched shoes, used condoms, torn pieces of fabric that might've been a shirt at one point, and a submerged blue tarp all stare back at me. They call to me. This is the place.

I look around, but there's no witnesses. I consider dropping the gun into the sludge, watching it disappear into the mud, but I can't get my hand to let go. Instead, I find myself, slipping down the slope, sneakers caking with mud, until I've made it to the bank. With careful steps, I creep farther under the bridge until I'm completely hidden from public view.

It's a private place, and yet I don't see any signs of a desperate soul using it as a makeshift home. The stench from the rotting creek probably keeps them from staying too long. Moving a few larger rocks, I nestle the gun near the top of the bridge and hide it with stones, dirt, and bits of trash until I'm sure no one will ever find it. A rush of relief crashes over my skin in a torrent of goosebumps. He'll never find it here. Crisis averted.

I try to relax my shoulders, telling myself the problem is solved, but deep down, I know it's only temporary.

If he wants a gun, he'll get another one. It could take a while, but he'll get one if it means that much to him. The thought looms over me like a dark cloud as I walk home.

He's on the bedroom floor, lying on his side and facing the wall, when I get back.

"I just want it to end. Let me do it, please, just let me make it stop." His voice is meek, a whimper that's lost all the bravado and confidence I'm used to hearing in that baritone register. My head spins and I want to run away again. It hurts too much to hear him reduced to this, and I don't even know what's wrong. Part of me knows he'll never tell me. He never lets me into those soft, injured parts of himself.

I sit down behind him, try to stroke his hair, but he pushes my hand away. Suddenly, I notice the sharp smell of booze rising off his skin. That half-explains it, but I wish he trusted me enough to talk.

"I got rid of it. And before you ask, no, I'm never telling you where it went. We can't handle having it here. Don't you see? We're too broken. Both of us. You used to say it was for self-defense but we both know we'll end up hurting ourselves, or each other, and there's nothing but regret down that path." I watch his face crumple, but he turns away before I can make out whether it's anger or pain swimming in his eyes. "I'm sorry, but you'll realize in the morning that I'm right. It's only because I love you so much that I did it."

I set my hand on his shoulder, but he pulls away, and when he turns, his face is a smolder of fury. "Don't you ever fucking dare try to tell me what to do again."

I watch helplessly as he stumbles to his feet and out the front door, car keys in hand. I know he's too drunk to drive, but there's no stopping him. The engine turns over and my stomach turns with it. All I can do is hope he comes back soon, safe and ashamed, but it's more likely he'll just shrug it off like nothing happened at all.

Birdie

It's the kind of night where I take out the old picture album and torture myself. When I was a teenager, I'd slice into my legs with a razor or a knife borrowed from the kitchen, but the flipping of thick, yellowed pages with the adhesive peeling at the corners is the only kind of self-harm I engage in anymore. Moving on to psychological torment only felt right when I realized how much more painful guilt, regret, and self-loathing are, no longer trying to dissipate the emotions, I know work to rouse them. I want to wallow in them so I remember why I deserve everything that comes to me.

The first dozen pages are washed out polaroids, the only remnants of my childhood and the only evidence my father ever loved me. There's a couple of me as a baby in my mom's arms, her face a mix of exhaustion and awe, but those ones don't make me tear up like the four nearly identical photos of a toddler-aged me sitting on my father's lap, mouth smeared bright red from the popsicle in my grubby fingers and his bearded face aglow with pride. Mom never would tell me why he left, and if I'm honest with myself I don't actually remember the man at all.

These photos are all I have of him. Sometimes I tell myself I'll save up and hire a private investigator to track him down. It'd be nice to know if he's still alive, if I have any siblings out there in the world, if he left because of me, if the responsibility was just too great, or if I'm right in my suspicions that mother's mood swings ran him off, but the fantasy always dissipates into nothingness, a flurry of gnats to push to the back of my mind. It wouldn't matter if I knew. It wouldn't change anything. He never came back. That's all I need to know about what kind of man he was.

The rest of the oldest pictures document my childhood and adolescence in less than twenty photos. There are no home movies on old VHS tapes in an attic somewhere, no box of kindergarten crafts and Mother's Day cards stashed in a closet at her house, and no graduation pictures proudly displayed on anyone's wall. There are only these few photographs that exist to document my life from age three to eighteen, most of them blurry or overexposed, and only two where I'm over the age of eight. Mom only appears in a handful of them, and in not one is she smiling. She'd never admit it, but I think I ruined her life. She doesn't have to tell me for me to know. The way she's always kept her distance, just out of reach, and the unenthused expressions whenever I make the effort to visit, at most a tired half-smile, at worst a dour sneer, tell me all I need to know about her love for me. That's part of why I tried so hard with Noah. I didn't want him to have a childhood like mine.

I can hardly stand to look through those last dozen pages, filled to the edges with bright, glossy photos of my little boy. I make it through the first few, Noah swaddled in a blue blanket and matching hat, newborn in the hospital cot, one little red hand poking up through the top with the tiniest hospital bracelet clasped around it, and the ones of Charlie holding him to his scruffy face, both mouths open in wide smiles, one full of teeth and one adorably gummy. Others document his first time rolling over, his first steps, and first trip to the beach in his teeny swim shorts and matching navy bucket hat, dipping his toes in the water. His first birthday, chubby cheeks pinched by the string of a conical party hat, and our old dog Jasper licking frosting from his cake-smashed smile. I touch the plastic covering the memories, attempting to smooth out the bubbles with the pads of my fingers, and remember every amazing moment with him. It hurts but I don't break down until I get to the last page.

There are four pictures on the last used page, though there are many empty ones that follow. The top two and bottom left are from Noah's second birthday party. It was Spiderman themed, everything blue and red, his smile peeking out from beneath a Spiderman hood that covered his eyes and a Spiderman-shaped pinata hanging from the big tree that hung over our house's driveway. The pain hits me like a wave, knocking me down and suffocating me with blow after blow, but I still force myself to look at the final photo.

His little powder blue casket rests on a white draped bier, a bed of calla lilies and baby's breath cascading out in a nest around the bottom. The lid is closed. They tried to fix him up to look like himself, but it wasn't him anymore. I couldn't stand for anyone to see him like that, so the funeral director kept it closed and secured for my peace of mind. A blown-up portrait smiles out from an easel, Noah's name and angel wings painted on by Charlie's mom, reminding us all of how beautiful and sweet he'd been.

I trace the image of the final bed for my sweet boy and wonder who thought to take this final photo. It hadn't been me, and I don't remember anyone giving it to me. Instead, I found it in a pile of sympathy cards weeks after the burial. It was a morbid relic, and I couldn't imagine what possessed someone to snap the picture, and yet I cherished it. Every time I needed to remember just how precious he'd been, just how much I'd lost, I knew this one photo would crush me back into the terrible reality I'm destined to live in.

"Oh Noah. Noah, Noah, Noah," I whisper in a sob-burdened whimper. His name tastes forbidden on my tongue, and I usually only spoke of him in private, keeping the two syllables just for myself.

My boy. My world. What I wouldn't give to have just one more day, one more minute, with you in my life.

BLOAT

BODY

I feel the time pass in a way I never could while alive. With nothing to do but wait and relish the ticking away of minutes, hours, days, I take it all in.

My eyes have deflated, the lids partially obscuring my view. I track the time by the light that filters through the trees down on me. My eyes can't move, but I can manipulate this cursed postmortem vision to look downward, at my own body, my belly a round globe that long ago pushed free of my sweater, pregnant with the gasses of decomposition that strain against mottled skin. They whip and whine in airy voices past the pale skin, blue and green veins mapped across the taut surface like spiderwebs. I know my smell must be unbearable to the living, except those scavengers who seek it out, and I wonder why none have found me yet.

If I were alive, the tickle of ants across my face would surely be torture, their tiny dancing feet scrambling across my lips, but I thankfully feel no urge to swipe them away. There's no fear, no terror, only a peaceful melding with the natural world around and the inevitable processes bubbling within. But why can't I leave this plane? I'm not afraid if this is eternity, but it doesn't make sense. There must be an end. How will I continue on when I've degraded past human recognition, eroded to the particles that make up my cells?

I try not to focus on those questions and just enjoy the peace. There will be an answer someday, and there's no use in worrying, trying to rush things along. Dying is fast, but breaking down is a slow, beautiful process.

I wish I could float above myself and see the gruesome decay I've become. I'm sure I'm still human-looking, but do I look like myself? Will they be able to identify me when I'm found? I wish I could remember my loved ones. I'm sure I have someone who cares about me, is out there looking for me.

Sometimes a liquid bubbles up and spills from my nostrils and down the corner of my mouth. Secret parts of me liquifying and escaping into the dirt and leaves. The parts of my arms I can make out, also swollen and pushed partially out of their sleeves, have a strange look as the skin slips away, exposing various layers underneath. I feel no disgust, only fascination. There's no point in dwelling on the unanswered and painful when this incredible transformation is happening to the shell that was once me.

And yet that mournful longing still howls inside me, and it calls out in its ever hoarser voice past the gurgles and belches that swirl in my stomach. Find me. Find me and then I can rest.

SPRING INTO SUMMER

Cami

The man had been waiting outside her house for hours, sweating in the summer heat while he sat in the bushes, only standing up now and then, just enough to stretch his legs and peek in the living room window near the back fence. The sky had slowly desaturated to a deep indigo before becoming a pure void of blackness, the lights from the neighborhood making it too bright to see a single star. Cami watched television, occasionally scrolling her phone. Based on all his reconnaissance, that's all anyone does when they're alone, and she was alone.

He'd found out her name was Camilla Watkins from snooping through her mail, and he knew she goes by Cami after overhearing her neighbor call to her during one of his causal scouting trips, walking nonchalantly by her house. His spying also confirmed some things he'd already suspected: she lived alone, followed a predictable work and social schedule, only really seeing friends on Friday nights and Saturday exercise classes. She didn't seem to be dating anyone, or at least nothing serious since he hadn't seen a man enter or exit her house since he started surveilling her. He'd peeked through her windows enough nights to know that each day she followed the same routine after work—dinner while she watched tv, worked on her laptop for about an hour, then a couple hours more of tv and phone until she fell asleep on the couch. The few times he'd stuck around, she'd wake up around one and head to her bed, looking embarrassed even though no one was around to judge her.

Careful not to make too much noise, he rose from the bushes and slid up against the side of the house, his face pressed in such an angle that he could scan the room again. The television was the only light, a jumble of blue hues flashing across the room and illuminating Cami. Her phone was on the table, dark and forgotten as she fell into sleep with a light snore, her head tilted back into the pillows and her arm hanging limply with her hand resting on the floor. Her eyelids twitched. She was dreaming.

After a moment more of watching, making sure she was deep asleep, he broke away from her embrace so he could begin the plan he'd rehearsed in his mind for weeks. Before he snuck to the back gate, he pulled on his gloves and scanned the darkened block once more for possible witnesses, but everything was quiet except for the faint sound of faraway televisions.

The gate's padlock was broken and hung open, and after moving slowly and steadily, to decrease the chance of squeaking hinges, he was in the backyard. It was modest, with a concrete slab patio, neglected barbeque, and an old tennis ball, an artifact of some long-gone dog. The patio door was a simple sheet of sliding glass, its flimsy lock easy enough to bypass, and right as he entered, the air conditioner switched on with a gentle hum, covering any whisper of noise he might have made.

The first room was her kitchen, aglow with the silver lights of the neighborhood pouring through the windows. A knife block on the counter caught his eye. He took the largest butcher knife, relishing the sharp sound as he withdrew it. He weighed it in his palm. He enjoyed the thought that she'd likely never considered this a weapon before as it flashed through his mind.

He navigated through a few dark rooms, then found her in the gentle glow of a forgotten miniseries, still slumbering. The sound was muted, and he took in a deep breath of the humming, cool air. It felt like the room was waiting for him.

His feet moved quietly across the carpet until he loomed over her. Her dark hair loose, the big soft curls framed her face on the pillow like a wreath. He loved how she looked: barefaced, innocent, natural. She stirred, as if she sensed someone there. He held his breath until she groaned and draped her arm across her eyes.

He struggled to control his breathing as his excitement began to build. His hand reached across his chest and brought the strap of his bag over his head, then lowered it to the floor. Crouching, he set the knife on the carpet and unzipped the bag very slowly to dampen the sound. Then he pulled out the latest addition to his fantasy: zip ties.

Taking the knife in his hand again, he stood. Several minutes ticked by as he watched her, listened to her breathe. A surge, like a high, ran through him as he thought to himself over and over that this breath, or that one, or this little snort in her sleep could be her last moment if he chose it to be. He cleared his throat and woke her up.

"Cami, open your eyes and don't you dare fucking scream."

Her eyelids snapped open and the dark doe eyes stared at him so wide the white showed all around. She looked back and forth between his face and the knife. He cleared his throat again and licked at his chapped lips.

"Good. Now get on your stomach."

She nodded, her eyes wide but confused, unsure if she was still dreaming. Following his directions, she got into a position where he could restrain her, arms behind her back. He pulled the zip ties tight enough to be uncomfortable but not completely cut off her circulation. She whimpered and squirmed, but still didn't fight or verbalize her complaints. She was almost frustratingly compliant.

She craned back her neck to look at him, but her hair kept falling over her eyes. He roughly pushed it back and grabbed a handful from the back of her head, forcing her to look into his eyes.

"Please, please don't hurt me. I'll do whatever you want. Just don't hurt me." Her whisper like a rugged scratch through the silence of the house.

"Shut up." He slammed her forehead into the arm of the couch, and she began to cry softly, then a little harder as he ripped off her pajama bottoms.

"Stop. Stop. Stop." She whispered this pleading mantra, but each time she let a muffled squeak pierce through, he pounded her head against the arm again and reminded her to shut up. She clenched her jaw until her teeth cracked against each other.

Her body relaxed awkwardly against the restraints as he limply fell out of her. He stood, stretched, and took his time making a slow circle around the living room. When he glanced at her, she was facing the inside of the couch, but as soon as he closed the blinds, she turned back to face him with terrified eyes behind the mass of tangled hair.

"I can tell you where all my jewelry is, and I'll give you my pin so you can take out all the money from my account. You don't even have to untie me. I won't tell anyone. I swear on my mother's grave, I'll never tell a soul."

"Hmm," he hummed as he pulled his lips between his teeth, nodding. Her face relaxed, eyes wet with tears of relief. Bending over, he set the knife on the table before opening his backpack again, and she listened in silence as he rifled through the bag.

"What are you doing?" She only realized she asked a question when she heard the words, as if someone else had spoken them. Then a deluge. Words tumbled uncensored from her trembling lips. "My boyfriend is coming over soon. He'll be worried if I don't answer the door or my phone. You need to leave."

"Shh, I'm not as stupid as you think. There's no boyfriend coming to rescue you. No one is coming." He stepped closer so she could see the rag hanging from his grasp.

Cami screamed and flung herself off the couch, but he quickly overtook her and forced the rag into her mouth, muffling her cries.

"I told you to shut up!" He bashed her head against the floor and then the leg of the coffee table until she ceased her struggle. She flinched but kept her head down, refused to look, her head facing away from him, even when he flipped her onto her back. Again, her hair fell over her face as she squeezed her eyes shut.

"You know, you can look at me all you like. It doesn't matter."

She shook her head in reply, keeping her eyes shut tight, holding onto the last shred of hope she could muster.

As the man strangled her, she struggled. The skin around her eyes became blanketed with petechiae. She searched the room for any chance of escape but found none. She writhed against her bindings, rubbing her skin into angry raw rashes, but there was no give and the plastic tightened as her wrists and ankles swelled from the friction.

At first, the pain was terrible, but it soon faded, her body going dead to sensation in a merciful final burst of natural opiate her brain stored away for such an impossible encounter. She rolled her cow eyes to the side and began to fade into nothingness.

As soon as it was finished, the man stood and walked to the bathroom to clean up. With a microfiber cloth he packed for this purpose, he attempted to wipe away any bit of evidence he may have left.

He exited through the front door, walking casually down the front steps, across the yard, down the quiet sidewalk, as if nothing out of the ordinary had happened at all.

Birdie

I don't know why I drove here. My hands quake with tremors, clasped tight around the steering wheel. I never come here anymore, and yet, today something brought me back. I can't take my eyes off the little brick and stucco house I used to own, a few houses down from where I parked, on the opposite side of the street.

Whoever lives there now hasn't changed much. The front door is still the ketchup red Charlie picked out, too vibrant for my taste but he loved it, so I kept quiet. The rose bushes I planted are still alive and trimmed. I'm glad they're tended to. I'd worked so hard on keeping the yard nice, it's a relief to see it's still loved, even if they covered most of my flowerbeds with barren wood chip mulch.

The curtains are different. I had sky blue ones, but these new ones are dark, almost dreary. Somehow that seems appropriate now. This place will never be as it was again, no matter how many times it changes hands or how the owners decorate. This house knows loss, it's felt the shudder of grief, and nothing can change that.

My eyes wander down from the front porch, the vacant spot where my porch swing once hung, down the driveway to the street. The dark gray river of pavement runs through the neighborhood the same as any other road. As if it didn't remember what I remember. What all the neighbors remember. What the house remembers.

I drive away before I start crying. I know if I break down now, I won't be able to drive home, and what I need more than anything right now is to go home. Maybe that's why I drove here on autopilot. Some part of me, deep down and hidden, still thinks of this as home. That thought nearly breaks me, but I power through, pushing down those feelings as I drive across town to my new home. The home I deserve.

The contrast is astounding. I sigh, thinking of how many times I've nudged Russ to fix the place up, and how I've even tried my hand at a few things, but I'm just not good at repairs. The trailer looks rotted and trashed, rips in the screens over the windows and the front door not fitting properly so that a half-inch of clearance allows any bugs that make it past the screen to come and go as they please. I've tried jamming things in there at night to at least help keep the air in, but it never stays. Sure, Russ always promises he's moving us somewhere nice eventually, but I doubt it'll ever actually happen. This is just another facet of my punishment, doled out little by little as the years roll by. I don't have the strength to fight it, and really, it's not so bad. At least there's a roof over my head, some creature comforts, and Russ to share it with me.

I pull myself together before I head inside. I can tell by the patterns of light that skitter across the ground through the gap in the front door that Russ is home, watching the game. Pulling down the visor, I rub at my makeup until it's back in acceptable shape. The smudged eyeliner almost looks intentional. Then I grab the snacks I picked up at the gas station and head inside.

"I'm home," I announce, trying to sound cheery, but when Russ turns, the look on his face tells me everything I need to know about how the game is going and the much more subdued level of happiness he'd appreciate. Biting my lip, I bring him the plastic bag full of various kinds of chips and a sleeve of Oreos, hoping that might perk him up, but he just digs through it and scoffs, setting it next to him on the couch.

I try not to take it personally. It was probably a hard day at work, and now with his team down by so much, he's understandably on edge. Instead, I do what always cheers him up and fetch another beer from the fridge, pouring it into the glass I stashed in the freezer last night so he could have that little extra enjoyment. He always argues when I say it, but it really is the small things that count. It's those small things that make him love me; make me worthy of his love.

When I set it down, he continues to pretend I'm not there, but when he wraps his hand around the glass, a smile curls up one corner of his mouth. "Cold glass. Nice touch, babe." The words make me blossom with happiness. To be noticed is what I live for.

I bask in his mild delight as he drinks the beer and his team scores. Get out the broom, clean up a bit, put away the dishes, and go out to the mailbox to grab the mail. I'm about to flip through the stack of letters, inevitably mostly junk, when he asks to see it instead.

Watching him go through each letter, either tossing it in a pile of advertisements or ripping it open and cursing at the owed total, spurs a spark of anxiety deep in my gut, but I try not to fan it into a flame. He'll be finished soon and go back to his game. It can still be a good day.

"What the fuck is this?" He holds out a letter, the envelope sloppily ripped open, the header in block letters staring at me: *Greenville Community College*.

"Hey, I told you to stop opening my mail," I say, grabbing at the letter, but he's too fast, yanking it up out of my reach.

"I'm going to keep opening your mail for as long as you think you can keep secrets from me. Now, why are you getting an estimated bill from the community college?"

"Russ, I've talked to you about this. Remember? I filled out all that financial aid paperwork, been working extra hours, all in order to be able to start school again. I'm going to try to get my associate degree and be a CNA. Really help people, make a difference. Come on, I know I've talked to you about this a million times. Were you seriously never listening?"

"No, there's no way you ever mentioned this before. And just look at this bill. We can't afford this. Not right now at least."

"Well, if you'd let me have it then I can look at it," I blurt out and Russ narrows his eyes, finally lowering the envelope close enough for me to snatch it back. I skim over the itemized list and feel a giggle bubbling up from my stomach.

"No, babe, this is totally within budget. All my hard work applying for grants and stuff paid off. With my savings, it's definitely doable. And it'll help me make more money, so it'll be worth it." I laugh a little through my words, relieved to see that there hadn't been some miscalculation on my part, but the laughter fades when I see he's still looking at me with the same, disgusted look in his eyes.

"Are you saying I'm too dumb to understand our budget?"

"What? No!"

"I think you've gotten it into your head that you're so fucking smart now that you've gotten accepted to this fucking college, and you think I can't see through your bullshit anymore. Is that it? I'm just some dumb blue-collar idiot and I couldn't possibly get that you're trying to pull the wool over my eyes, huh?"

"No, it's not like that at all." I can't believe what he's saying, but the intensity in his eyes and the snarl on his lips tell me that he's dead serious. "I just want to better myself. You know this has always been my dream and now—"

"Since when has going to college been your dream? Stop lying. You just want—"

I surprise myself when I interrupt him. "I've always wanted to be a nurse. Ever since I was a little girl playing with my dollies. I want to help people."

His eyes cut me, razor-sharp, with something like hatred, but it can't be. He can't hate me for this. I didn't do anything wrong. He stands, throws the plastic bag of snacks at me, and I brace for impact but it's thankfully soft, only bouncing off my shoulder. My jaw drops open, quivering, as he storms out the front door, slamming it behind him.

"I just need some air. Don't you dare fucking follow me," he shouts back at me, with the wagging finger of an authoritarian father. I nod, shrinking under his pale, mean eyes. Then the car is humming to life, and he's gone.

I look again at the letter in my hands. He'll come around. He must've just been a little embarrassed that he misunderstood. It'll all work out fine. I have to tell myself that or else I feel I'd turn into a thousand useless gnats and flutter away forever.

Juliana

It's not until I'm driving home from work that I remember what day it is and grimace. She's acted so happy and normal all month, texting me about how nice the warmer weather has been or calling me to chit chat about the peonies she planted and how lovely they're blooming after she was sure they wouldn't come back from that frost last year, it had completely slipped my mind that it was May. And now here it is, Noah's birthday, and I haven't heard from her in days. I rush over, my heart jumping up my throat with a trembling thrum the whole frantic drive.

The windows are dark when I pull into the driveway, gravel crunching under the tires, and for a moment I think she's not home, then I think something worse and swallow the bile that rises in a nauseous burn up my throat.

"Hello?" I pull open the screen and call through the front door, lips nearly touching the wood, trying to make sure she hears me. "Birdie? It's Juliana." I pause, hating myself, clenching my teeth then adding a defeated, "I didn't forget. Well, I almost did, but I'm here now."

With my ear pressed to the door, I make out a slight shuffling of feet against carpet. I know she's in there, listening.

"I'm sorry, Birdie. Really, I am. But I'm here for you. Please, come to the door."

I hear her get closer, soft, muffled crying just audible through the door.

"Please?"

My last plea is rewarded with a turn of the knob, a sliver of darkness from within revealed, but Birdie stands out of sight.

"Come in," her voice creaks from the shadows, the soft drawl rusted into the ragged bray of a crone from what must've been hours of crying. It prepares me for the swollen eyelids and slicked red skin that await when I move inside and finally see her face.

"I know," she says with a dry laugh, "I look terrible. Couldn't help it, I guess. I had to call in and everything. You'd think it'd be easier each year, and yet, somehow, it gets harder the farther from him I move in time." She laughs again, shaking her head. "Listen to me. I don't even know if I'm making any sense at all."

My hand lands gently on her shoulder, squeezing it as I hold back my own tears, more for my friend than her son. She crumbles slightly under it, her eyes glassy beneath their heavy hoods. I can't help but wrap my arms around her, feeling her exhale against my neck, fresh tears already running down her face and soaking into the space between my neck and shoulder.

"No, it makes sense. I can't even imagine how hard it is for you."

I hold her for a long time, swaying back and forth a little, letting her decide when to break the embrace. When she finally takes a breath and pulls away, there's a little more life in her face.

"What can I do to be here for you, Birdie? Do you want to talk about him or would you rather I distract you? We could watch one of those cheesy movies you—"

"I want to talk about Noah," she interrupts. "Please, there's nobody else. Russ, well, he's not good at these things. If we could just sit, let me gush about my little boy for a while, that's what I'd like more than anything."

I nod, following her to the couch where we sit turned toward each other, kneecaps kissing.

"How old would he have been today? Is it five or six?"

"He's five. Old enough to be starting kindergarten in the fall." The smile threatening to break across her lips shatters. "How can he be five already?"

Her face is blue-black in the dark room, my eyes only barely adjusted enough to make out the detail of her face, and I contemplate opening the blinds, pulling back the curtains. A little light might help with the gravity of the day. Maybe seeing the beautiful day outside would help her understand that Noah wouldn't want her to spend all day crying on his birthday; he'd want her to be happy. But then those impulses settle into my stomach as I realize how comforting the dark must be for her.

Last year, she slept all day and all night for two days, the day before and after his birthday, only waking enough to sip some water or use the restroom a couple times. She'd stayed at my house in the guest room, needed to be away from that fucker Russ. I remember she'd told me the dark kept everything from feeling too real, being too clear. Time seemed to slow in the shadows, lose itself in the fabricated night, so I let it be. If this was what she needed, I'd give it to her. Despite her flaws, Birdie had been my friend for eight years, and I cared about her more than my own sisters.

"Every year that goes by... I just feel like I'm forgetting him."

"Jesus, Birdie, I wish I had been around more back then. But I do remember when I first met him. He was so little, just a tiny little wrinkly red potato." I laughed through my nose, wiping the tears from my lashes with the back of my hand. "Do you want me to tell you about when I first met him?"

A weak smile wriggled across her mouth, and she nodded.

"I'd like that."

"Well, you were so paranoid about visitors those first couple weeks, so I didn't get to meet Noah 'til he was about a month old, but damn, that boy was a chunker!" We both burst into giggles.

"Yeah, he was a big baby, but he thinned out later," she says warmly, the memory obviously vivid in her mind.

"True, but he was just a whopper of an infant. And you've always been so petite, so I was especially surprised you'd pushed out that big baby," I laugh again, but then I notice she's nestled back into her grief a little, so I pull back. "He was just the cutest little thing though. And always trying to latch onto everything. Remember when I tried to kiss him and he started sucking on the tip of my nose?"

I watch the memory flood Birdie's face. She beams, her arms instinctively coming together as if she were holding her baby again before she realizes and lets them drop again.

"I remember," she says, color climbing her cheeks and neck, and tears matting her lashes.

"I'm so sorry that I didn't make more time for you back then. Work kept me frazzled back then, always on my feet and bitchy as hell, but I shouldn't have been so selfish. You needed me. Even with Charlie and his mom and all that, you still needed more help, and I let you down. You don't know how much I wish I'd seen him more. Then I could help you keep him with you."

"I wish you'd known him better too, but there's nothing to be done about that now. No need for you to feel guilty. We were both younger, always busy, and innocent to the true wickedness of the world," Birdie says with a resigned sigh, her hand on mine. "Thank you for being there for me now. Sometimes I just feel so alone in this, you know?"

I hold her as more sobs quake through her frame, but she fights them, trying to regain control, wiping at her face again and again until it's a bright raw red.

"No more talk of regrets or anything like that. This is Noah's day. I only want to think about him, how he was. Perfect." She takes a deep breath then her eyes light up. "Oh, I have a special treat! Come over here."

We walk together to the kitchen where she brings out a box of Zebra Cakes, Noah's favorite. She unwraps the flimsy cellophane and jabs a blue candle in the middle, but her hands are shaking too much for the lighter. With gentle hands, I click the flame to life and cup it as the candle finally catches. Offkey and holding back sobs, we sing the birthday song in her dark kitchen for the son who'll never get to be five.

Tallulah

The lights were on in the house.

Even with the blinds closed, the man could see up into the room where Tallulah sat at her computer, scrolling through pages of items, filling her virtual shopping cart with a slightly downturned mouth and determined eyes. She was absorbed in her mission for dopamine and didn't notice the feeling of being watched. Even when the man tripped and the delicate inner branches of the shrub that concealed him broke in a hundred tiny snaps, Tallulah didn't look out her window. In the suburbs, so close to her neighbors and with mounted motion sensor lights, there was an illusion of safety. The biggest threat she could've imagined was a rabid raccoon rummaging through her garbage. She couldn't fathom the man that watched her from right outside her window.

She clicked and sent another slinky black dress into her shopping cart, another body shaper, another eyeshadow palette, then clicked over to observe the total. Several hundred dollars deep, she sighed and shut off the computer, purchases left in limbo, likely to be emptied in the shame of morning when her head was clear, and her brain didn't ache for any ounce of pleasure she could muster. Exhausted, she didn't bother taking off her makeup or even brushing her teeth, burrowing under the bed covers and wrapping them around herself. She entered a dreamless state of relief, snoring lightly, within minutes. The man still watched, now from the crack beneath her bedroom blinds, peering into the dark of her room.

Around the back, he kept close to the wall and didn't mind when the motion light caught him, stilling in a crouch until it went out again. She was sleeping so he knew she didn't notice, and his scouting of the house earlier that week had revealed there was no outdoor camera. He was still dressed in a baggy outfit and made sure to pull up his hood before approaching, just in case.

He was always careful. Care and calm were the keys. A killer only gets caught when he gets sloppy, and that only happens when he's scared. No, he was fearless when he popped the flimsy lock on the backdoor and stepped inside. The quiet of the house was comforting. A dull hum from the refrigerator, a ticking grandfather clock in the living room, and the occasional snore down the hallways were the only night noises.

The wooden floor squeaked in a few places as he made his way across the house. He heard her in the main bedroom, but first explored the other rooms. Slowly opening a door to reveal a home office, the same computer he watched her waste precious minutes of life chasing a fleeting surge of excitement and faux happiness. He walked to the center of the room, breathed in deeply through his nose, and smiled. Cinnamon and vanilla mingled in the smoke of a just extinguished candle.

The man moved to the bathroom, observed himself in the mirror, shadows cast across his face by the orange glow of a nightlight. He smiled. There was no fear in his movements as he quietly opened the medicine cabinet, closed it again, opened a drawer and removed a scrunchie, savoring the velvet feel on his fingertips before stuffing it in his pocket.

Tallulah still snored, as softly as a puppy, through the open doorway at the end of the hall. The man took a deep breath and walked with infinite patience as the floor adjusted under his weight—each step deliberate, applying even pressure. If she'd been awake, she still would never have heard him coming. His years of practice honed his skill to an unearthly ability.

He was a shadow on cat feet across the carpet of her room. She stirred in her sleep, her unconscious body sensing his presence, but she didn't wake up.

He stood over her. Watched her breathe. Relished the way a strand of hair swayed in front of her parted lips with each exhalation. Admired the ripple across her closed eyelids as she dreamed, tumbling deeper and deeper into slumber. He reached out a hand, felt her breath hot. In a steady, delicate movement, he took the wisp of hair and placed it behind her ear. She ascended from the depths of dreams to near consciousness, her hand darting up and brushing at her ear and the spider web tickle there. Then she plunged back down, still unaware of her watcher.

The man stepped forward, slowly bent over her, and brought his lips to her ear in a featherlight kiss. He breathed out, a look of supreme pleasure spreading over his face as his breath penetrated her, filled a secret place, and she shuddered.

His steps were hurried but still feline, nearly floating, as she shook and rubbed her eyes, waking in her room, alone.

"Hello?" she asked, her voice groggy but still painted with terror. She knew something was not right, but her sleep-addled mind couldn't pull together any reasonable scenario. As she awakened more, her breath quickened, her heart leapt into the back of her throat and lodged there, throbbing painfully. A whimper escaped her lips while she cocooned herself in her blanket, pulling it over every bit of her except her eyes. Those needed to stay exposed in case the threat revealed itself.

The man stood in the hallway, listening, for twenty minutes. Thirty minutes. Forty-five minutes. Perfectly still, shallow breath, always listening. When she was finally back in a deep, safe sleep, he made his way out of her house, his fingers on the velvet scrunchie in his pocket. Not tonight. The foreplay of suspense made it all the more sweet.

Birdie

I take the twin bluebird magnets and stick the paper to the fridge. I smile and it smiles back at me with its line after line of passing grades. I've never felt so accomplished since elementary school, when Mrs. Riley would stick a gold star on the corner of an exceptionally well done worksheet or scrawl a lop-sided smiley face with a grape-scented marker on one of my stupid stories. School was never easy for me, but all the long nights, studying under the yellow, half-dead kitchen lamp, and long days, attending class before or after grueling shifts at the store, were paying off. The success tastes sugar-sweet on my tongue and I savor it, staring at the sheet.

I know Russ won't notice. Of course, I secretly hope he'll see the paper, tear it from the fridge, magnets flying, and run to me grinning, pick me up, spin me around, whisper proud little snippets between kisses. But it'll never happen. Maybe he'll see it and say a little congrats.

That'd be enough, I think as I sip at a glass of wine, stirring the potatoes as they come to a boil. Part of me is afraid of how he'll react. He just doesn't get it, and that's fine. College isn't for everyone, but it is for me. I take another longer drink of the tangy, cheap wine.

When he gets home, I'm putting dinner on the table, and that gives me a different taste of accomplishment, a slick, polished one like a strong IPA. His smile and kiss on the cheek fill me with fluttering joy and I sit across from him, serving him a slice of meatloaf with the ketchup crust he adores.

"Mmm, good job, Birdie. This is delicious," he says between bites. I nod, burrowing into myself warmly with the compliment, storing it away to bring out later when I need to combat the nighttime anxiety.

"Thanks," I say, and then the white slip on the fridge catches my attention again. Pride snakes through me and I can't help myself. "So, I got my grades back for the semester."

"Huh," he says, the fork slowing between bites.

"All A's except one B, but that teacher is known for being a tough grader."

"You know, now that you bring it up, I've been meaning to talk to you about this school stuff," he says and my heart drops into my stomach with an acidic hiss. As it deflates inside me, I already anticipate what he's going to say, but I don't want to believe it. "I know you've been working real hard, and I'm proud of how well you're doing, but did you ever step back and see if this is just too much for you right now?"

"No," I spit out the words, my lips already trembling. "I think I'm handling it all just fine, to be honest."

"It takes so much out of you, what with all the studying and trying to arrange your schedule around classes—"

"I've got a handle on it, don't worry."

"Babe," he takes my hand, eyes puppy-dog wide, and something inside me snaps like a rubber band. "Maybe it's time for a break. What do you think? Take a semester or two off, then pick back up when things are a little easier for us. I'm looking to make a good amount from that job coming up in a couple months, and we could set some of that aside so you could work less hours when you go back."

"But I just started, and I'm doing fine. Yeah, I'm tired a lot, but it's always going to be hard. And my grants and scholarships don't work like that. I'd have to apply all over again. It just wouldn't make any sense. Plus, I'll be making so much more once I'm a nurse, and the program does its best to set you up with a job when you graduate, so if we can just hold on until then—"

His grasp tightens around my hand, constricting like a python's hug and tears spill down my face. I know I'm a goner. He's my everything and he knows it.

"I know, I know, and I don't want to come across like a bad guy here, but I don't know how else to tell you." His ice-blue eyes spear into mine. "It's just not the right time for us, hon. You understand, don't you?" Then his own eyes mist up, and I give up. "I need you at home when you're not working. I *need* you, you hear me, Birdie? It's been so hard. So lonely."

I crumple over my plate, tears mixing with ketchup in a salty, sweet paste. Russ sits looking at me, I can feel it without raising my eyes, but finally goes back to eating. There are no words spoken while he clears the plates, rinsing them off and loading the dishwasher. I'm grateful that at least I don't have to clean up. He even wets a rag and wipes down the counters. Such a sweet man. I'm lucky. Really, I am. Not everyone has someone like him to take care of them.

We make love, but I have to fake it because my heart isn't there. He says all the right things: how I'm the only thing that chases away the sadness, that I'm his whole world, that I'm the sexiest woman he's ever seen, but I can't get out of my heat. Instead, my thoughts shattered, piercing pieces of dreams that won't come true. I want to believe him, that I can glue them back together and start again in a year, but I know what he meant. And I agreed. Because it made him happy.

When he's snoring facedown, pillow wedged under his arm, I sneak into the yard and walk out into the striped shadows of trees. I pick up a handful of white pebbles in a sliver of moonlight and drop them as I walk, letting go of my sadness a little with each soft clatter of rock against rock, or nearly silent thud once I make it to the tall grass. When I'm far enough away from the trailer, I sit down and cry. I sit with myself in grief for a long time, but finally, I pick myself up and walk back.

On the front porch, I lay sprawled on the lawn chair and pull out my phone. The ringing goes on and on, but I keep trying. Juliana's voice is husky and dark, full of sleep or maybe exhaustion, but she's not upset.

"What's up, girl? Couldn't wait until the morning?"

"I need to talk to you about something, but you can't get mad. I can't take it if you get all flustered, I'm in a bad place already. I just need someone to listen so I can get it out. Is that okay?"

There's a long pause, then she answers, "Yes. I can do that." Her voice is heavy with expectant anger, held back in her throat, but I know she'll keep her word.

"Russ asked me to drop out. I mean, just temporarily, but still, it really hurts..." It all pours from me, but I don't cry or scream. I surprise myself with how calm and distant I feel from it all, and though the silence on the other end of the phone is thick with hatred for the man I love, Juliana's a good friend and she keeps quiet, just letting me get it all out. When I'm done, she waits to make sure there's nothing else ready to bubble up, and when it doesn't, she answers.

"I love you Birdie, and I hope one day you learn to love yourself because this isn't it. It just isn't it."

"Goodnight Juliana," I say, feeling satiated and empty.

"Goodnight." The phone goes quiet, and I sit in the still night air for a few more moments before curling back in bed with the man I love more than life itself.

Birdie

I scan the front yard. Plastic dinosaurs are strewn across the lawn, their mouths stretched wide, displaying teeth in silent roars. The purple toddler bike that my sister passed down when her daughter outgrew it lies discarded on the driveway. Noah runs and jumps over the mess of toys, in black sweatpants, a little too short after his sudden growth spurt, and a blue striped shirt he'd picked out from the last trip to the thrift store, already permanently marked by his signature mustard smear.

He's beautiful. Absolutely perfect. His blue eyes the exact same shade as the summer sky and his hair, a straw-colored mop that's broken two combs with its thick stubbornness. The strawberry mark on his neck has nearly faded away in the two years he's lived makes me smile. I always gave it my third kiss at bedtime. Two on the cheeks. One for each year I've loved him. *Momma, stop it.* His giggle sparkling bright in my ear. And one more just because that's how much I loved him. *I love you too Momma.*

Noah. Looking just like his daddy. Loud and full of joy. The love of my life.

Jasper is barking his head off, running back and forth across the yard while Noah runs after him. I shake my head, thinking it's cute but a little annoying, especially with my head pounding as I try to finish my coffee, already gone cold.

I sit on the porch swing, my phone already buzzing in my pocket. It's early. Just past nine. I hadn't expected a message from him already. It takes my attention from everything important.

My thumbs type as fast as possible; my attention completely absorbed by the phone. George has sent a flurry of steamy texts, punctuated with hearts and winky faces. A hot flush radiates over my face, my heart palpitating along with the electric nervous tap of manicured fingernails against the screen. He'd been a high school flame, reconnected through a reunion planning group. We haven't met up in person yet, but it's more than flirting. We both know. The way I instinctively hid it from Charlie was all it took for me to realize I was falling in too deep. Staying up all night, my husband snoring in our bedroom while I sat on the couch, texting away, telling my life story, every stupid thing that came into my head, to this man.

The way he talks, it makes me glow. Charlie barely looks at me anymore, though I know it isn't all his fault. He's on the road so much with his new job, it's hard to stay connected, and of course Noah makes things even harder.

A secret smirk creeps over my lips as I type out flirtatious replies, hearts back and forth between us. Jasper's still barking, and Noah's laugh seems far away, on another plane from me, as I'm only half-aware of their existence while my cheating heart gushes a word vomit of limerence.

I glance up, just long enough to see they still exist, both wide-eyed as a squirrel makes his way down the big oak, takes his chances on a run to the bird feeder. I don't think anything of their increasing volume other than that the cacophony makes my headache nearly unbearable. Eyes back on my phone, I know the noise meant they've teamed up, chasing that damn squirrel around the yard, and I wish for the briefest moment that they'd disappear. All the yelling, barking, the unending mess and noise. I want them to leave me alone; to let me pretend I'm young, beautiful, and in love again.

There's a blur of action beyond the focus of my screen. They both know not to play near the road. Charlie trained Jasper as a puppy, making sure he knew never to set one paw on the dark asphalt at the end of the driveway unless he was on his leash. I'd tried to teach Noah, but he was harder to control. He could be forgetful when something sparked his interest. Unlike a dog, trained to halt for fear of my husband's wrath, Noah has a penchant for rebellion. He follows the squirrel as it darts between two parked cars, scurrying across the road to the safety of the neighbor's yard. Noah has only made it halfway when the car whirs around the corner, going too fast for a neighborhood, manned by a half-awake morning commuter.

I hear Noah's laugh followed by the screeching of bad brakes. Then a sickening thump as his life is torn from his delicate body. The sound echoes in my skull, bouncing against bone in a disgusting imitation. The sedan skids as it struggles to stop, dragging my baby's body for a moment. He's already gone.

I run to his mangled body, every movement around me in an adrenaline-soaked slow motion. The sounds slow and distort; Jasper's low, loud bark dragging on for an eternity. The phone shatters on the concrete corner of the steps as my feet flew under me. I'm on the road in seconds, following after the car as it forces his tiny body over itself, breaking him apart before releasing its lethal grip. My breath burns through my lungs like acid, every step eating me away from the inside out until I reach him, hollowed out, to be forever empty.

The car pulls over, a confused and weeping woman rushing to render aid, but I'm already huddled over my baby, refusing to move as my body arches over him, trying to protect him, but it's too late.

The screaming is mine, yet it isn't. It's some faraway sound, muffled through layers of cotton and fog. I press the pieces together, trying to make him whole again, human again. He is broken. His tiny femur has splintered and pushed its way free, jagged and glistening. His jaw sits unnaturally in his mouth, shattered and caving in, teeth spilling out when I grab him, hold him to my chest. For a moment, he shivers, twitches. The doctors and therapists will tell me it was normal, something that happens often with a body violently killed, and that he was already gone. Just dying nerves. It haunts me, the lifeless shaking in my embrace.

Thank God his eyes are closed. I couldn't have lived another moment if he looked at me, even if unseeing, like the glazed marble orbs of the dead I'd seen in animals and my own father. His body is difficult to move, a sack of flesh burst open inside so that blood weeps from any opening it can find, but I still hold him. He was my everything and now he's gone.

The driver's clacking heels and stink of expensive perfume mock me. I yell at her to keep her distance. Call her a murderer. Tell her I'll kill her for what she did to my baby. But below the pulsing adrenaline and pain, I know it's my fault. There is no one else to blame, no matter how reckless the driver, no matter how blind the curve. *My fault.*

I wake with a stifled scream burning in my throat. As reality blurs into focus around me, I cuddle my pillow, imagining it's Noah, pretending I can pick up his long-gone scent on my own arms. It hurts, but I know why I dream of him. My mind wants to remember him, to warm my hands by the effervescent glow that was his beauty and wonder. To remember why I'm alone and cold. It's my fault. No one else.

No one understands. Russ is right. I deserve to be punished.

Tallulah

Sitting at her computer, finishing up an overdue expense report, Tallulah felt eyes on her. She'd had an unsettled feeling for weeks now, and nightmares of a stranger watching her sleep haunted her, feeding her insomnia. The little sleep she'd managed to get had been wrought with fear, sweat, and stifled screams into her pillow. The doctor tried prescribing a sleep aid, but she didn't want to be sedated into dreamless sleep, so he'd relented and given her an anxiety medication to take before bed, hoping to dampen the midnight feeling of impending doom. The bottle sat by her keyboard, and as soon as the feeling of an unseen observer fell over her, she shook her head, bit her lip, and popped open the little orange bottle.

The bitter chalky residue lingered on her tongue even after downing the rest of her water bottle. Still, a strange calm surrounded her like a cloud, cushioning her from the gnawing anxiety that tried to bite through. She hated needing a medicinal crutch, but she had to admit that it did help.

Her fingers danced across the keys, completing the last few entries, and then she began her nightly ritual of social media scrolling, but just a few minutes into the game of envious comparison, something scraped against her window. A bolt of icy terror shot down her back. She turned to the window, noticed the blinds were slightly parted. She could see nothing past them but the reflection of her screen in the glass. Just as her heart began to settle back to its usual steady beat, the scrape came again, and she scrambled to her feet, half-falling out of her computer chair and knocking the empty water bottle to the floor with a loud clunk of metal against wood.

Her mind brought up every possible cause of the sound, turning them over and examining every angle, but the worst scenarios burned neon red behind every reasonable explanation.

It's the stranger from my dreams. It's the killer on the loose.

She shook her head, trying to knock the thought away, and tightened the closed blinds so that every strip of window was hidden. She switched off the computer, pulled on a sweater, and rushed to first the front door and then the back, making sure they were locked securely. Every window was shut and latched, her phone was fully charged and waiting at her bedside table in case of the need for an emergency call. Still, she couldn't settle her nerves. In the kitchen, she took a knife from the block and brought it to her bedroom. First, she tried tucking it under her pillow, but the fear that she'd accidentally stab herself in her sleep was too strong, so she settled on keeping it in the nightstand drawer, still close at hand but infinitely safer.

In the bathroom, the water sputtered on and she took handfuls of it, rinsing her face of the second cleansing product in her routine. A bit of waterproof mascara still clung to the rims of her eyes even after her vigorous washing, and she sighed, giving up on it for the night. She was sure it'd come off in her sleep and she could start fresh in the morning. Rubbing the serums and creams into her skin, waiting between each layer for the previous one to absorb, she couldn't stop looking into the mirror and checking the door frame behind her, making sure it was still unoccupied. Finally ready for bed, she slinked under the covers, her silk pajamas sliding against her moisturized and pampered skin, but the fear still lingered. Past the fog of medicated calm, there was still an animal warning blaring in the depths of her mind.

Someone was watching. She didn't know who or how or why, but they were there.

She forced herself to flip the lamp switch and darkness swallowed the room. Sinking into her pillow, she willed her eyes to close, but they refused. Instead, they searched the impenetrable darkness, trying to make sense of the shadows and shapes they conjured in the void. The air conditioner clicked and whirred to life, cool air pouring into the room, and she became aware of the sweat that had gathered across her brow and upper lip, wiping away the cold dampness with her silken sleeve. Though the blasting air was necessary to cut the late summer heat that had thickened and gone stale throughout the house, she hated how loud it had to be. Any sound in the house that she might have heard before was now hidden behind a wall of white noise.

Turning on her side, Tallulah tried again to close her eyes, but just before she forced her lids to shutter her vision, she saw something in the dark.

No.

Every nerve in her body sparked to life, a static shiver running over her skin and pushing each follicle of hair to attention. Her intestines knotted and she involuntarily pulled in a rush of cold air, her lungs ballooning painfully against her ribcage. The stranger was there. In her room. Watching her.

She couldn't make out any details, but she didn't have time to try. Run, run, run. Her heart pounded the command again and again, pushing blood to her extremities. Her body moved on instinct as she jumped from the bed and ran to the corner opposite the strange figure in the doorway.

"Calm down, Tallulah," the man said in the voice one would use to approach a frightened dog but hearing her name in the strange man's voice only elevated her fright to a new, unstable level. "There, there. Now be good and I'll be out of here before you know it."

He approached as she spoke, hands empty and outstretched. Each step closer pulled the strings of desperation tighter in every fiber of Tallulah's being. She needed to get away, but he was in the path of the only exit. *Escape, escape, escape,* her heart boomed.

As he closed in, she knew she had to do something. With the shriek of a Valkyrie, she summoned all her strength and ran at the man with her hands out. He jumped to the side just enough for her to push past and careen toward the door. Her hands reached out, and she clutched the doorframe for one second, trying to propel her body out into the hallway, find her way to freedom, but hands were on her, pulling her back.

"No!" she screamed, thrashing and snarling as the man forced her to the floor. Her face rubbed against the carpet, burning with tiny tears against the fibers. He was beating her, but every punch was dull and far away as the rush of adrenaline kept her fighting.

"Stop it! You stupid bitch," the man grunted, each word broken with exertion, but she didn't stop. A punch to the nose caused a torrent of blood to pour down her face, hot and sticky against her skin, filling her mouth with salty syrup and the smell of old pennies. He ripped at her clothes, short, jagged fingernails digging down her back, and she sobbed through the blood until she was sure she'd suffocate.

When he finished, he shushed her like a baby. She'd gone limp, let him do what he wished as she tried to comfort herself, hiding away in the safety of her own mind. But as he continued his futile attempts to reassure her, something new sparked in the core of her animal brain. A new flashing warning screeched through her. He tried to flip her onto her back, but she wriggled and he stopped. Then his hands brought themselves around her neck and she knew. He was going to kill her.

A surge of power raced through her veins, and she pushed herself to her hands and knees. The blood from her nose had drenched her neck and she felt his hands slip. A flicker of hope pushed the air back into her lungs. This was her only chance.

With no regard for the pain it might cause her, she thrust her head back and felt it collide with his as he yelped, his own nose now a faucet of blood, covering her back. She was on her feet in a fraction of a second, not letting him register what had happened. She panted, keeping herself going as she sprinted down the hallway. She could hear him right behind her. She couldn't make it outside. With a shriek, she darted to the right into the bathroom, slammed the door shut behind her, and flipped the lock.

The handle jiggled and he was cursing as he pounded on the door, ordering her to open up, but she ran to the tiny window and pried it open. Though she could never fit through, she had a different plan.

"Help! Help! For the love of God, somebody fucking help me!" Her piercing screams echoed through the quiet suburban night. Again and again, she shouted for help, every sense gone blank as she concentrated every bit of strength she had left into her cries.

A light across the street sprang to life, bathing the driveway in white. Then another light, and another. Tallulah collapsed against the wall, sliding to the floor, her voice still straining with screams for help that seemed to come from some other plane, not her own body. She looked behind her to the door, but the handle was still. Her assailant's frantic pounding had stopped. His voice, full of rage and bristling with murder, had been replaced by silence. Now only her screams rang through the night, but she was frozen.

Neighbors knocked on her door, shouted back to her. Blue and red lights illuminated the night, spiraling through the bathroom window and alternating their colors across her broken, bloody form. Even when the police rapped on the bathroom door, their voices kind and ready to help, she couldn't move and had to watch from her faraway place as they broke down the door and rushed in to save her drained, exhausted body.

Birdie

"What the hell is on your face? Is that makeup? *My* makeup?" I laugh, walking toward Russ with my arm outstretched, but he evades my touch. "Why are you wearing foundation?"

"I'm not!" he shouts, turning away to hide his face, but I've already seen the streaky mess that's too pale for his skin tone blotched under his eyes. And his nose, there was something wrong with it.

"Turn around. What the fuck, Russ? Look at me. You're acting so weird."

I force him to face me, nudging his shoulder until he gives in with a grumble. A gasp slips out before my hand slaps over my mouth. Not only is there a creased splotch of concealer under each eye, desperately trying to cover the still visible purple-blue crescent bruises, but his nose is swollen twice its normal size, the nostrils crusted with dried blood.

"What happened?" I ask, my hands clutching his arm with a tender concern I can't help.

He doesn't answer, only tugs his arm free and scowls before heading to the kitchen. I know better than to follow right away. Could he have gotten into a fight? Usually, he'd be proud to tell me all the gory details if that were the case.

He got home late last night, after I'd already fallen asleep. What had he been up to? He'd texted it was just some beers with the guys, but suddenly my heart races with the sharp twinge of suspicion. *Not again.*

A sizzling accompanied by the smell of burning butter finally brings me to the kitchen. I walk in just as he's fishing bits of shell out of the scrambled eggs he's struggling with.

"Let me take over, honey," I say, and he relents. "Now, come on, tell me what happened to your nose?" I can't help but giggle at his slanted frown, the ballooned nose adding to the cartoonish look about him. "And if you want help covering up those shiners, I'll gladly blend that out for you, but it's not gonna hide that someone decked you good."

"Just drop it, Birdie."

"Did you get in a fight or something?"

"I said to leave it alone!" he shouts, storming into the hall, the bathroom door slamming behind him. Behind the door, a faucet spurts to life and I know he's washing off his sad attempt at camouflage, which is for the best. If any of the guys at the site saw him like that, they'd tease him so hard, I'm sure he'd quit. I stir the eggs, picking out the last couple bits of shell from his careless cracking, and mull over why he won't talk about it. It really must've been something embarrassing for him to be this sensitive. *Or.* My stomach tenses at the similarity to a situation two years prior where the girl he was messing with turned out to have a big, jealous boyfriend.

When he comes out, the makeup is gone and the bruises give his eyes an eerie look with their bright blue irises staring out from veiny sclera and dark hollows. Most of the blood from his nose has been washed away, but the swelling looks even more pronounced, probably from the agitation of washing. I'm sure Russ was anything but gentle, even with his own injured face.

"Babe, just tell me what happened. I won't say anything."

"It was some guy from the site. New guy. Talking shit. He looked ten times worse, don't worry." He says all this with a nonchalance that feels like a lie. "Now fucking drop it, alright?"

"Okay, fine. Whatever. Here's your eggs."

I slide the plate to him and watch him inhale the eggs, chug the mug of coffee, and head out the front door without so much as a goodbye. As soon as I hear the crunching gravel beneath tires, I head to his laptop. I log in easily. His password was incredibly easy to guess, and he's never changed it beyond adding an exclamation point at the end, even after I found out about Kirstin two years ago. But maybe he figured he didn't need to change it. I didn't snoop often, even when he came home with a "bruise" that looked more like a hickey or a sheen of glitter on his lap. I knew that he and the construction guys went out to strip clubs and flirted with every girl they saw when bar hopping, but Russ just liked to look, maybe take it a little farther, but not cheat. No, he was mostly faithful. Only Kirstin, that girl he messed around with from work when he had to stay overnight near a job so he wouldn't have to drive too far. But after he almost lost me, he cleaned up his act. He knows not to take it too far or else I'll outta there. Although, I still get tested every couple months, just in case.

I scour his social media inboxes and text history. He never bothered to delete anything so it would be easy to find everything I need, but I start to feel silly for doubting him. Maybe it was just a fight after all. Was I being paranoid? Nothing incriminating in his browsing history beyond the usual porn. No fake contacts I can sniff out, and nothing lewd was shared in the depths of his messages except the same sexist shit he and the guys always sent each other. I sink into the desk chair and suck my lips, trying to dispel the feeling that I'm missing something.

"Hello?"

"Hey, can you talk?"

"Um yeah, sure, I can talk for a bit while I get ready. Don't have to go in for another hour but you know me." We both laugh and a bit of the fluttery discomfort settles. Juliana always makes me feel better. "What's up? You okay?"

"Well, I'm not sure. Russ came home really late last night. I know, nothing unusual about that, but then I saw his face is all bruised and messed up, like he'd been in a fight."

"What? I thought he stopped doing that dumb shit."

"Right? Like his nose is swollen up and he's got double black eyes. Somebody whacked him hard."

"Ouch. Did he tell you what happened?"

"No. He won't say anything about it, and I caught him using my makeup to try to cover the black eyes."

"What!" Juliana shrieks out a laugh.

I can't help but giggle along with her. "It was really weird, and it looked terrible. I made him wash it off so the guys wouldn't tear him to shreds over it."

"Jesus, that is so strange. Why would he try to cover up black eyes?"

"Well, it's making me feel a little sick, ya know? It's so out of character, it's giving me flashbacks to the whole Kirstin situation."

"Oh shit. I can totally see that."

"But I couldn't find anything on his computer. Dumbass never changed his password." I glance back at the computer, glaring as if it's purposely hiding something from me.

"Well, maybe he was just trying to hide it because he was embarrassed he got hit. I mean, I'm always the first to say trust your intuition, but maybe there's really no affair this time. Or maybe it was something like him getting too handsy with a dancer again, had a bouncer knocking him around."

"Yeah... that honestly sounds more plausible. He knows I'll leave if I find out about another thing like last time," I say, finding myself compulsively standing up and pacing the room.

"If you couldn't find any evidence, it's probably not an affair. Russ is too messy to get away with that stuff."

"You're right. I don't know. It's probably nothing."

Juliana takes the chance to change the subject, and after some of her own venting about her terrible boss, she has to go and I'm alone again. It isn't quite silent. The refrigerator buzzes a quiet white noise and there's the occasional scritching I can never locate but I'm sure it's a rat in the wall. Still, it's quiet enough that I'm left with the rumble of my own thoughts and memories.

I sit in the stripe of light that cuts across the couch from the broken blind, watching the alien dance of dust particles. Before I know it, hours have crawled by, marked by the elongating shadows of furniture and the green digital face of the microwave, just visible around the corner in the kitchen. Somehow another day has slipped through my fingers, and I race to work, only half made-up with frizzy, wild hair.

"Busy day?" Lucinda asks when I come out from the employee lounge.

"Yeah, guess so," is all I could say. Her eyes burn as they rove over my messy look, but what does she care anyway? I'm kempt enough to stock shelves and even man a cash register if someone calls out. She's always nosing around in everyone's business, and it makes me uncomfortable.

The afternoon shift drags on forever with hardly any customers. I find myself reading the headlines on the magazine racks to pass the time. The tabloids have always been my favorite. I chuckle at their ridiculousness. *Alien-dog hybrid discovered in Arizona. Princess Diana spotted in the Philippines: Massive Coverup or Ghost Sighting? Keanu Reeves and Marilyn Monroe Time-Travel Romance: Photo evidence!* But then the smile runs away from my face as I glance at the block letters of the front page nearby. *Serial Killer on the Loose: Police Warn Residents to Stay Alert.*

My blood crawls through my veins like a million ants and I scratch at the growing goosebumps on my arms. A serial killer? Could that be true? Sure, there'd been murders I'd heard mentioned on the news and fear-mongering posts on social media, but the idea they were connected chills me with a fear I'd never felt before. When I leave through the back door after locking up, I rush to the bus stop, darting from streetlamp to streetlamp like a nervous child. I feel a little safer when under their halo and wait there for the next bus instead of sitting in the dark on the bench like usual. I wish there was someone to wait with me, some old lady or even that man who talks to himself. Anyone to help keep my fears at bay. I feel like I can't breathe until I'm home and behind my own front door.

"I didn't know you were working the late shift," Russ says from the sofa and I startle, stifling the scream rising in my throat. "What's wrong, babe? You look scared shitless."

"Nothing. I'm fine," I say as coldly as I can muster with the whoosh of blood in my ears deafeningly loud and my heartbeat pulsing painfully in my jaw.

He can't stay away from me, staying willfully ignorant that I'm icing him out. Even when I start chopping vegetables, he's hanging on me, kissing my neck, stroking my arm.

"Babe, you're seriously acting weird. Tell me what's going on."

I step back and stare into his pale blue eyes, searching for the truth.

"No, *you* tell me what's going on. Don't act like I didn't catch you trying to hide those black eyes this morning." I take a deep breath and prepare myself for the truth, forcing my back as straight as I can. "Are you seeing someone on the side again? Did her boyfriend catch you? Is that what it is?"

"Birdie! What the hell? No, it's nothing like that. Jesus Christ. Okay, yeah, I was embarrassed. I got into a stupid fight after having a few too many last night and got my ass kicked, okay? God, I can't believe you made me admit that shit. And on top of that, you're accusing me of fucking around? Two terrible fucking nights in a row." I watch his jaw move as he clenches his teeth, and I might be mistaken, but his eyes seem to mist up. "What do you want me to say? You want me to tell you I'm depressed? Because I fucking am, alright? Is that good enough for you?"

Guilt floods through me like spilled wine across a linen.

"I'm sorry. I didn't mean—"

"You're not sorry. You're only happy when you see me groveling. I was so excited for you to come home, but then you act like this?" His eyes narrow, sending a shiver through my bones. "You're lucky I love you, you know that? Because when people get to know you as well as I do, they're gone. You're not as easy to love as you think you are. Actually, after what you did to your son, I doubt anyone but me could ever love you. And that's only 'cause I'm fucked up too so I can see past it, almost understand."

The words cut deeply. I feel lightheaded and vomit a stream-of-consciousness slew of apologies and declarations of my love. It's not until we're wrapped in a nest of sheets, Russ snoring away in postcoital bliss, that shame lifts its weary head, and I know I've given in to him again. But he knows my secret: I'm unlovable. It's true. He's seen me at my rock bottom and took pity on me, nursing me back to something human again. I can never leave Russ because without him, who else would I have?

PUTREFACTION

BODY

The insects come in waves, covering me and disappearing into every orifice, sometimes creating new entrances through their own frantic burrowing. Blowflies, maggots, and so many others. I welcome their companionship. A melancholic loneliness has descended over me as time loses meaning and I've learned to embrace their visits. They're part of the process as I slowly liquefy into the wet mulch around me. I feel them nestle in and lay their eggs in the moist hiding spaces they've found in me, and I thank them for their part in my disintegration back into the earth.

I was only bothered when my scalp sloughed away, leaving my skull unsheathed and bare. I don't want to be discovered like that. It's certainly too gruesome for anyone who once cared about me to see. A few of my fingernails have also fallen away, resting in gluey puddles beneath my mottled, wrinkled hands. I don't look human anymore. I'm sure of it.

I can feel my eyes have shriveled and fallen far into their sockets, but my otherworldly vision remains unchanged. My belly has lost its rotund shape, now caved in on itself, the skin blistered with patches of green and black. Greasy, yellow-gray wax and bursts of dark blue and red bruise add to the marbled rainbow of my decay.

Every tissue has softened and drooped away from the bones that try their best to maintain a semblance of structure. The organs that had swollen have burst and deflated like balloons over the days, sometimes temporarily scaring away my insect visitors, but they always return. I'm a beacon of safety for their young, a food source, a treasure in the forest they cherish and worship. Their tickle in the base of my lungs spurs no fear, but instead a faraway warmth. I am still useful. Still loved.

I've heard someone walking along the path a few times. I remember it's not far away from where I lay, and I recognize the crunch of gravel under hiking boots from memories buried somewhere deep and barely accessible of my life before. I wish I could call out to them, to let them know that I'm here, waiting.

Are they looking for me? One time I heard a group, several people walking together, but they didn't speak. Were they a search party? Am I missed? There must be a reason why I'm still here, waiting to be found. I don't know much about my life before, but I was young, happy, loved. I had a life ahead of me that was stolen in a moment of violence. There must be a reason I stay, and I think it might be justice. Or something bigger than that. To stop the dark blur that took my life from taking others. There are young, happy girls out there in danger, and they don't know. He could be stalking them right now. Biding his time to turn them into masses of flesh and moisture and insects, barely human, like me.

A great sadness falls over me, and I cry out into the void where only my mind exists. Please, find me. Help me. I need to be found before there's nothing left, nothing human to give closure to the loved ones I'm sure I had. I whisper through the wind that carries from me on the buzz of flies' wings with a sickly scent and a desperate plea.

Find me. Find me. Find me.

SUMMER INTO FALL

Birdie

The phone rings again and again before a click followed by a robotic female voice telling me that the voicemail of the number I'd called is full. *Fucking Russ.* Why doesn't he ever delete his messages? I hang up, tossing the phone onto the bed next to me. Twenty phone calls today. I know it's too many, but I can't help myself. Probably close to fifty since he left four days ago. Not once has he picked up. Hasn't answered any of my pathetic texts either. I sigh, rub my eyes so hard that bright stars momentarily appear behind their lids, and hate myself for worrying so much when he's done this to me so many times before.

As I pick up the phone again, my thumb hesitates, shaking a little as I hover over a different contact. Might as well give it a try.

The line rings for an eternity, but just before I'm sent to another voicemail box, there's a click and the connection goes through.

"Hello?" Mom's voice is cracked, craggy with age and strained by self-inflicted hardships. I regret calling her almost immediately, but I can't hang up. Not when she finally answered. If I do, she'll likely use it as an excuse to never make contact again.

"Hi Mom."

"Why're you callin' me?" Her question sizzles through my eardrums, static and acid, but I shake it off.

"Just missed you, I guess."

"Hmm." The air goes dead between us though the sounds of a television or radio cut through, barely audible, now and then.

"Well, how have you been?" I venture the question, but she only responds with a heavy sigh. "Anything new? How's Bert?"

"Moved out."

"What? Last I heard, y'all were engaged and everything."

"Didn't work out. Fucking bastard."

"Oh." I pull a breath through my teeth. "Sorry to hear that."

"No you ain't."

The line is silent for a moment before I force my creaking voice forward.

"How's Tamara?"

"She's fine."

"And the kids?"

"Don't you worry 'bout your sister and her family. They're doing just fine without you. And so am I. Not that you actually care how we're doing."

"Mom, I don't hate you. I want you to be happy."

"If you wanted that, you shouldn't have killed my grandson. Just leave us alone."

Despite the slurring in this final sentence indicating she's heavily intoxicated, despite her anger being valid, her hatred of me deserved, I can't help myself. I hang up the phone, bury my face in the pillow, and scream. I cry for who knows how long and would've kept on crying if my phone's tinny chime didn't snap me out of it.

You okay? Haven't heard from you for a bit.

It's Juliana. I rub my eyes and answer.

Russ still isn't home. I'm not good.

The phone dings again right away.

What!? Coming over.

Part of me wants to tell her not to bother, let me wallow in my mire of worry and self-pity, but I know she's right. I can't keep torturing myself like this.

By the time she's arrived, I've pulled myself together a little, dressed in clean pajamas and wet hair drips down my back, fresh from the shower. I don't care how Juliana sees me, but I don't want her to smell my grimy depression stink. That's the kind of thing someone never forgets, I think as I rub my hair with a towel and answer the door.

"I brought the party!" she says, rocking her hips and raising the two bottles of cheap white wine over her head. I can't help but giggle, the smile painful as the muscles are forced up for the first time in days.

Cups filled to the brim with the oversweet wine, we talk about nothing and everything. Well, anything but Russ. She's too smart to bring him up. There is nothing we could do to make him come home, and we both know I'll just dissolve into tears again if I think about him too much, so she keeps it light and playful. She waxes on about her husband's new hobby and how he's spending too much money, about how her job sucks and she deserves to be paid way more, how the washing machine's on the fritz again and her brother tried to fix it but just jacked it up more. When she sees my brows knit together, the worry cutting through the chit chat and alcohol despite her best efforts, she suggests a movie.

The television blinks to life and a blonde woman in a tight blazer and teased hair blabs on about local news. I turn away, looking at Juliana as she brings the glass to her lips.

"I know he's probably fine, but I can't help–"

"Wait!" she shouts, interrupting me and jumping backwards into the cushions. "Uh, is it just me or does that look like Russ?" Juliana's eyes are fixed beyond me on the television, lids pulled back so that they bulge slightly, and a tremor of terror contracts in my chest. I whip my head around to see a police sketch plastered across the screen. At first glance, I see what she sees, a man resembling Russ too close for comfort, but as I take in the details, I relax slightly. Those lips are too thin, forehead a little too high, jaw not defined enough. Most of all, there's a hardness, a rage in the clenched teeth, that I've never seen in Russ, even at his worst. It couldn't be him.

"I mean, kind of, but not really," I say with a shrug, but Juliana side-eyes me, her mouth screwed up to the side.

"You've gotta be kidding me. That dude looks *exactly* like Russ," she says, but I only half-hear her as I focus on the news anchor's exaggerated lilt outlining the case.

"This suspect is wanted for questioning regarding a sexual assault that occurred last month in an East Riverview neighborhood. The police are urging anyone who thinks they may know this man to reach out to their tip line below to help with this investigation. Now we go to Randy with this week's forecast. Randy?"

"You really don't see it?" The scorn is palpable in Juliana's voice. "Maybe I ought to call it in, you know, just so they can rule him out right away. There's no way other people won't be thinking the same thing when they see that sketch."

"Don't even joke about that."

"I'm not joking! You saw it clear as I did. It looks just like him. You don't think he could... be capable of something like that, right?"

"Shut up. I cannot believe you are seriously asking me that."

"I mean, he can be a bit volatile. Even you've got to admit that." She steps over the words delicately, but each one still pierces.

"No, if you have to ask, I don't think Russ could do something like that. Sure, he's not always the best partner." She raises her eyebrows. "Okay. Yeah. He fucks up a lot. But that still doesn't make him a goddamn rapist."

"Okay, okay. Whatever you say."

"You're not going to call, right?"

She looks into my eyes, past the swollen red from hours of crying, past the pleading pupils. I can feel her gazing directly into me, as if she's trying to read my mind, or pry her way inside my brain, nestle in among the worries and fears and love all tangled together in there.

"Fine. I won't call. Not now at least," she says with a resigned sigh. "But I can't promise I won't do it if he gives me more reason to, you hear me?"

"Yeah." I settle back into the couch cushions. "That's fair."

Thankfully, the news has moved far past the unsettling story, but the sketch stays in the forefront of my mind. I trace over the details again and again, sometimes seeing the uncanny resemblance and sometimes nearly no likeness at all. Juliana notices my mind is elsewhere and clicks off the television so our ghostly reflections stare back at us.

"That's enough TV, don't you think? How about we play a game?"

"Yeah, that sounds like a good idea," I say, forcing myself from my own uneasy eyes staring through me.

"Awesome! I'll go crack open that other bottle while you pick one out."

Russ shows up as the morning sun peeks between my blinds and sends my head spinning with a dizzying nausea. I sit up with a start when I hear the slap of the screen door. My hands dart to the left, ready to wake up Juliana, but there's nothing but a slight impression from her sleeping form, the sheets disrupted and no longer warm. *Fuck, I told her not to drive home*, I think, hoping there was no unfortunate encounter with a cop on her way back. Checking my phone, I don't see a message from her and my heart sinks until I remember angrily setting my phone on "Do Not Disturb" after ranting about being left on read. I flip it off and the reassuring text telling me she made it safe and sound pops up. Russ enters the room just as I set my phone back on the nightstand.

"Wow, you look like shit," he says before flopping onto the bed in the empty space where Juliana had slumbered.

"Thanks," I say, rolling over closer to him. "Where the fuck have you been? I've been worried sick."

"I had a job. It was far so I just stayed at a motel. I'm sure I told you; you must've just forgotten."

"No, you didn't," I fume, but he shrugs, closing his eyes and pulling the sheet over himself without bothering to undress. "I almost called the police at one point. That's how fucking scared I was."

His eyelids flip open as his expression morphs immediately to extreme agitation.

"Why the fuck would you do that? You know I hate cops. They're always lookin' for a reason to lock everyone up."

"I don't know! What if you were dead somewhere? You don't get it. I was insanely worried."

"Is that why you stink of booze and your face is swollen and red? 'Cause that doesn't seem like worry to me. Seems more like the mouse was partying while the cat was away."

"What? No. Fuck you." Rage bristles over my skin that he would dare accuse me.

He pulls the sheet to his nose and sniffs deeply. His eyes dart to me, brow furrowing deeply.

"Why does the sheet smell like a goddamn whore?"

"What?" I stammer, dumbfounded.

"Here." He tosses the sheet at me, and the faint scent of perfume wafts over me. "Smells like a slut and I know just which slut it was."

"Ugh, don't be like that, Russ. She just drank too much and crashed for a while until she sobered up. That's all."

"Sure, it's not at all that you cheated on me with that little bitch friend of yours."

"I didn't!"

"Don't lie. I know you love eating her out. You're probably fucking her behind my back every chance you get." The rage was building in him, his arm tensing under my hand.

"That was one time, forever ago, and afterward we decided we were better as just friends. You got that? *Just friends.* That's all. Nothing has ever happened between us since then." I throw off my comforter and stand up, my hands compulsively combing through my hair over and over. "Jesus fucking Christ, I wish I'd never even told you about that. I didn't think you'd hold it over my head forever."

"Well, I mean, how am I supposed to trust you around her after knowing that?" He laughs a dry, viscous snort. "And you're over here worried about me? But having your little girlfriend in our bed? Disgusting."

"I didn't say I thought you were cheating, I thought you were dead, for God's sake! And I don't know how to get it through your thick head that nothing happened!" I was yelling now, struggling to lower my voice as I see the fire roaring behind his irises.

"Listen. I work way fucking harder than you and I can't help it that sometimes it's out of town work. You need to calm your stupid ass down and realize if anyone should be angry, it should be me. You had that whore in my bed and then you're telling me you almost sent pigs out looking for me when I was just fucking working?"

When he mentions the police, the unsettling sketch suddenly fills every corner of my mind. Maybe it's my mind's eye distorting it, but as it comes into focus, it looks more like him than before.

"You know it was nothing. You *know* that." I wait a moment before I push the topic forward, knowing he'll be angrier, but I can't stop myself. "Hey, have you seen that police sketch going around by the way? Some people think it looks a little like you."

"*Some* people? You mean your filthy fuckbuddy," he scoffs. "If it's the one I've seen, then y'all need to get your eyes checked because it looks nothing like me. Actually, you know what I think?"

"What?" I cross my arms.

"I think your little girlfriend hates how hard I've been working, all the nice things I've gotten for you with my hard-earned paycheck, and she's jealous as fuck. She wants us to break up so she can have you and be miserable and poor together."

"That's stupid and untrue. Juliana—"

"It's not like you haven't fucked her."

"Come on, Russ! It was years ago, before I even met you, and we were drunk. I'd never do that to you, and Juliana and I aren't like that. She's in a relationship and so am I. You always think I'm being unfaithful when—"

"Yeah, because you don't earn my trust. Otherwise, the bed wouldn't stink of that slut. What else am I supposed to think? And then you go accusing me of being a criminal. Fucking disgusting. You know, I don't have to take this. I'm going out. We'll see if I even come home again." He doesn't look back once as he leaves the room.

"No!" I shout after him, but there's no stopping his stomping footsteps, the front door slamming behind him. My fingers reach out toward the ghost of where he'd stood a moment ago and I whisper an apology. Maybe it is wrong of me to be friends with Juliana after what happened, but it was so long ago. She's my best friend.

Curling up on the bed, I think about all the ways I could join Noah tonight. The family-sized bottle of ibuprofen, whatever else we have lying around in the medicine cabinet, and the full handle of vodka in the freezer to chase it. A long, hot bath with a scented candle and the sharpest kitchen knife against my wrists, vertical cuts so they can't stitch me up even if I get scared and call an ambulance. I think of Russ's gun and wonder if it's still down in the creek. How painful would a bullet to the brain be? Would it hurt for even a fraction of a second? I drift to sleep before I can decide. I'd like to think it's because I don't really want to do it, that my life is worth living, but deep down, it's more likely I'm just a coward.

Sydney

The man watched Sydney as she rolled her cart down the aisle. He was just another stranger at the supermarket, minding his own business as he gathered necessities and maybe a few treats. She was too tired to notice that he'd passed her three times as she zigzagged the store, drowsily collecting the items on her scrawled list. The overtime was hardly worth the sleep deprivation that she was forcing herself through as she completed her last couple errands. She couldn't wait to pass out on the couch, watching some shitty Hallmark movie, and sleep a blissful, dreamless five hours before her alarm went off.

While she dreamed of this upcoming comfort, he passed her again, watching her drop a box of microwave popcorn into her cart. This time he kept his eyes on her longer, to the end of the lane and as he turned the corner. She sensed something off, scrunched her nose, and looked around her. They locked eyes, his pupils pinpricks in a sea of cornflower blue, and then he was gone. A shiver tickled down her spine and her stomach warbled to her, unsettled, but she shook it away. He was just some creep checking her out. It happened more often than she'd like; it didn't matter that she looked half-dead and was still in her dingy uniform, mascara smeared under one eye. Creeps don't care. In fact, they seemed to like it. The more pathetic and vulnerable, the better.

She tried to forget it as she swerved into the next aisle and picked through the varieties of microwave dinners. By the time she made it to the checkout line, she'd completely forgotten him. Stepping into the crisp autumn air outside brought her out of her daydream trance, but it wasn't until she was halfway home that she noticed the red car following a little too close.

When she squinted, focusing as hard as she could in the rearview mirror, she just made out through the tinted windshield that same face. Her heart sunk into her stomach, dissolving in the acid to a sickly salve that coursed through her, nausea and sudden vertigo taking hold. She needed to pull over to vomit and find her bearings, but if he was following her, that seemed like handing herself over on a silver platter. She wanted to believe she was wrong, that it was just a coincidence, but every part of her intuition told her to fight through the panic. Keep going. Test him.

She took a slow breath, her hands trembling as they clutched the wheel, and took a right turn at random into a neighborhood. She watched in the mirror with bated breath. He turned behind her.

"Fuck," Sydney shouted, slamming her hand down against the steering wheel. Just to make sure, she passed a few streets and took another right turn. The red car followed. A myriad of terrible scenarios, each one worse than the last, invaded her mind, soaking every last nerve in a serum of complete terror. The animalistic brainstem impulse gnawed into her, panicked whispers of *get away* beat against her eardrums.

A surge of bile climbed her throat and coated her mouth, but she swallowed it back down. Going home was the only thing she craved, but to lead him there would be stupid. Even if she made it into the building and he didn't know exactly which apartment was hers, he'd still know where she lived and could case it, wait for her to emerge again, or even worse, sneak in behind some tenant and find her. She shuddered to imagine looking through her peephole and seeing those eyes. She'd have to lead him away. She tried to remember the way to the nearest police station or firehouse, but her mind was blank. Finally, after a few more turns through the neighborhood and getting back onto the larger street, she had a plan.

Every breath was cobwebbed with anxiety as she pulled into the diner parking lot. The bright wall of windows faced the parking lot. The red car turned in, but as Sydney pulled in broad view of the eyes of every patron and server, the blue-eyed man tucked his car between two dark SUVs, the shadows of early evening nestling him in obscurity.

Sydney bolted into the restaurant, panic racing through every synapse. The car idled in the parking lot. Watched through the glass door, it waited a moment then eased out of the space, back onto the road. He was gone.

"Are you okay?" a waitress asked, startling Sydney who turned with a gasp.

"Oh, yeah. Sorry."

"What's wrong? Do you need help?"

"Uh, I–I don't," she stammered as she held herself in her own tight embrace, swiveling from side to side in an attempt to self-soothe, "I don't know. A man. He was following me, I think. I don't know."

"What? Did you get his license plate?" The server waved down another, both nervous and staring with furrowed brows.

"We can call the police for you," the second server said, pulling out his phone.

"I didn't even think to–" Sydney didn't get the rest of her sentence out before her emotions crested and crashed over her in a tidal wave of sobs and unexpected tears. The servers reached out with hesitant hands, a gentle squeeze of her shoulder, a half hug. Embarrassed, Sydney broke away from the contact. "No, I'm sorry. I think I'm just confused. I'm so fucking tired."

"Let me get you a coffee, on the house," the first server offered, her voice bubbling with the prospect of being helpful, settling this uncomfortable situation.

"Thank you. I think I need it before I drive home. I feel like I'm losing it." Sydney tried to laugh it off, but everyone's smiles were forced on like masks as they festered in the jarring, surreal moment like insects under a magnifying glass.

Birdie

Noah's headstone glistens, the gold specks in the granite like glitter in the sun. The corner of my mouth twitches up in a smile for just a second. He'd always loved glitter. Any kind of arts and crafts we made, he'd insist on a finishing touch of goopy lines and droplets of Elmer's glue covered in glitter. At the time, I'd moaned and dreaded the cleanup after he'd finished his dazzling mess, but looking back, I cherish those moments more than anything. Everything about Noah sparkled and shone.

I set the bundle of blue hydrangeas and a little green matchbox car along the stone before lowering myself to the ground. With one arm hooked around the cool granite, my bare legs pressed against the manicured grass, and my eyes shut tight, I pretend that I can feel him there. If only I could hold him one more time, tell him I love him, plant a soft kiss on his little forehead, apologize for everything.

"What are you doing here?" the voice startles me, but I recognize it without opening my eyes.

"I'm allowed to visit our son, Charlie."

"You know I visit him on Fridays. We agreed you wouldn't be here then." The way his voice hisses through clenched teeth, I know exactly the look of rage on his face, but I still don't open my eyes.

"I'm sorry. I didn't even realize it was Friday. My schedule's been so hectic and—"

"Just leave. I want to be alone with my son."

A bolt of anger surges across my shoulder blades and down my back, the muscles contracting and seizing painfully. I open my eyes, turn to glare back into the hatred waiting for me.

"He's my son too. You don't get to order me away."

"Don't start. We both know why I asked to never see you again, and I'm not bringing it up here, in front of him. This is a peaceful place. A place to remember my *son*. Just leave." There's no anger, only a devastated broken man, with tears rolling down his round cheeks.

He looks so different from the last time I saw him. He was always solidly built, but now the muscle has softened and drooped. The hairline I remember as a widow's peak has receded back too far to call it anything but balding. There are deep lines under his eyes, at their corners, and between his brows, giving him the appearance of someone much older than his early thirties. Lines that only formed during these last couple years as our lives became nothing but a thin veneer of acceptance, guilt, and regret.

Still, despite these changes, some of Charlie is the same. His hazel eyes, whether filled with tears or rage or love, always glisten in their entrancing multicolored way. Even as he scowls, looking like a different man than the one I'd once called my husband, I see the young man I fell in love with behind it all.

"Charlie, I'm sorry. I didn't mean to upset you." I stand, my shoulders slumped forward as I cave into myself, trying to disappear. "I'll leave." I walk a few steps away before everything crumbles, and I'm crying, hunched over as I try to force my body to leave. "I just miss my baby so much."

I didn't mean to say it. I'm sure Charlie will think it's a guilt trip, a shot of manipulation for trying to get me to leave, but it's not. There's nothing truer than the words that slipped free.

There's a hand on my shoulder. Then arms wrapping around me, embracing me, hands grasping me tightly. He's crying on my shoulder, his head buried in my blouse. We lower ourselves in what feels like slow-motion to the ground, crying together the way we did at his funeral, and for hours in our living room after everyone had left.

When we've both cried out every last tear there could be squeezed from us, we're left two awkward, desiccated husks, leaning against the other for exhausted support. He's the first to stand. His fingers wrap around my arm, tug me to my feet next to him. We don't speak, but all the anger has left his eyes, and he pats my shoulder twice before turning to walk back and sit with Noah. I understand, but it takes all my strength to lift my feet, one step at a time, and leave the cemetery. Noah will still be there tomorrow. He'll always be there. Even knowing that, I feel like I'm abandoning him, and though my face contorts to cry, scrunching up in red gasping breaths, there's nothing left. I drive home a ghost.

Russ is on me right away with his bloodhound nose. Somehow, he always knows if I've so much as smiled at another man.

"Who is he?"

"What are you talking about?"

"Don't try to deny it, Birdie. You smell like cheap, shitty cologne. Who is he?"

I stammer through some nonsense syllables. The truth is innocent, and yet impossible to get out. He never understands my visits to Noah. I know he thinks I should just forget about him, move on with my life, but it's not like that. Life doesn't work like that.

"Who the hell were you out fucking?" he shouts, bringing his face so close to mine that I can smell the hint of a cigarette behind the freshly brushed teeth, our noses nearly touching.

"No, it's not like that. I wasn't fucking anyone. Jesus Christ." I back away a step, but he follows, his aggressive breathing hot on my face. "I went to see Noah, and I forgot it was Friday, so Charlie was there—"

"Oh, I see. I see how it is. Goddammit!" He stomps the floor so hard I'm surprised it doesn't go straight through the linoleum to the crawl space below. I startle but refuse to back down.

"Stop it! I didn't do anything wrong."

"You're asking me to believe that you just ran into your ex at your kid's grave and through that briefest of interactions, you now stink of him all over like you've been rolling in his fucking bed?"

"No, I...see, it's just—" Once again my words fail me, and as a consequence, I've made myself look guilty. I feel the rage rising in Russ like a kettle coming to a boil.

"How could you? After all I've done for you? You're just out there fucking whoever you want. No. Worse. You're fucking that scumbag that treated you like absolute shit. Is that what you want from me? Would you fuck me more often if I treated you like that?"

"I didn't fuck him. I just started crying, and then he was crying, and we ended up hugging for like a minute. It was no big deal."

"I'm supposed to just believe you? You come home over an hour after your shift ends, I'm here worried sick about you, thinking you might've died in a fucking car crash or something, and you're telling me you were just hugging and crying with your ex-husband? Listen to yourself. You're fucking unbelievable, you know that? I'm outta here." He pushes past me, but I grab onto his arm, fresh tears having formed behind my eyes now slipping down my face.

"No, don't go. I mean it! I wasn't fucking anybody. I just missed Noah. That's all. I swear to God, that's all it was." I hate the way I become a worm, lashing myself around him, cowering and pleading for him to stay. "Please, don't leave! I'm sorry!"

"Let go of me," he says, pulling his arm free of my desperately grasping fingers. "Fine, I won't leave. I need a fucking smoke." And just like that, I have to let him go, out through the screen door, and pray he doesn't walk out of my life forever.

I hold my breath as he walks onto the porch, takes one step down toward the truck, and then stops. He pulls the smashed pack of cigarettes from his back pocket and takes one between his teeth, lights it, and as the smoke leaves his lungs, I feel the tension break just a little. Enough for me to breathe again.

On quiet, hesitant steps, I make my way to the door frame and watch his back as he smokes, trying to read his emotions through the way his muscles tense and any tiny shift of posture. Each puff spreads out halo-like around his head before dissipating into the air around him. I wait until a feeling of safety, nebulous and undefinable, settles around us. Then I approach him, stand next to him, and finally take his hand in mine. He doesn't pull away, but he also doesn't look at me.

"I don't know if you're telling the truth about the cemetery or lying, but I know either way, you won't be making that mistake again." His tone has the hard, gravel quality of a man attempting to be stern, but it's broken by the slightest hints of the hurt beneath his words.

"I won't. I promise." I cuddle against his arm, nuzzling it like a cat.

"You'd better not, or else I'm outta here. And I mean it."

I nod and I believe him. I don't deserve a man who loves me so purely, so profoundly.

Juliana

When I pull up to Birdie's trailer, she's waiting outside, her arms wrapped around herself in a tight hug. A deep sigh eases out of my lungs. *Here we go again*, I think, watching her slide into the passenger seat.

"Thanks for picking me up. Russ forgot I needed to grab some groceries when he left, and I hate taking all those bags on the bus, it's such a pain, and—"

I cut off her breathless, apologetic rambling with a soft smile and hand on her shoulder. *Oh Birdie. Birdie, Birdie, Birdie.* I mask my disappointment with a veil of pure sympathy. *When is she going to wake up and see this fucking mess she's in?*

"Hey, no need for all that. It's not a big deal. I needed a few things anyway, and you're on the way." I watch her shoulders relax, a timid smile creeping across her lips. "Plus, you know I love the company."

"Still," she looks me in the eye, "Thank you. I appreciate it."

"Of course."

By the time we're in the produce aisle, she's calmed down and chatting away about some series she's halfway through that Russ won't watch with her even though "it's incredible." Her hands dart around in her usual dramatic way of acting out everything she says when she's excited, and her laugh comes easily, yet I can feel some kind of anxiety or fear bubbling just under the surface. Something she's dying to tell me but not sure how to put into words. I know her so well, I anticipate exactly when she's going to bring it up, and I'm spot on. As soon as we've loaded the groceries in the back, she's biting at her cuticles, and the second I put the truck in reverse, it all comes pouring out, exactly as I'd expected.

"So, I ran into Charlie when I was visiting Noah."

"Oh?"

"It was awkward, but kind of…I don't know…nice?" Her eyes shimmer with a sheen of tears and I swallow my words. Now is a time to listen.

"Hmm," I hum with a nod, trying to keep my face as neutral and sympathetic as I could so she can get it all out, but I already feel that there's something cruel lurking in the rest of the story, and that thing is Russ.

"When I got home, Russ knew. I don't know how, but he did. Said he smelled him on me. Fuck, maybe that's true. I have no idea." Her eyes refuse to meet mine, and my heart breaks for the shame hidden under that curtain of dark lashes. "He thinks I've been cheating on him. Even after I swore it wasn't true, he let it go, but I can still feel a strain between us and it's killing me. He's so suspicious, and I haven't done anything wrong. Have I?"

"Girl, you know you haven't." My hand shoves the stick into park again. I need to give her all my focus right now. "Listen, yeah, most people wouldn't like their partner hanging out with an ex, but this is different. Charlie is the only other person who understands the pain you have about Noah. He's the only one who knew him like you did. Russ needs to realize this and support you. As long as you're not actually fucking Charlie, I don't see how he dare get jealous like that."

"But I was hugging him. Crying on his shoulder. I probably did smell like him. Fuck. You know Charlie always wears that strong cologne. I feel terrible. Maybe he was right to be mad. I just–" But she can't continue. Tears choke the rest of her words from her throat.

"You love Russ, and there's nothing I can do to change that, and maybe he even loves you too, but you need to take a step back and realize this isn't healthy." I tiptoe over the words as gently as I can, but I feel her pulling away, closing up in defense. "I'm not telling you to break up with him, mainly because I know you won't." I laugh to break the tension, but it doesn't work, so I continue. "Seriously though, you need to go on a solo trip and really work through this on your own. Maybe you can go see your mom? Or sister? I know you're not close, so maybe not, but even staying by yourself or with me for a few days, just to look at everything with a clear mind, I think it'd do you wonders."

"No, I can't do that. Mom doesn't give a shit, that's why I don't talk to her, and Tamara completely cut me out. And you know I can't afford to stay at a motel or anything. Money's already so tight." She glances up at me and then back to her lap. "And I love you, but I know you'll just try to convince me to leave him, plus Russ'll know where I'm at and come looking for me. He'd never let me do that."

"Don't you hear yourself? That's not right." I mean the words to be gentle, but they are pure venom, and I regret them right away. Birdie closes up like a clam.

"Please, just take me home. I can give you a little money for gas."

"No, it's fine. Like I said, I needed to go anyway."

We drive back to her home in silence, but I know she's not angry. She knows what I said is true, but she's too beat up and broken to do a thing about it. Someday, I won't be able to stand to watch her fall apart like this anymore. My life gets more complicated and I get more tired every year. I know there'll be a day I lack the energy to shake her loose from his spell, show her a glimmer of the truth behind the lies. But not yet. She needs a friend and I'll stay that for her. Poor thing needs love, and the world just spits on her every chance they get, but I wish she didn't welcome it, basically beg for it, like she does.

She opens the car door but hesitates for a second.

"Can I call you later? Just to chitchat, you know?" There's a desperation in her voice that shatters any tinge of negativity I'd ever felt toward her.

"You got it, girlie. Hope the new recipe turns out good. Can't wait to hear about it."

She smiles and pushes the door closed so softly it barely latches. I watch her walk to the door and slip inside, holding my breath as if I could stop her if I concentrated hard enough. Closing my eyes a moment, I pray that she figures out her worth before it's too late, then I pull out of the gravel driveway and head home.

Sydney

The man was waiting in his car for hours before Sydney pulled into the parking garage. Her tires swooshed quietly through the puddles slowly collected from the day of drizzle, climbing each ramp slow and deliberate, with her never knowing what was waiting on the third floor.

He looked out the tinted window, knowing he was concealed. Watched her sit staring at her phone for several minutes behind her steering wheel, oblivious to his gaze. Once, she looked up, her head quickly checking out both windows, as if a bubble of fear in her stomach had alerted her, but she batted it away with a few blinks. Back to scrolling, her shoulders set a little higher she tried to disappear into her own world. But he was watching. Waiting.

She scanned the garage around her again when she grabbed her purse and finally exited her car, but there was nothing out of the ordinary about the line of cars on either side, their interiors dark and empty. Her heels clacked along the concrete, gingerly stepping over a puddle, when she heard a car door close. She paused for a second. Footsteps, faster than they should be. She glanced over her shoulder as she forced her legs to keep moving her forward. A man in a navy sweatshirt, the hood pulled down low, obscuring his eyes, was gaining on her. A tiny yelp escaped her throat and bounced against the damp walls.

Still, she wasn't sure he was after her. That seemed like something in a movie or that happened in the bad part of town. Not here in her high-end apartment complex. Her mind raced, urging her to take in every possible escape route around her. A red emergency exit sign glowed over the door to the stairs, next to the elevator that always took so long to arrive. And around a corner, she saw a sliver of the door that led to her floor, a maze of glossy hallways. Three turns and she'd be at her doorstep. But would he follow her there? Her stomach cramped at the decision in front of her.

The man panted, his footsteps slapping through the puddles she'd carefully avoided. *No. It couldn't be true. And yet it was. He was after her.*

She made her choice, bolted toward the door into the apartments. Even if she couldn't make it home, someone would hear her scream. They'd stop him, call the police, do something, *anything* to help her. A rattling wail gathered in her vocal cords, held back by ropes of anxiety that threatened to choke her with every step. Her hand closed around the handle, wrenched it open, and she thrust herself through it. Her feet flew over the stairs, landing on every other step as her hands grasped for the handrail, pulling herself onward.

But he was right behind her.

Closer.

And closer.

The wail broke free like the whinny of a wild mare. Her heel caught on the edge of the next step and her ankle twisted under her weight. She kept going, gritting her teeth through the pain of her weight on the hobbled foot, but she had to continue. He was there. Behind her now. Reaching out for the railing, her legs failing her, she felt his fingers at the tip of her ponytail as it bobbed up behind her.

"No." It wasn't a scream, only a whimper as she tumbled down the flight to the next landing. Her knees burned as they scraped against the dirty, rough floor, but she ignored it as best as she could, attempting to scramble to her feet. He was there, wrapping his arms around her, confining her. Again, a whimper fell from her lips, splintered into shards of soft sound on the ground below them. "No."

He took his time, confident from his previous stakeouts that the stairwell was rarely used, and she made little sound to draw unwanted attention. There was only the softest pleading through thick sobs, followed by the terrible gurgle of asphyxia, which made his eyes reel back in his head with wild pleasure. He timed his own release with hers. A brutal, feral moment shared between them, of man's two basest drives.

The difficult part was the cleanup. He'd never killed somewhere so public before, and as soon as the glaze of euphoria faded, a mild panic he'd not expected crept into his throat. But he'd planned the whole scenario down to each minute detail as he'd done before, so he put faith in his plan, dragging the corpse down the stairs as quietly as possible, her shoes making a soft thud as they limply landed on each step.

The trickle of rainwater slowly draining through the seams of the building was the only sound that greeted him when he peeked out from the doorway. The rows of cars sat in silent reverence, foreboding in their dark emptiness. Not a sign of life anywhere. He let his adrenaline lead him through the process he'd rehearsed meticulously when he lay in bed at night, staring at the ceiling. The whistle of an approaching storm cut through the quiet, but it didn't startle him. He continued, methodical and detached.

He carried her like a bride over the threshold across the garage. She was heavier in death than her small frame would appear, but he gritted his teeth through the ache in his bad knee, exacerbated by the rain.

The metal bin in the corner of the garage was rusted at the corners and streaked with unidentifiable sludge of brown and black. He opened the door and shoved the body inside. Refuse tightly wrapped in white and black plastic bags awaited Sydney, a bed of pillowy garbage, and when the man looked down at her body, arms and legs splayed out, head turned to the side, hair billowing out like a golden halo, eyes closed, relaxed, even peaceful, he wished he could reach to check her pulse because he could've sworn she was only sleeping. But as he furrowed his brows, searched her beautiful, young face, watched her chest to see if it rose and fell in the slightest indication of life, he observed the dark mottled rainbow encircling her neck, and he was reassured.

With a bang, a new bag was added to the pile as it fell through the chute, landing to half obscure her face. He didn't close the doors. The key was left in place for any tenant to use, an obvious lazy, safety hazard, but it sparked a flicker of delight in the man. He could watch.

The metal plate pressed against Sydney with slow, unstoppable force. The man watched as she became less than a person, compressed into the bed of garbage. Bones snapped and tore through skin like tissue paper, blood weeping out in thick, gelatinous red so dark it was nearly black. He wished he could see her face, but it had been buried right away, so he settled for salivating over the mangled remains. When the plate pulled back, it was stained by the shameful job it'd been forced to carry out. The man closed the door on the mess he'd orchestrated, wiped the handle with a cloth even though he still wore gloves, and walked back to his car.

Birdie

Russ sets his hand on my thigh as he drives. His eyes are on the road, but he's smiling. I know he always loves that soft, thin cotton feel of my sundresses and I love the warmth of his hand through them. He hasn't touched me in days, so it's electric and sets my head spinning, giddy like it's full of iridescent bubbles. It's a good day. The kind that makes it all worthwhile.

We're way out in the country, driving through rolling hills of green with the occasional cow grazing beyond endless fences before Russ starts to nod the way he does when he's remembering something. We must be nearing the special spot he had in mind for our picnic. When I notice a shock of trees planted close together at the bottom of a hill, a frog pond to one side and no buildings in sight for miles, I'm sure that's where we're heading.

I smile to myself when he pulls off the highway and says, "There we go. The perfect spot for our date."

We leave our shoes in the car. Soft grass under bare feet is a grounding feeling unlike anything else. It makes me feel like a child again, and the way he hurries me along to just the right spot overlooking the tiny scenic view he picked out, makes me giddy and lightheaded. The red checkered blanket bellows out like a balloon before drifting down into place. I didn't have a picnic basket, and the backpack ruins the ambiance a little, so I unpack the treats right away and hide it under the corner of the blanket.

Russ doesn't mind. He's brushing my arm with fingertips, leaning against me, holding me to his chest. He doesn't talk much, instead using his touch to tell me everything I need to know.

He smiles but there's a sadness written in the lines on his forehead. Still, I languish in the way he props my chin up with his fingertips, leaning in but lingering a moment, our lips so close that the spark of excitement seems to leap between them before he kisses me.

I melt. In these tender times when he gives me his heart, makes me feel that I'm all his and he's all mine, there's nothing he could do to ever lose me. He pulls away and takes my breath with him. The same quietly sad smile flickers across his lips.

"Do you remember that gun? It was several months ago, but I had it in—"

"Of course I remember. Why are you talking about that?" Reality snaps back sharply into focus, but he's just toeing the soft earth like a sheepish boy. A mild anger boils in my gut that he would ruin this moment for us.

"I've just been thinking about that a lot and wanted to say thank you for getting rid of it. You know those dark thoughts I get sometimes, and I've got no business owning a gun. When you took it, got rid of it for me,

I knew you really loved me. Sometimes it just feels like nobody cares, like nobody ever fucking cared, but you, Birdie, I know you care." He kisses me again, not hard and passionate like he wants me, but soft as if I'm made of spun sugar. It's a kiss that brings me back to when we were first dating.

"Babe, you know I care about you and would never want anything bad to happen to you, not ever!" I plant my own kiss on his lips and feel its sloppiness ruin the moment. I always do that. "We're meant to be together until we're old and gray, rocking on some front porch, holding hands and drinking coffee every morning."

Then he looked at me with a startling clarity, his eyes so pale blue that they were like holes straight through to the sky behind him, and his voice got deadly serious.

"I don't wanna live to get old and fall apart. Hurting all over and half outta my mind like my grandaddy. Never gonna be like that." His honesty penetrated my soul, sending a cold shiver through me, but I couldn't look away. "No, not like that. See, I know how I wanna die, but that's why I need you to have the gun, not me, otherwise I'll make a rash decision and end it all too soon. But someday, and it's probably a long way off, but you'll know when it comes, I want you to get that gun back, and you just blow me straight outta this world into the next. Do you understand?"

I could hardly form my question, my voice stuttering against my shaking jaw. "What?"

"You're gonna walk outside with me on that day, and it's gonna be a beautiful day, just like this one. Not too hot, not too cold. All blue skies and puffy white clouds, sunshine pouring down on us. Absolutely gorgeous. And then you're gonna shoot me in the face. Just take me out, pow, just like that." He closed my open jaw with his fingertips the same as he'd done earlier, gentle and calm, like he didn't just say the craziest thing I'd ever heard.

"I'd never do that. I can't believe you'd joke around like that. It makes me sick."

Imagining the gun in my hand, his lovely face looking at me, urging me to do it is too much. I struggle to catch my breath.

"Aw, come on. You'd do it for me."

"No!"

"Yes, you will. Because you're the only one in this whole fucking world that understands." The rough skin of his palm grazes down my bare shoulder. "You're the only one who loves me enough to put me outta my misery, babe."

"Stop it. No, I wouldn't, Russ. And I hate you even talking like that. I don't get it, and I don't want you to ever talk about dying and death and all that shit again." I'm so worked up, I raise my lip like a dog and spit into the dirt, not even caring that I don't look cute for him. The audacity of bringing up this strange request when things had finally felt normal again sends me into a fury. "Jesus, I can't believe you would even suggest something like that."

But he's laughing as I finish speaking, and a flush of foolishness roams over my skin, turning me red and patchy. Had he been joking?

"Eh, you know what, just forget I said anything," he says, wrapping his arms around me and kissing me before I can say anything else. Still, I can't get it out of my mind. Even as his hand slips its way past my skirt, fingertips brushing against me with tickling pressure, I keep imagining a gun in my hand, muzzle pressed against his cheek, and him smiling, framed by a blue sky, a crown of fluffy clouds, before I blow a hole in him, pieces of skull and brain matter fluttering around us in slow motion. I pull away.

"No, I don't want to. Well, just not yet. I need a minute. My stomach feels weird."

"What? You love it when I touch you like this," he whispers in my ear, breathy and full of playful lust, but as I pull away again, his tone changes. "Are you serious? Stop being weird about it and come here."

"I just don't know why you have to say things like that. Now I can't get it out of my head."

"Fine." He pushes me away and as I nearly tip over, I watch the regret move like a shadow across his face. With the snap of a synapse, he's back to his caring, confident self, every trace of contempt washed from his face, and he's grabbing my waist, pulling me close. "Careful, my clumsy baby bird."

My hair tumbles loose down my back and over my shoulders as he releases it from the clip that'd held it in place. Soft lips pressed against my neck, but no more roving hands. I hold him close, my hands pressing him to me by the shoulder blades. I know it's his way of apologizing. I know every bit of his personality, the complicated nonverbal language of his love, and the way to make him feel how he wants: loved, but never not in control. I let him think he controls every bit of me because I love him so.

I meekly protest with giggles before I give in, starting as a performance of sighs and moans before finally summiting my own climax after I let the words from earlier fall away and immerse myself in the physical moment, his panting hot in my ear. When we're both satisfied, we put ourselves together enough to bask in the sun and enjoy the picnic I'd painstakingly curated that morning. All of his favorite treats, even the marmalade they only stock in the spring and the little crackers he loves it on. I'd squirreled some away back then, saving them for a special occasion, and when he surprised me this morning and told me to pack a picnic lunch, I knew it was the right time to dazzle.

"Where'd you get these? You always say they're out after April," he asks, crumbs flying out of his mouth, but I brush them away from the blanket before he gets embarrassed or any ants notice.

"My little secret."

Things feel good again. He's all over me, and I don't try to fend him off. There's no need for more games. We make love again in the grass, in full sun and full view of anyone who might wander by, but nobody does. We are completely ourselves, animalistic and in love, the scent of hot skin and sweat filling my head until my thoughts are a jumble of uninhibited ecstasy.

Russ always knows these beautiful, remote spots in the countryside. He points them out when we're driving sometimes and tells me we're going back there. One that looks nice for a picnic, one that looks nice for an impromptu lover's lane, one that would be a good camping trip, though it's private property so we'll have to come late so no one notices. He's so observant, and the memory of an elephant. When he points them out, I see something compute in his eyes, like he's memorizing the coordinates for later. It's a strange talent, but perfect for getaways like this one. Yet another thing I love about my Russ that the world doesn't get to see. I wish he'd open up to more people, especially my family. Then they'd understand why I stay, even when things are hard. The good parts are always worth it. I always say, his love is stronger than the flowery stuff everyone else gives. His love is like a precious metal, hidden under layers of dirt and grime, but once you wipe it clean, maybe even crack it open, the glitter inside is invaluable.

When we're finished, he rolls away and cleans himself off with a cloth napkin while I bask in the glow of afternoon. A breeze ripples across the hills, the grass bowing under it, until it reaches my naked body and sends a shiver across my skin for a second before the sun warms it away. I pull my dress down over my head, rubbing my arms and letting out a sigh.

"Not many days left like this. Fall will be here any day now." I glance at him, but he's looking far away, over the hills, past the horizon. "Did you feel that? Definitely blowing in soon."

"Why do you stay with me?"

"What?"

"You heard me. You're not dumb like the other girls, Birdie. I don't get it. You know I'm a bad person." He turns and our eyes lock. There's something broken and brimming with sorrow in his gaze, unlike anything I've ever seen before. "Please, just run away. Run away from me. I don't want to hurt you."

"But... I love you." The words fall out. I couldn't think of anything else to say.

He's on me, pouncing like a tiger, knocking me to my back against the soiled picnic blanket. Kissing me hard. Too hard. His teeth knock into me, bite my lip and pull it like a puppy, a hint of copper dribbling onto my tongue. His hands rove up my body, but they are not his hands. These hands are rough, wild, ripping my dress at the seam, and then they reach my neck and encircle it. He pulls away enough for our eyes to lock again, and I recoil at the coldness there. But it only lasts a second.

He collapses on me, burying his head against my bosom, nosing under the fabric as if he wanted to hide his head in my dress. His back trembles and I feel the tears forming a river between my breasts, puddling wetly where my dress cinches at the waist. I wish I knew how to comfort him, but my mind's gone blank. Rubbing his back and shushing him like a mother calms an infant back to sleep, I feel him cry soundlessly against me for what seems a long time.

When he's finished, he sits up, his eyes rimmed red and swollen, and my dress soaked but his face dry. He sniffles a little and sits back next to me, looking down at the tiny forest and its miniature pond at the bottom of the hill.

"Don't you dare ever leave me." His tone is surprisingly harsh, not a plea but a command. I nod, but he doesn't turn to look. He waits a moment and repeats himself. "Don't you dare ever leave me, you hear?"

"Yes, I hear you. Don't worry. I'm not going anywhere."

This seems to satisfy him, and his shoulders relax. I want more than anything to ask him what that was about, but he'd never tell me. He's not big on sharing his feelings, forever intensely private. I probably know him better than anyone else on Earth, and yet I hardly know him at all. If he doesn't divulge it of his own free will, there's no knowing what's on his mind. But that's okay because he needs me. We need each other.

Ava

The man doesn't cause alarm when any of the women he follows first notice him. At least, not any more than any other man would. He's attractive, in shape, tall, a man who works with his hands but dresses a bit above his station, like he hopes to climb the ladder into a cushy white-collar job before middle age sneaks up on him. His smirky smile and ice blue eyes are first striking, then disarming. Most women smile back when they see him. Some likely because they've been trained to smile at strange men to ward off danger, don't look too eager but polite enough, but others are flattered, maybe a little interested in the good looking man smiling their way.

The second time Ava saw him, in the darkening evening after a long day at work, she was a little more uneasy. She felt him watch the fear flicker across her face. Alarm rose in her belly, but she didn't want to jump to conclusions. *Isn't that the same man as before? No, I must be mistaken. Just hurry along. Don't stare. You'll just egg him on.*

She scurried to her car, trying to walk calmly but knowing by the clacking rhythm of her heels she was moving noticeably too fast. *He knows I'm scared. Does that matter?* The thoughts flashed through her mind as she pulled out her keys and got into her car, tapping the door lock as soon as she was safely inside.

Ava looked over where the man still stood, staring after her. A shudder ran down her spine, but she tried to play it off. *Always anxious, it's so silly. Maybe I should talk to my doctor about adding anxiety meds to the usual cocktail.*

She started the car, sipping in a long breath, but when her eyes rose from the dash back to the man, she jumped. He was slightly closer. Only a step or two, but definitely closer. He was also still smirking. Was there something hostile in it or was her mind playing tricks on her? He raised one hand in a wave of acknowledgement, telling her he knew she was watching. She gave a quick wave back and hated herself a little for being so damn nice. Then it was over. She drove home, but the interaction haunted her for days.

The next time she saw the blonde man with the bright blue eyes at the agency, she looked up from the mockup she was working on and there he stood. He was in a delivery uniform, speaking with Jody at the reception desk, laughing and leaning forward in an obviously flirtatious way. A small part of her felt almost jealous, but mostly she was relieved. There was something about him that gave her a queasy nervous feeling despite his good looks, and she was glad someone else was dealing with him. *It'd be so awkward if he brought up their strange exchange in the parking lot.* She blushed to think of it, shook her head to banish the thought. *It's alright. Jody's got it.* Still, she hunched slightly over her desk, ducking away under the low-walled cubicle so he couldn't catch a recognizable glimpse of her and remember.

A few minutes later, she'd nearly forgotten he was there until Jody came to her and gently tapped her on the shoulder. When she turned and removed her earbuds, she was struck by the way both Jody and the man, still at the front, were staring with expectant, excited smiles.

"Yes?" she asked, drawn out long and slow, her brow furrowed.

"You have a secret admirer," Jody said in that infantile sing-song voice she hated. She could feel her face turn ashen and her heart dropped into her stomach with a painful thump.

"What?"

Brandishing a huge, annoying smile, Jody brought up a trio of tiered boxes wrapped in gold foil and tied together with a red ribbon. She set it in front of Ava, who stared wide-eyed, pushing her chair away from the chocolates as if she'd set a poisonous snake in front of her.

"What the hell?"

"Yeah, that delivery guy just dropped these off. I know, I know, I'm too nosy, but I read the little card and it just says 'from a secret admirer' and now I'm all invested. Who do you think sent these? Ava! Did you get a boyfriend and not tell me about it?"

As Jody rambled on, Ava's eyes darted to the front counter, but the man was gone. Her intestines twisted and cramped as she excused herself in a mumbled whisper from the gushing Jody. As soon as she'd made it to the bathroom, locked away in the privacy of a stall, she burst into tears. There'd been no one for months. Who would have sent that? Was the man stalking her? She dried her eyes with toilet paper, blotting her makeup back into place as well as she could, and tried to compose herself. She was making too big of a deal of it all. That man *could* just be a delivery man. A coincidence. Who did she think she was to have a stalker? She couldn't even get a date. With a deep breath, she emerged from the bathroom as close to normal as she could manage.

The chocolates sat on her desk all day, untouched, and just before she left, she slipped them into the trashcan when no one was looking.

Ava didn't see the man again for a few days. Her guard lowered with each day. She regretted not taking the chocolates home and eating them in the bath as an indulgent treat, though she still couldn't figure out who might've sent them. She narrowed it down to a few clingy exes, guys she only saw a couple times before ghosting. They were the most likely suspects. The more time that passed, the more she let herself believe it was all in her head. An overreaction from being paranoid after listening to too many true crime podcasts.

When she got home after a particularly grueling shift, dog-tired and ready to slap on a green tea facemask and down a bottle of wine, she barely registered the lingering smell of a cigarette outside her front door, and didn't notice the already unlocked back door, even when she opened it to let her cat, Sprinkles, out.

A woman's raspy voice sang the blues along a smooth baseline from the speakers as the microwave beeped to alert her that the frozen meal was ready. She took it out, dumped it in a bowl and peppered it a little, trying to doctor it to look a little more appetizing, like the unrealistic picture on the packaging. She didn't hear the footsteps, so slow, so careful with even pressure, sneaking up behind her.

The spicy warmth of the Syrah coated her mouth and throat. She took another sip, set the glass down, and leaned back into the cushions. Something above her caught her attention. She looked up and saw burning-bright azure eyes, hard as diamonds, cutting into her. The man brought the cord around her neck, immediately tightening it.

Ava instinctively tried to spring forward, but the cord dug deeper into her neck. Her hands became claws, fingers prying to make room under the cord and give her a chance at another breath, but the cord held tight. She grabbed behind her. There were the man's hands around some sort of stick, a mechanism that tightened harder than brute human strength could allow. She scratched blindly at his hands, at where his face should've been, but he'd considered her nails and positioned himself away, just out of reach.

The man spoke to her, but the sound of blood pooling against her eardrums was too loud for her to hear.

She wanted to curse herself for not trusting her instincts, for not noticing that something was off, but there was no room for those thoughts in her brain. Instead, every bit was filled with the pounding drumbeat of survival, the darkness encroaching with every passing second. Somehow, she managed to stand, but the man brought her back down in an instant, falling face-first into the cushions. Her eyes bulged, eyelashes scraping against the microfiber as they frantically fluttered. She stared into the dark green of the couch, the clouds of black coming in from all sides. Ava thought of everyone she'd ever loved as her brain shut down and settled into an eternal sleep. She thought of her father last and wished she had called him more often. Then the darkness consumed her.

Birdie

I'm stacking sodas on the shelf, my lower back aching and thinking about what to make for dinner, when I see Charlie walking down the aisle towards me. Instantly, a chill runs through my body, my sweat-soaked pits and temples freezing. I scramble to do something with my hands, but the cardboard cases suddenly feel awkward and too heavy.

"Birdie, hey. God, I'm sorry. You look so frazzled," he says as he reaches me. I hate him for saying that. It's made me simultaneously sweat and shiver even more.

"I just didn't expect to see you here. You *know* I work here."

"Yeah, that's why I came actually. I just... well, honestly, I feel like a total dick for what happened at the cemetery the other day. I've been going through a lot of stuff, but one thing I've been focusing on with my therapist is forgiving you and that wasn't very forgiving of me to act that way to you. I know you loved Noah too, despite everything."

We stand staring at our feet, not daring to look each other in the face in case we start wailing or kissing. There's a warmth between us even after all of our history, and I know that warmth is the memory of Noah.

"Listen, I have something for you." I watch as he digs around in the shopping bag strapped across his chest. He seems to find it as his eyes dart up to me, hard and serious. "Now don't be mad at me for keeping this from you because I'm giving it to you now. When Mariah and I were cleaning everything out of the house, I found this and I've kept it in a box all this time because I just couldn't handle seeing it, feeling it, god, even smelling it. It still smells like him."

Charlie's hand emerges and I gasp. He's holding Rover. Noah's small plush dog, made of blue terrycloth with black bead eyes and a crescent smile of thread across his muzzle. It's Rover. I thought he'd been lost forever.

"I looked everywhere for him." The words are only a whisper choked out through my throat, so tight I can't get enough breath to my lungs and the world whirls around me. "Rover was his favorite."

"I know." Charlie holds the toy in a tight grasp, and I want to grab it, pry it from his hands and bring it to my face, smell the faintly dusty scent with a hint of Noah's skin, but I don't. I wait, my eyes glued to the toy, my bottom lip quivering. "A part of me thinks you still don't deserve this, but after seeing you the other day, and talking with my therapist, I decided to dig ol' Rover out and give him to you. If I'm never going to hold him and smell our sweet boy again, then at least someone should." He holds the dog out to me, his hand shaking just perceptibly, and I snatch it. The smell is there, just like he said, just like I imagined. Tears run down my face as I sob into the stuffed dog and breathe in my Noah, after all these years.

"Consider this my olive branch, okay? The war is over. Let's just agree to respect each other's space and mourn our boy in private."

"Yes, yes. Of course. Thank you," I force out, the words thick with snot and grief. Charlie nods, his face relieved but graver than before as he turns and leaves. I stuff Rover in my back pocket, his head sticking out, and check to make sure he's still there every few minutes for the rest of my shift. There's an unexpected comfort having him back, like a piece of Noah is with me again.

After clocking out, I tuck Rover into my purse and think about how to explain his resurfacing to Russ without flaring up his jealousy. He hates Charlie, blames him for everything, and I know he'll be furious that we spoke, especially without him there to protect me. My mind ticks along with the beat of the blinker and suddenly I'm home without any memory of the commute. I feel inside my purse, making sure the dog is still there, and sigh. I'll figure it out later. For now, he can remain a secret.

Russ is already home, and some white truck is parked poorly right up against the porch, so I know he's entertaining some friend from work. There's also a dark tinted car across the street, but it grumbles to life and slinks away before I have a chance to get a closer look. I hear shouts and crackling laughter in tar-filled lungs as soon as I get out of the car. That's alright. Russ needed a good distraction, and he sounds in a good mood, that's all that matters.

By the time I have everything chopped and on the stove, the friend has headed home to his own family and Russ is beer-buzzed and watching the news with the volume too loud. I don't like to hear about that stuff, all the fearmongering gets to me and unravels my nerves, but I don't want to risk his good mood by asking him to turn it down. The reporter talks a while about the un-seasonably warm weather, global warming and coming years of unbearable heat, but then they change gears to local crime, and I actually let out a little breath of relief. At least crime feels like something preventable.

"You hearing this, hon? There's a madman on the loose," Russ shouts from the other room over the blare of the tv. I tune into the reporter's voice and try to pick up the details. It's more about that serial killer in the city who's targeting young women; police warn to be careful when walking alone, carry mace, travel in groups, never answer the door for a stranger, all the precautions every woman already knows.

"Scary stuff," I say, stirring the soup, and Russ grunts in reply. He might have his faults, but I know he'll keep me safe at least.

I bring the soup over to him and he slurps it down with greedy gulps, the bowl under his chin where it can catch any drops that slither down. I set mine on the cof-fee table, letting it cool a little.

"Can you believe there's a monster like this in our own fucking city? Makes me wanna move. I've been thinking about that a lot lately. There are places that are safer and have more construction jobs that pay better. We could have a fresh start. Then you wouldn't have people going off on you when they hear about the thing with your son or giving you the stink eye and talking behind your back. I know they still do that." He gives me a sidelong glance and I shrug. "It'd be fun to get out of here, like an adventure. Yeah, the more I talk about it, the more I like it. I'll start checking out places soon. Find us a nice, new landing spot. Safe and full of fresh opportunities."

"Whoa, slow down there. I don't know if I want to leave. You can't just make that decision for us."

He stops eating and stares at me, his mouth twisted in an ugly way and I know he's surprised I spoke up against his decision at all.

"Why the fuck would we stay here? There's nothing for us here. It makes the most sense for us to get outta here."

"But what about Noah?" The words float around us like a ghost. A young child's ghost. The silence is suffocating but I refuse to speak again until he does. He finally does, a sputtering disbelief in his voice.

"What about him?"

My lip rises as I feel the unspoken words on his tongue, moving across his teeth behind closed lips so I can't accuse him of being heartless. The words *"He's dead."*

"I don't want to move away from him. I like to visit him."

"Visit his grave, Birdie. Not him. He doesn't know you're visiting, so would it really be that different if you only came back and visited a couple times a year instead of all the time?" He seems to realize how harsh he sounds, a flash of panic flying over his features, and adds, "It'll be healthier for you if you try to move on a little. Not forget him, no, not that at all, but just move on a little bit from seeing him so often."

An emptiness, hollow and nauseating, moves over me like a shadow. He must see it in my eyes because his brows crease with something like shame. But it can't be. He's not ashamed because he doesn't understand. He'll never understand.

"Let's table it for now, but just think about it," he says, turning back to the television so he doesn't have to look at the hurt inhuman thing I've become. When we talk about Noah, it reminds him of what I really am. It reminds me too.

I excuse myself and rush to the bathroom, making it just in time to vomit in the sink. I wash it down, directing the water flow to pick up every last bit of dinner and push it down the drain so he doesn't see the evidence. Even after all this, I know he'll make a comment about wasting food. He'll never understand, and I force myself to forgive him of his ignorance. I stay in the bathroom a long time, but I can't stand to look at myself in the reflection. There's a risk I'll catch the light in just the right way and see Noah, and I don't think I could continue on if I see him right now.

Instead, I splash water on my face, carefully avoiding my eye makeup so it doesn't streak, and roll the idea around over my tongue, seeing if it might melt into me and become an acceptable reality, but it doesn't. It only leaves the taste of bitter ashes, the same taste that hadn't left my mouth for nearly a year after losing him.

When I return to the living room, there's a definite change in the atmosphere. The embarrassed, cold electric spark in the air has been replaced by a suffocating heat. I know before he even turns around that Russ is seething, and I prepare myself for whatever conflict he's manufactured to turn the tables back on me. I shouldn't be surprised. It's been his usual modus operandi for as long as I've known him. His ego can't support even a grain of guilt, so he has to push it back on me. A deep sigh churns in my lungs but I keep it in. No need to provoke him further.

"Finally felt like joining me again, huh?" The way his smile curls in a knowing sneer makes the bile creep up my throat all over again, but I swallow it down. "You gave me so much time to think that I figured it all out. This isn't about Noah at all, is it?"

"What?" There's more venom in my tone than I intended, but I can't help it. I'm already building up my defenses.

"Who is it?"

"Who is what?"

"Who is the guy you're running around with that you can't bear to leave?" He slams his hand down on the coffee table and I swear the whole room shakes. Bloodshot eyes burn into me like lasers, tearing through me, searching for any hint that his ridiculous suspicions might be true.

"Russ, you're acting crazy! You know there's nobody but you. I'd move in a heartbeat if it wasn't for Noah."

"Shut the fuck up! You know that doesn't make any fucking sense. Tell me who you're out there fucking so I can kick his fucking face in!"

I watch as the anger in his eyes boils over into a pure hate-driven rage, and I realize I'm shaking all over. I want to run out the front door, drive away and let him cool off, but I'm frozen to the spot. My mouth trembles as it opens and closes like a fish, not able to form a word or produce a single sound except a staggered breath.

"Yeah, that's what I thought. Stunned that your stupid boyfriend would figure this out, huh? Just because I didn't go to a fancy-ass school like you doesn't mean I'm dumb. In fact, I'm smarter than you, fucking little whore," he says, his lips baring gritted teeth, the corners curling into a disgusting smirk. That's when I notice his hands reach down to the couch and lift up the small, blue dog. *Rover. He has Rover.*

"Give that back!" I shout before I even realize the words are pouring out of me.

"No. You don't need some shitty cheap love trinket from whatever jackass you're fucking and I'm gonna–" I watch as his fingers dig into the terrycloth while he speaks, ready to tear it apart.

"That was Noah's! Don't hurt him!" I scream, tears stinging my eyes so I can barely keep them open. I watch as Russ looks back and forth between me and the stuffed dog, chewing at his cheek as if he's trying to decide if he believes me. I know he's noticing the worn ears and scratched beaded eyes, the faded color from my little boy's cuddles, the fact that the dog looks much more like a well-loved children's toy than a gift from a paramour, and yet I know Russ. He doesn't like to admit when he's wrong. My legs still won't move, so I find my voice again and plead, "Please. Please, don't. That's Rover. Remember? I told you about him. I thought he was lost. He was Noah's favorite."

"That doesn't make any sense. How the fuck did you find him now?"

My face tingles and glows red as I force myself to tell the truth, knowing it'll piss him off even more, but I need that part of Noah more than anything.

"Charlie found him and brought him to the store. He knew I'd want it, so he just showed up and gave it to me. Barely talked to me really, more like shoved it at me and left." Right away I regret giving those extra details. They sound fake, like I'm trying to hide something.

"Okay, so you're telling me you're fucking Charlie again?" The anger simmering in his eyes again, his fist clenches Rover and my pulse beats a rhythmic headache behind my temples.

"No, I'd never do that to you. You know that! And especially with Charlie." This plea is so earnest, even Russ can't help but soften. "It was just like I said, he was only dropping off the toy because he knows how much I wanted it. Please, give it back."

"Fine." He tosses the dog at me, its soft body hitting me in the face before I have a chance to react. He's already outside, the screen door screeching back into place behind him, as I bend over to retrieve the toy. I cuddle the dog to my chest while the truck roars to life, letting my legs bend beneath me until I'm puddled on the floor, nose in the soft terrycloth, remembering a boy I loved with corn silk hair and cotton candy breath. I could never move away from here and leave him.

It's late when he comes back home. Really late. I don't check the time, but I can tell by the intensity of the dark silence outside the window that it's well past even the neighborhood night owl's bedtimes. Whiskey and cigarette smoke waft around me as the sheet lifts and cold air tickles my bare legs. Heavy breathing in my ear and soft kisses on my neck, he slides into bed, naked warm skin against mine.

"You awake?"

"Mmmhmm," I murmur, still half-dreaming.

"Babe, I'm so sorry about earlier. I don't know what I was thinking. You'd never cheat on me, sweetheart. I know that." His arms snake around my waist and pull me closer, but I stiffen, keeping my hands by my face, Rover nestled under my cheek.

When I don't respond, he goes back to kissing my neck, his fingers dancing up my back to knead the sore spots in the depths of my shoulder blades. I can't help but melt a little under his touch. I don't want to, but I forgive him.

"I love you, Birdie, and if you don't want to move, then maybe we don't." He buries his nose into my hair, and I cuddle backwards, into his lap.

"You get why, though? I can't leave my baby."

"I know, I know, and I'm sorry I suggested it, honey pie. I've been thinking while I was out there by myself, and I want to take you on a trip, like the old days when things were always easy and good. Maybe camping. We used to do that all the time, and how long has it been since we last went?"

"Too long," I sigh under his embrace.

"Let me take you on a trip. We can have fun again. Play around together like we did before."

"I can't just take off work…"

"It doesn't have to be for too long. We'll make it work."

"And you won't make me move away? Because I can't leave—"

He interrupts me with a kiss. "No, no, no. Never. You can stay near your baby, and maybe," his voice lowers to a comforting rumble, low like thunder, as fingers caress down the soft curve of my stomach, "it's time for another baby in your life."

I hold back the tears, my head swimming with a wave of fear, excitement, confusion, and enchanted lust, as I try to imagine the life we could have together. Then I'm fully smitten; his, all over again.

ADVANCED

DECAY

BODY

I marvel at the changes that have taken place over such a short period of time. To think I once looked pink and supple, with blushing skin and silken hair, beautiful. Alive. There's a kind of beauty in this new appearance, though I know past-me wouldn't have been able to appreciate it. The swarms of insects have dissipated, their young having already hatched inside me and wriggled their way to the surface.

A vulture and a coyote have both inspected me, but by the time of their arrival, I wasn't of much interest to them anymore. They each tore my degrading tissues a little, rummaged inside, and left with precious few bites, slightly spoiled organs swallowed quickly down their gullet. I could see the regret in their hungry, tired eyes, exhausted from the fight to survive another day, that they had not found me sooner, when I was fresh with so much more to offer. I felt sorry for them, but what could I do? I just lay bare and open for them to take what they wanted.

Now my visitors are few. Beetles gnaw through rotting tendons and cartilage, a few flies visit now and again, and a trail *of ants cross my strewn innards as a shortcut, tiny feet parading over the broken, spilled intestinal lining and flesh dark with rot.*

My skin has blackened, wrinkled and thin as burnt parchment. The yellow of bones has begun to peek through where the flesh has fallen away. My eyes were long ago lost, but I witness from empty sockets the rapidly changing seasons of my physical form.

I've heard many people along the trail now, but none seem to be looking for me. There was a helicopter two nights ago, its long beam searching through the trees, but it didn't find me. I'm camouflaged by my discoloration, blending in with the earth around me, becoming the soil and moss that slowly consume my remains. I want to let it happen. I want to give myself up completely to the process that's called to me since my very conception, but an urgency, far away and distorted by time, lingers and keeps me here.

Find me. Find me so I can be free. It's the sole thought that vibrates through the consciousness I'm cursed with. I remember less of myself each day, but I know I was a person and that I was loved. Something terrible happened to me. I need closure before I let go.

Time is running out. I know this limbo of lifeless, deathless slumber is fading every day. If I'm not found soon, I'll be lost to history. Forever missing.

Find me. Find me. I'm waiting right here.

AUTUMN INTO WINTER

Birdie

Strands of hair fall over his eyes, and even though I know Russ thinks it looks sloppy grown-out like this, I'm glad he's pushed back his haircut for an extra couple weeks. With the two-day growth of stubble and his heavy brows, the untamed look reminds me of when we first met. I lean over, pressing my hips down against him as I kiss the corner of his lip, the prickle of his beard tickling me.

"You know how to drive me wild," he says between kisses. "Always sweet as honey with a hint of fire underneath. Damn girl, you're a goddess." His fingers tiptoe down the curves of my body and I shiver under his touch.

"You're my everything, Russ. How do I keep us like this? Like how it used to be? All the fighting, sometimes it wears me down and makes me forget we can be happy like this." His strong, calloused hand brushes across my scalp and gently down the length of my hair. "How can we stay like this?" I press my lips to his, the smell of his cologne engulfing my senses so I'm dizzy when I pull back for air. "Just like this."

"I don't know, but you've got to understand, that's all I've ever wanted too. We're so good together, good for each other, we have to keep the peace. I need you, sweet girl. You're the best thing I've ever had in my life, but when we fight…I'm just so scared of losing you."

He lights up a cigarette and falls back into the pillow, letting his words swirl around us in the curls of smoke. With his eyes closed, he looks as chiseled and perfect as those marble statues they have in museums. How did I ever get so lucky?

"Yeah. Things have been kinda rough lately, but I always know you love me. I'd never leave you, not after all we've been through together."

"How do you know that?" he asks, the blue of his irises peeking out barely between his eyelids.

"Know what?"

"Know you'll never leave me."

"Russ, stop being weird." I bat him with a pillow, but he only turns away, taking a long drag on his cigarette before he sits up. "I just wouldn't, okay?"

When he doesn't turn, I watch the muscles of his back ripple slightly and my stomach drops. Is he crying? The room is absolutely quiet, and I don't hear a sound from him aside from the slow exhale of smoke, but I can't shake the feeling something's wrong. My hand reaches out, touching his shoulder blade with featherlight pressure. He immediately recoils.

"What's wrong, hon? You were fine a minute ago."

Sidling up against him, I watch him take one more puff before tapping out the cigarette in the nightstand ashtray. He doesn't seem to be crying, doesn't make a sound, no jagged shudder in his breathing, and yet his eyes are red and wet. All my happiness from before melts down me, puddling around us on the bedsheets, and we're left exposed in the stark light of the unshaded bedside lamp.

"You're going to leave me. You'll realize I'm human trash and toss me out of your life. I told you, Birdie, I'm a bad man. I just need you to put me out of my misery." Tears roll down his cheeks before falling onto his bare legs, but his voice remains stern and unemotional.

"What?"

"Tomorrow, you need to go out and get yourself a gun. That's the way it has to be. Just like I told you before. And you've gotta be smooth about it. Don't let me know it's coming. I need you to understand that this is the *only* way things can get better." The steel blue eyes seize me in their stare. "Tell me you understand."

"Babe, that's just your depression talking. You're a wonderful man and I promise I'll never ever leave you." I pat his shoulder gently but he pulls away. "And all this talk about..." I can't bring myself to say it. "Well, I think you might need to see somebody if you can't get those kinds of thoughts out of your head like that. You know, those medicines, they're not a forever thing. Remember, I was on some for a while after what happened to Noah. It's just a tool, a little burst to get you through the worst parts and then–"

"I'm not taking any fucking meds, so you can stop right now."

My mouth hangs open, lip still quivering in anticipation of the next word, but my throat closes off any sound that tries to escape. The way he snaps at me isn't the usual, frustrated tone but instead something darker, rumbling with rage and yet concealing a deep wound he doesn't want me to see. He wipes away the tears and straightens his back. When he stands up without looking at me, I sigh. The mask is back on. I doubt he'll tell me anymore. All I can do is hope my presence is enough to let him know he's loved. I promise I'll never leave.

Birdie

That bitch Janine. I can't stand her. I've been working my ass off for this promotion and she only just started three months ago. What does she have that I don't have? The thoughts pulse through my head with migraine intensity. The rage is so raw, it feels more like a nightmare than real life. My face burns, tingling with a prickly flush as I bring out the cart and stock the shelves of vitamins and weight loss drinks. There's a flash of sound, a giggle from the backroom, and my sight turns red for a split second.

No, I must have imagined it. I won't let it be true.

Even when I see the narrowed eyes and plastic smiles of Janine and Sheena, hear their whispers that I can't quite make out, I shrug it off. But still, the hours drag by slower than usual, and it feels like an eternity before Juliana pulls up to get me.

"Thanks. I really appreciate the ride. I wasn't up for the usual bus bullshit today," I say as I climb into the passenger seat.

"Of course, girl! I can't believe they picked the new girl over you. It's blatant favoritism, and it's just because she's a kiss-ass. You know that, right? It has nothing to do with you." She waits for me to nod before continuing. "In fact, you need to start applying elsewhere because they don't deserve you and your work ethic. You work your ass off every day for them and they repay you like this? Oh hell no, fuck them! We're finding you something better."

I smile a little. Juliana always knows the right thing to say to cheer me up, and after a couple beers at Toby's, I'm feeling better. I talk her down from her stance that I have to quit right away, but I also let her talk me into looking around for something new. I've been at the store so long, it'd be nice to have a change anyway. By the time she takes me home, I'm feeling better about the whole situation.

"So, you have a girl's night out or something?" Russ says as soon as I'm through the door.

"I texted you. Hours ago. Did you see it?"

"Yeah, but I didn't think you'd be out this late."

I glance at the clock. "It's only eight-thirty."

"Well, you're pretty fucking drunk for eight-thirty, don't you think?" He's smiling like it's just a playful joke, but his tone tells me it's anything but.

"Actually, no. I only had three beers. I feel fine."

"Tell that to your slur and the way you're propping yourself up against the wall." His lips part, a toothy, snide smile snaking across his face, but I don't care to argue. I haven't told him about the promotion, and it does seem out of character for me to go drinking on a Wednesday night. He has every right to be suspicious, maybe even a little hurt. My heart softens for him, and I try again.

"I'm sorry. I should've texted you what happened, but you remember how Regina told me I was moving up as soon as a spot opened? Well, she lied. That new girl Janine got the position and everyone's acting like I shouldn't be surprised. I don't know why everyone hates me so much. I work so hard, and nobody cares." As the tears slip down my nose, smearing my makeup down my face, I realize maybe I'm a little tipsier than I'd thought.

I wobble to the kitchen table, and just as I sit down, Russ is behind me, wrapping his strong arms around my chest, his stubble tickling my neck as his face slides against my shoulder.

"I'm sorry you had a rough day, babe. I didn't know."

I bask in the warmth and compassion. When he kisses my cheek and starts to pull away, I cling to him.

"Wait, stay with me. I need you."

He sits across from me, the old wicker chair creaking as he leans back. With a long sigh, he rakes his hand through his hair and I watch the expression on his face slowly change from sympathy to something else. Something I can't put my finger on.

"Of course you do. You always need me to help you through this kind of stuff, and that's why Regina skipped over you. Don't you see?" The velvet of his voice confuses me, and I just look at him, my brow wrinkled and lip dropped open.

"What?"

"Honey, you and I both know not everyone is meant to climb the corporate ladder." He takes my hand and I'm too stunned to pull away, the coarse calloused palm scratching into me. "You've excelled at stocking and maybe that's just your place in the world. It's okay to be thankful for what you have and not always be coveting what other smarter, more ambitious people are achieving. You're doing just fine, and I'm so proud of you."

"You don't think that–that–" I can't even finish my sentence before he's shushing me like an overeager toddler.

"What I'm saying is that you're excellent at your job and you should be glad you've found your niche. Hell, look at me, working construction all my life when I could've been so many things. I've got the brains, the talent, but no drive. You know me, I hated school, so here I am, wasting my smarts on heavy labor, but that's life, ain't it? At least you're where you should be."

"You don't think I could be a manager, a fucking cashier?" I stand, my voice rising. "Juliana was helping me find places to apply that would appreciate my work ethic and pay me what I deserve, and you just think Regina's right and I should be happy with the shit they pay me? Just be happy for the rest of my life stacking boxes on shelves? Fuck you, Russ! You don't think I can work a goddamn cash register?" Before I know it, I'm flinging the plastic vase full of fake flowers across the room. When it hits the wall, it fails to shatter dramatically, instead just cracking before clattering across the linoleum.

"That's not what I meant. You totally misunderstood!" Russ shouts after me, but I've already stormed to the bathroom, the only door with a lock that works. He leaves me alone for a while, but then comes pawing at the door like a puppy.

"Babe? Come on. I just wanna talk to you."

"Go away." I'm sitting on the lid of the toilet, my legs pulled up to my chest, rapidly sobering up and wishing I had another drink to numb the wave of emotions battering my skull, pulling me in every direction. Part of me fears he's right, but I hate that part of me, so I try to ignore it. The more I push the thought, the more it balloons somewhere else. Maybe I'm not even good at stacking boxes and bottles on shelves. Maybe that's why I never get anywhere in life. Here I am, always blaming Noah's death and the rumors surrounding it, but maybe it's never been that at all. Is Russ right?

"Please, come on, Birdie. You're totally twisting my words. You always do this. Just open up and we'll make up like we always do." His voice is gentle again, silky smooth, and I can't help myself. I open the door. Walk into his arms. Accept his half-apologies and let the words shrivel away like they were never spoken at all.

Charlie

I was on my way upstairs when I saw the shadow swaying through the glass. My heart leaped up my throat. Was someone casing the place, hoping nobody was home? I watched the shadow, standing like a ghost, not knocking or ringing the doorbell. Anger and unease compelled me forward and I swallowed hard as I opened it, ready to confront whoever was waiting outside.

My ex-wife was standing just past the awning, rain pouring down so hard she couldn't keep her eyes open. She was sopping wet, looking like a drowned kitten that showed up at my door in the middle of the night.

"What are you doing here?" She didn't answer. Just stood there like she couldn't hear me, eyes closed and teeth clattering so loud I could hear it through the wind. "Well, don't just stand there. Come in."

She shuffled in behind me and I grabbed a towel, tossed it to her. She didn't so much catch it as let it fall over her, taking a second before reaching up and drying out her hair. I couldn't bring myself to kick her out when I saw that. I knew she was probably here looking for sympathy, most likely something about that asshole she was shacked up with, but what if it was about Noah again? I couldn't just throw his mom out. He'd loved her so much, too young to realize who she was deep down. I tried to swallow the lump stuck in my throat. *I loved her blindly too, kid. Now look at us.*

She stood in the foyer, swaying as if in a daze, half-dried off but still dripping, until I took over. I didn't feel a thing, stripping off her clothes and wrapping the damp towel around her pale, goose-pimpled flesh. I tossed the wet stuff in the dryer and put the kettle on. She was still standing there when I got back, so I took her arm and led her into the living room, sat her on the couch, then set myself in the armchair opposite.

"Well, what the fuck are you doing here, Birdie? It's almost one in the morning and you just show up at my door, unannounced and uninvited? Did that jerk kick you out?" My voice lowers into a protective growl I can't help. "Did he hurt you?"

Her eyes very slowly raise to meet my own and the sorrow there is so deep and palpable, my chest tightens, and I have to force myself to remember what she put me through or else I would've taken her in my arms like the old days.

A quiver on her lip kept her words in for a moment, then in a whisper so quiet I could scarcely hear it, she said, "I just miss him so much. I thought it'd get easier, but it hasn't. Not at all." Tears spilled down her face, but her voice stayed soft and clear. "Is there any future out there where we start again? Have another child, no, never to replace Noah, but to try again? To let me try to be the kind of mom I should've been for him?"

I felt myself wither and age decades under her glassy gaze. The memories we never made flashed in my mind's eyes, some with Noah, some with some golden-haired child that never was but could've been, and some just us two, curled up in bed or on the couch in front of a forgotten movie, lovers sharing secrets and her hot, comforting breath on my neck. She had no idea how much time I'd wasted grieving what could never be, trying to forgive her, pushing myself to move on.

"You already know the answer, Birdie."

She nodded and we stared into each other's eyes for a long moment. I wanted to run away and hide, but I couldn't break the contact. Something in her sad eyes fed the grief in my belly, nourished the pain that tears every fiber of me apart but that I'd never willingly give up. *My Noah. My baby. How can life be so beautiful and so cruel?*

"Is it okay if I stay here a little longer? I don't want to go... home yet." She hesitated before the word. We both knew there was no home anymore. Never would be again.

"Yeah, that's fine." I got up and headed toward the stairs. "I'm going to bed. Just be gone by the morning, got it?"

"Goodnight," I heard her meek voice call to me when I reached the top of the stairs, but I bit my tongue and pretended she'd already left. I'd promised myself years ago that I wouldn't shed any more tears over that woman, and so I swaddled myself in a cocoon of blankets and told myself it was just a nightmare, again and again until I fell into a dreamless stupor.

Maeve

The man was already hidden in the closet when Maeve got home from work. She'd heard the same news everyone else had about a criminal who stalked women and slaughtered them, often in their homes, and while it had given her a shiver when she heard about it from a coworker, she hadn't given it much thought since. Those crimes had all happened in a city nearly two hours away, which might as well be on the other side of the earth. She thought she was safely outside the boundaries of the supposed serial killer's realm and didn't need to worry. But she'd left a window cracked and a man she'd seen four days before at a gas station, a stranger who'd eyed her up and down and given her the creeps, had checked every door and window each day since he followed her home, even though it meant a long commute and he had missed work to do so. She was beautiful and lived alone, and he wanted her all to himself. Now that man was in her house.

Maeve grabbed her purse from the passenger seat and slid chapstick across her lips before heading inside. Her throat dry from artificially heated air at work, she tossed her things on the kitchen counter, retrieved a sparkling water from her fridge and took a long swig, before sitting down with a book.

As her eyes scanned the lines of text, blurred with exhaustion, she sighed and decided maybe a long bath and an audiobook were better plans after such a hard day. She didn't hear the soft padding of the stranger's shoes down the carpeted hallway. Before she could get up from the couch, something heavy crashed into her head, and a sickening crack accompanied a devastating, split second of pain before the world went black.

She didn't know how long it'd been when she began to regain consciousness, her head pounding with an intensity that the world seemed tinted with red agony. A sticky puddle spread out from where her head rested on the carpet and she knew without looking it was blood. Duct tape held her lips closed, and she struggled to break the bindings wrapped around her wrists and ankles, digging into her skin and making her extremities tingle as blood fought to circulate. In darting glances, she tried to take in the situation and make sense of it, but it was surreal beyond comprehension. Her vision blurred in and out. A sense of impending dread had slowly settled over her in the moments since she awakened, and now she was sure she needed to escape or she would die.

A strange man sat on the sofa, looking at her with a seething rage just visible in the snarling quiver of his upper lip. His jaw tightened as he clenched and unclenched his teeth over and over, but he didn't say a word. He just stared at her, face as blank and empty as a mask. Waiting.

There was a familiarity about the stranger, and Maeve spooled through her memories, trying to identify him. If she could just place him, maybe this would make a little more sense. She was desperate, thinking through every coworker's husband, each man she'd snubbed at a party, every profile picture from the dating app she swiped through after too many glasses of wine. Then it came to her in a burst of clarity. With a shudder, she recognized the man as the one from the gas station. *How had he found her?* Panic swirled through her mind with electric blue static. Her mouth filled with bile, but it couldn't push past the tape, only drips sputtered past her lips and into the adhesive, so she swallowed it down.

Maeve knew she had expressive eyes. She'd been told that all through her drama classes and failed casting calls. Never quite right, but so expressive. Focusing every bit of her concentration into her eyes, she gazed at the man with a plea for mercy, but as he stared back into her desperate eyes, his own glowered with a spark of anger that ignited and spread across his face with burning fury.

"You're all the same. Always begging, if not with your voice, then with your fucking eyes. Let me guess, you'll do anything if I only let you go?" He sneered, his upper lip quivering and pulled back like a snarling dog. Maeve nodded furiously, sticky strands of her hair plastering to her face and leaving lines of blood when she shook them free.

"Not gonna happen, got it? Never. Ever. Ever." The man laughed but there wasn't an ounce of joy in it.

Maeve cowered against the carpet, fighting the futility closing in like a shadow ready to devour her whole. She watched as he moved across the room with the casual nature of a houseguest, opened the fridge, took out a soda, and popped it open. He proceeded to take out cheese, deli meat, and mustard then went to the pantry to grab some bread. She couldn't believe her eyes. It was as if her tied up and bleeding was the most ordinary thing in the world to him, and she knew she should be more horrified, but somehow the surreal nature of it kept her from being swallowed by despair, the denial keeping her head just afloat, and that gave her hope. Not much, just the slightest sliver of hope shining like a lighthouse through a storm.

"You know, Maeve," he said, shoving the slices of bread down into the toaster and her heart stopped at the sound of her name on his tongue. "If things had been different in both of our lives, we might've been lovers. You're just my type, and I could've made you so happy."

Quietly, trying not to draw his attention, Maeve worked to free her hands from the bindings. She hoped that even if she couldn't break them, she might be able to slip her hands free if she could get them in just the right angle. The terror and effort had built a film of sweat across her palms and she maneuvered her wrists round and round, trying to use it as a lubricant and slip free, but it was no use. They were much too tight, and she could just feel the hard plastic tail, identifying her binding as a zip-tie, something she was sure she couldn't loosen.

"It doesn't matter now of course, and it never would've worked out anyway. You never would've submitted to me the way I need. Why do you bitches always think you deserve so much, anyway? I give and I give and what do you do? Spread your legs and lay there? You're all the same."

He spoke between bites of his sandwich and when he finished, he chugged the soda and carefully placed the can in a black backpack she hadn't noticed before. She watched as he calmly washed the plate in the sink, dried it, and put it back in the cabinet. His shoes padded softly across the carpet of the living room until he stood over her, straddling her, staring down with those eerie ice-blue eyes, full of seething wrath. She slowly turned onto her back, staring back, her gaze no longer a plea but full of her own hardened wrath. He laughed and nudged her in the ribs with the toe of his shoe.

"Now be good and wait here. I've got a surprise for you."

She could do nothing but watch as the man grabbed the backpack and strode down the hallway, with a relaxed back and not a hint of urgency.

The moment she heard the click of the bathroom door, Maeve set to work. In a blind panic, she crawled on hands and knees across the carpet. She tried to move quietly, even attempting to control her breathing, but her lungs felt full of glass shards. He called her a worm and that was what she would be, using her elbows, knees, and all her core strength to inch her way toward the sliding door that opened into the backyard. She knew the front door would be a better option, as the chances someone might see her were much higher, but she'd have to pass the bathroom and the man would surely hear her scraping across the carpet. She couldn't risk it. No, she had to make it outside. In the backyard, she might be able to hide, or maybe drag her mouth across the rain-wet grass to soften the tape so she could rub it loose and scream for help, or even writhe her way to the front yard through the broken gate that would fly open with even the slightest breeze. If she could just get out, there were so many options. So many chances at escape.

And just like that, she was at the backdoor. Adrenaline and determination had brought her this far, and she looked into the yard, the early evening painting it in shades of blue and midnight green. She was so close; she could taste the cold air on her trapped tongue.

Pressing herself against the door, she forced herself to her knees and nudged her head against the flipped down switch lock. Blood smeared across the glass as she tried again and again to push the lock upward. And then a click. Her heart stopped. She'd done it. A new surge of adrenaline drove her to work faster, replenishing her depleted strength as she dragged her head against the handle and felt the door inch open, a rush of night air spreading goosebumps across her skin. *Almost there. Almost there.* She repeated this over and over, not letting herself lose the momentum the small victory had gifted her.

The door was now open enough for her to slip her torso through, and she did, shoving it even wider as she tumbled out onto the freezing concrete of the patio.

"Where do you think you're going, sweetheart?"

The calm question solidified Maeve's blood in her veins, and she turned to see the man standing over her again, his hands now in blue medical gloves as they clutched the doorframe. She tried to scream as he dragged her back inside, but it was only a muffled sound behind the silver tape. She closed her eyes and collapsed into herself, a cavern of defeat and sorrow, as she heard the whoosh of the sliding door closing and the tiny click as he latched it.

There were no tears when he flipped her onto her stomach and tore off her pants, ripping them as he left her exposed, nor when he slipped the cable over her head and she felt it tighten against her throat. She'd already left her body by then, floating nearby and watching with surprising apathy until the scene of carnage ended and she could fly away, untethered.

Birdie

"Why don't you leave that alone? We're supposed to be relaxing," I say, watching Russ poke and prod at the fire, the shadows dancing ghoulishly across his face. "Come sit and cuddle with me. I brought the stuff for s'mores. Your favorite."

He looks up, attempts a smile, but the orange firelight distorts it into a strange grimace. Still, I smile back. It's been so long since we had a getaway. I want to savor every moment.

"It's colder than I thought it was gonna be. Goddamn forecast's always wrong," he grumbles.

"Yeah, it's a bit chillier than I'd thought, but that just means we'll need to snuggle up together more." I give him a quick peck on the cheek as I settle down next to him by the fire, but he pulls away, his face still hard and unreadable. "What's wrong, sugarpuss?"

"Don't call me that. You know I hate that fucking nickname."

"I'm sorry, I forgot."

"Okay, whatever, Bernadette," he says with a mean sneer, and I can feel the romantic vibe I'd tried so hard to curate dying around us.

"Touché." I try to make it sound cute, breathe a little life back into the conversation like the banter we used to have when we were first together, but it just comes out as bitter as him.

Resigned, I start to roast a marshmallow, not even offering any to him because I know he'll just say something else hurtful. We sit in silence for far too long, just staring at the fire. When he takes out his phone and starts scrolling mindlessly, I decide enough time has passed to try to start again.

"We should wake up early and try fishing again. Maybe they were just spooked by so many lines out there. If we go early enough, there won't be so many people and—"

"God, do you ever shut up?"

My jaw drops open, but I snap it right back. Of course he's going to ruin this trip that I planned for so long. I even took off work and bought little details to make it perfect: s'mores, two six-packs of his favorite beer, a new lipstick, lingerie hidden away as a surprise. All of it ruined because he feels like throwing a fit. The boiling sensation fills me up, making me clench my hands into fists and bite my cheek, and this time I'm struggling to swallow it down. The words slide up my throat without my permission, vomited out between us like the disgusting sludge they are.

"Why do you have to ruin everything?"

For a moment, we're both frozen, shocked that I would dare say such a thing. I pray and beg the universe to let me take those words back, shove them in my mouth and choke them down so they only poison me, churning in my acidic juices until they dissolve back into the ether of things better unsaid, but it's impossible.

Then the unthinkable happens. His hand rises and my adrenaline spikes. I barely have time to brace for contact as it slams against my cheek. My head is forced to the side, and my face stings and burns in the cold air. Before I can register the pain, the back of his hand swipes across my other cheek, sending my face in the other direction. Tears pour out immediately, though I don't know if they're from pain or shame.

"You bitch. You're the one who ruined *my* life."

He lunges, closing the space between us. His face is painted in shades of orange and red from the firelight, shadows dancing across his forehead, over his nose, dappling his brow, drawn together with a rage beyond anything I've seen before. Hands clasp around my neck, tightening until my ballooned lungs threaten to burst and my head is full of throbbing, a flurry of blood roaring in my ears.

Let me go, but the words can't be spoken. Instead, my mouth can only gape open and closed like a suffocating fish. I stare up into his eyes and I see a stranger. Feral, consumed by anger, with bulging eyes and every muscle straining, he's become a monster.

My fingers claw at him indiscriminately—his hands, arms, neck, face. The points of my manicured nails dig into anywhere they can find, tearing through hair and scratching at skin. Blind panic controls them, there's no thought in my attack, only the need to be free.

It lasts only a few seconds, then he releases me. Gasping and rubbing my neck, I scurry to get away, tripping and still pushing myself backward through the crinkle of fallen leaves, dripping with a cold sweat of terror.

"Fuck. I'm sorry. I'm so sorry," he mutters, reaching out for me, but I scoot further, a scream trying to escape my throat but only coming out as a scratchy squeak.

He stands, pacing by the fire as I watch with wide, blurry eyes, a stream of unending tears flowing down my face. A strange noise, like a stuttered version of a chipmunk's squeals, fills my ears and it takes so long before I realize it's me.

"Birdie, I–I don't—please," he tries to approach me again, but I put up my hands and squeeze my eyes shut.

"Stay away!" I try to shout but it only leaves my throat as a strained whisper.

"I'm sorry! I don't know what happened. Fuck!" He's shouting, eyes wild and filled with fear. "I'm going to take a walk. I'll be back soon. I'll make it up to you. Fuck. I promise, Birdie, I don't know what happened, but it'll never happen again."

I notice his own cheeks are stained with tears, his eyes not only fearful but truly scared, and I begin to thaw. It was just a mistake. I pushed him too far. It was so stupid, so cruel, to say something so hurtful that he had to lash out like that.

"Okay," I say, muffled through my snot and sniffles, and watch him walk away, down the trail and into the dark.

The second he's out of sight, I miss him. I want things to go back to how they were before. If only I could erase this memory, we could go back to happy and in love. This was supposed to be a romantic getaway and it's become a nightmare. I can't let this define us. I love him. I've given everything for him and his happiness, and I know he feels the same for me. We must get past this.

Pushing down every negative feeling, every bubble of fear, anger, and even hatred, I force myself to return to the blank face that hides it all. Finish roasting my marsh-mallow. Brush my hair. Hum myself a little song to keep my mind empty and present. The more time passes, the easier it is to forget, or at least pretend to forget. *I love him. I love him. I love him.*

Time ticks by slowly and I wonder what he's thinking out there, alone with his guilt in the cold and the dark. I forgive him because it was a mistake. He'll never do it again. If only he'd come back, and I could show him that I still love him.

I change into the slinky nightgown I packed when I thought this weekend would be sweet and cute, even sexy. I feel like a fool sliding into the extra-large sleeping bag alone and in lingerie, piling the extra blankets on top of me and shivering. Why do I have to romanticize everything? And why do I have to push his buttons all the time? I could've just stayed quiet, played the good, doting girlfriend, and everything would have been fine.

Scrolling through social media, I'm tempted to post the selfie from when we'd just finished putting up the tent, my cheeks pink with the natural blush of exertion and his hair mussed the way I love it. It feels so fake to post a happy moment when he's out huffing around, trying to get over his anger, but then again, everything rings false on social media. I post it anyway, rub my neck, and shut my eyes, pretending to sleep.

The wind whips against the tent and I start to doze off right when I hear the zipper. A blast of cold air hits me, but I pretend to sleep. I don't know why, but I don't want him to know I'm awake. His breath is loud and shaky as he undresses and slips in beside me in the sleeping bag, his cold skin pressing against my warm, sleepy body. Despite the cold, I push back into his embrace and let him spoon me. I knew we'd make up and things would all be okay again.

I'm surprised when I feel his hot tears seeping through my silk nightie, sticking it against my skin. He tries to stay quiet, but deep, quavering blubs quake through his arms and head into me. I think I hear him apologize, maybe say a declaration or two of love, but I can't be sure. It's too distorted by tears and obscured by silk, but that doesn't matter. I understand. I've been in his place so many times in my life, wishing I could rewind time back to a happy normal. I shed the lingering layers of anger and fear from our fight and lay there, completely open and honest for him.

"There, there," I say, and my own tears flow quietly down my face as I hear the same voice I used to comfort Noah all those years ago. "There, there. It's alright. Cry it out and you'll feel better. Shh, it'll be okay. I forgive you. I know you didn't mean it. There, there, my love."

Aubrey

Aubrey felt something was off as soon as she rounded the bend, but she didn't trust herself. Years of burrowing into herself when she felt anxious in a so-called "normal" situation had left her reckless and open to the worst of the world.

What are you nervous about, he's our neighbor for Heaven's sake.

Don't be shy.

You're embarrassing me.

Are you really going to cross the road because of him?

Mace? Really, Aubrey?

I'm sure he meant it as a compliment.

Not all men are bad, you know that right?

Her mother's, her father's, her friends', her boyfriend's words all mingled, jangling together in discordant keys whenever she tried to trust her gut, so the instinct faded. Maybe the world was safe after all. Her doctor gave her

Xanax, and when things were really bad, alcohol usually helped. Tyler had cracked open a beer for her as soon as they'd set up camp to help "calm her nerves," as he always put it. She drank dutifully, not wanting to mess up their trip with her hypervigilance and anxious stomach aches. Even then, deep inside, a tiny, almost inaudible voice cried out, "Danger! Danger!" but she swallowed it down and kept living with the abandon everyone expected of her. Things like *that* just don't happen to the average girl.

Until they do.

"I'm just going to go for a walk. I think I had a little too much," she'd said, but really she needed some space. Things had gotten heated when she'd brought up his wandering eye, but he'd blown it off and then she'd walled up like usual. A nice moonlit walk, alone with her thoughts, sounded just right.

"Aw, come on. Just come in the tent and sleep it off." He smirked the stupid shit-eating grin she hated so much, probably just to piss her off more. Bubbling with anger, she already knew what she wanted to do, but some time alone would reassure her it was the best choice, that things were over after almost two years.

"I'll be back soon. I'm just gonna head down to the lake, throw some stones in. It's always breezy down there, I bet that'll make me feel better."

"Well, I'm not staying up and waiting for you. I'm beat. Try not to wake me up when you crawl into your sleeping bag, okay?"

"Yeah. Got it." She had to turn away or else he'd see the contempt on her face. Just a short walk down the lake. There was nothing to worry about, especially with so many campsites around. Still, that cautious voice called out inside her. She smothered it, blocking it out as best as she could.

The man was leaning up against a tree, not looking at her, eyes fixed on the ground, and yet she felt him notice her. His entire energy wrapped around her, slithering into every crevice with penetrating violation, causing a violent shudder to travel down her spine.

"Hey," his voice called out to her, barely above a prickly whisper, "Ma'am, excuse me. You got a second?"

Aubrey kept walking, faster than before, pretending she hadn't heard him. Every fiber of her hoped that he would believe she hadn't noticed him, accept that she wasn't going to interact with him, wait for the next person to walk along the path or leave altogether. A dark veil fell over her mind as she realized that she might need to find an alternate path back to the campsite, just in case. She was now around a bend of trees and the man didn't seem to be following. For just a moment, she allowed herself to breathe a tiny sigh, her limbs numb and lips pursed with tentative relief, like a scared child the moment they've scurried back to the top of the basement stairs.

But he was there. He hadn't needed to call out again. She could only get out a yelp, more the sound of a frightened dog than a human cry for help, before he had tackled her, gagged her mouth with the crook of his arm clamped tight around her face.

Her hands became claws, grabbing and tearing at his clothing, but he was so much stronger. There was no breaking free. She tried to kick him, but as he picked her up, carrying her between trees, deeper and deeper into the forest, she realized how much harder it was to kick someone holding you than she had imagined.

Her mind flashed back to her mother's warnings, her worry, and the fear in her burned with the rageful force of a wildfire. She couldn't let this happen to her, to her family, to her mother. The burst of adrenaline through her blood gave her just enough strength to wrench her body sideways, a violent shake of her head freeing it from his grasp. Landing on the ground in an explosion of pine needles, she gasped and scurried to her feet. Crouched to avoid his arms that swung toward her like clubs.

"Help! Help!" Only two screams made it out, trill and raspy, before he was on top of her, her mouth quieted as it filled with dirt and forest floor. She squirmed, panting and spitting out foliage, but he grabbed her, flipped her onto her back with a force that knocked the air from her lungs. He struck her head again and again until the world spun around her.

His hands coiled around her neck, constricting tighter and tighter. Frantically, her eyes darted across his face, taking in every crease, the sunspot dark against the amber of his left eye, the yellow of his teeth, the few days growth of beard that sprouted black from his tawny jaw. She tried to memorize him in case she could get away, but the pain and pressure were too much. She couldn't get her hands to do anything but claw at his grasp, couldn't command her feet to do more than scrabble against the ground. Her body seemed beyond her control, fear its only master.

Her vision blurred and darkened, a rim of blackness closing in from the periphery. Her mouth gaped open, willing air to force past her restricted throat, eyes bulging and the thick congested feeling filling her ears, but to no avail. There would be no relief.

Nobody heard me. Tears bubbled up and streaked down her face, into her ears, matting her hair in mud against the soft earth. He was striking her again, her head warm with the flow of blood then cold as it was chilled by the night air. He grabbed something and hit her harder. Her eyesight failed completely when something shattered.

As life left her, the failure to escape haunted her with an intensity that magnified the pain thousands of times over. Would her mother ever find her? Would he be caught? Would they know she died full of love for them? *Please, find me. I'm so sorry Mommy.*

Birdie

I want to pretend I don't notice, erase it from my brain, but I can't. There's no ignoring it. My eyes are drawn to it so much so that I have to fight my instinct to stare or else he'll notice and get angry again.

There's blood on his shirt. A long stripe of dried blood down his sleeve. More than just a little scratch or regular camping accident. I know it's not mine. His violence against me was bloodless. What could he have been doing last night to get blood on his shirt? Was it from my fingernails? Had I scratched him that badly? I look at the underside of my fingernails, but there's no blood pushed deep inside. Not even that much dirt despite all the outdoorsy activities.

I examine him from afar, take note of the damage I'm sure came from my nails, but then I notice deeper slices along his neck in downward slashes, their full length obscured by his collar. There's no way I scratched him that hard. I would've felt the flesh under my nails. How could they have gotten there?

"What do you think it is?" The way he asks, it's almost like a dare. He wants me to pry so he can justify taking his anger out on me, but I'm not as stupid as to walk into that trap. He'll never tell me anything, so what's the use in asking?

"I was just worried I'd hurt you last night. That's all," I say, shirking away into myself, trying to disappear, but he won't let me. He draws me out again, his finger under my chin, pulling my face toward his own.

"Maybe you did hurt me. Maybe I was out there in the cold just trying to be tough like you want me to be." His face changes suddenly, as if he remembers what he's done, and I watch it smooth into something timid, apologetic even. "God, I don't know what's wrong with me. I'm sorry. I guess I'm just stressed, I'm taking it out on everyone. I never want to hurt you." He takes my hand, caresses the back of it with his thumb, and I forgive him all over again.

Tearing down the camp is nearly silent, and the drive home is just as quiet. We rarely speak, only when necessary, and the music is kept low, more a white noise to drown out our thoughts than something we actively listen to. I stare out the window at the forests, then the countryside and finally the outskirts of our city where our trailer park is tucked away, where no one has to see it unless they purposely go looking. I try to imagine what kind of people live in the houses in each place we pass. What kind of family resides in that cabin up the long driveway nestled among a grove of pines? What kind of people live in the big farmhouses with iron gates and what others live in the rundown shacks way out in the pastures, with the cows and a couple horses roaming in their expansive yards?

But when we get to our trailer park, I don't have to wonder what kind of people live there. People like Russ, and people like me. I used to be a different kind of person, one who lived behind a white picket fence in a house with hardwood floors and a security system that beeped a warning when any door was opened. But I was not myself back then. I had to be humbled, smashed like a worm under a shoe, and I smile thinking about how I'm slowly building myself back. I can build myself to be the woman I want to be, not one I *had* to be. I think of Noah and tears blur my vision, but they don't fall. Even in death, he gave me a gift. He was my whole world, and still is, in a different way.

"I'm going to go have a couple beers to unwind. Hop out and grab the camping gear," Russ says, not turning his head but staring straight in front of him.

"Can you help? That shit's kinda heavy," I ask, but he doesn't answer. Just keeps staring through the windshield at our modest home, the screen door flapping in the wind and banging loudly every so often. I sigh, open the door and get out. "Okay, I'll get it."

As soon as I've dragged the gear out from the trunk, he's backing up. I curse under my breath, watching him peel away when I haven't even finished dragging the bundle of sleeping bags, heavy duffel bags full of supplies, and blankets across the yard to the poured cement we call a patio. I don't bother to put everything back right away. I know I have hours before he returns, and I'm exhausted, so the heap stays in the middle of the living room, still smelling of campfire and evergreens.

I try to relax, watch a little trash reality tv for a bit, but it just makes me feel agitated. I click over to the news, watch some feel-good story about the adoption fees being waived at the animal shelter next weekend, and then that sketch of the wanted rapist is suddenly plastered across the screen. Russ is right, he doesn't really look anything like him, and yet I still can't stand to look at those charcoal eyes burning into me through the screen. I switch it off, close my eyes, and try to nap, but again, a nervous energy keeps my muscles tight and conjures a pulsing headache in my temples.

The phone rings and rings, and when it clicks over to voicemail, I hang up and try again immediately. It takes until the third try for her to pick up.

"Birdie, what the fuck? Is everything okay?"

"I don't know. I just...need someone, I guess." I stumble over the words, realizing that I didn't even know what I would say when Juliana picked up.

"I'm at work for fuck's sake," she snaps, but after a deep sigh, she adds, "but I get off at three. Can it wait until then?"

I glance at the clock. It's nearly noon.

"Yeah, I think so. I'm just feeling, I don't know, off. I really need a friend is all."

"Don't worry, girl, I got you. I'll come by after work, okay?"

"Okay." I let my arm fall to the side as soon as we hang up, the phone slipping onto the carpet. A heaviness sits on my chest and weighs down my limbs like sandbags, but I force myself to move through it.

I'm nothing but a shadow as I walk around the house, shoving the camping supplies back in the closet, vacuuming and dusting to kill time. I bury myself in my thoughts, wondering what Russ is really doing, wondering where that blood came from if my nails are clean, and wondering what Noah would think of the person I've become.

When I hear the horn outside, I shake my head and force myself out of this half-dead mode I've been stuck in. Juliana smiles at me with her bright red lips, her long dark hair tied up in a French braid.

"Get in, I'm taking you for an ice cream. It's time to cheer the fuck up, girl. I can tell your camping trip didn't pan out, and if that asshole doesn't make you feel special, I'm gonna celebrate you instead."

A smile flickers across my lips as I slide into the passenger seat.

"I love you, Juliana. You're the best friend anyone could have."

"And don't you forget it," she says, winking as she throws the gear in reverse and takes me away from this home that feels like a prison.

Paulina

Paulina jogged along the shoulder of the highway, the same route she took nearly every day. An EDM song kept her going and her pace consistent. Her blonde ponytail bobbed behind her, tucked through a baseball cap, and her windbreaker jacket swished around her arms as a cold wind nipped at her. She was going to need to start dressing a little warmer soon, she thought as she caught the smell of approaching winter carried by the wind.

Cars whizzed past, some slowing when they passed her, others completely disregarding her. She'd learn to block them out enough to not let them disturb her run. There'd been a few instances where someone had catcalled or whistled, a couple times some especially bold man or group of men slowed and begged for her number or to give her a ride or "just a smile." Those were harder to ignore, but she knew that if she kept her eyes ahead and didn't acknowledge them, they'd always leave her alone. So, she didn't think much of it when the red car slowed, and she felt the man's eyes rove up and down her body.

"Need a ride, sweetheart? It's warm in here. Take a little rest," the man said, loud enough to be heard over the wind and the electronic rhythm her feet pounded to, and Paulina kept her head forward, but let her eyes sneak a glance at this rude oaf in her periphery. He was surprisingly attractive with burning blue eyes that startled her with their uncanny lightness.

"Come on. Don't just ignore me like that." Even though she could barely make out the words over the noises, she could sense the growing agitation in his voice, and prepared herself to dodge another case of projectile spit. This man would need to show her his ego wasn't bruised, and so she readied herself for whatever stupid thing he would do to prove it.

Still, she was surprised when he fell back, still following her but slowly, right behind her as he pulled onto the shoulder, the gravel crunching beneath tires. Paulina's breath quickened and there was a pinch in her chest right over her heart. She pulled out her earbuds and tucked them into her jacket pocket, her shaking fingers nearly dropping them as she did.

Then the scratching sounds of gravel stopped, and she knew without looking behind her that he'd parked. It didn't take more than a second for the fear to light up every nerve in her body and force her body into a sprint. *Run. Run. Run.*

She breathed through the pain as her muscles ached and cried for mercy, having already finished five miles of jogging against the hard ground. Adrenaline dumped into her bloodstream and brought a burst of speed to her body, and she was sure she could outrun him. She was a trained athlete, practicing every day, rain or shine, and she believed in her abilities. This creep wasn't going to get her. *Run. Run. Run.* She urged her body forward, feet flying over the loose rocks with long-legged leaps like a gazelle.

But then the rustling sound of tires against rock again. *What was he doing?* She wrestled with her thoughts, not sure if he was giving up and leaving or something much worse. Her feet barely touched the ground with each step before pushing off again as she practically flew. Every part of her burned and begged her to stop, but she kept her body moving at a full sprint. She couldn't stop just yet. Not until he was gone.

The car rammed her and sent her soaring several feet ahead where she crashed to the ground, skidding along the gravel, feeling it dig into her skin along her legs and side of her face, burying into deep, bloody scrapes. Paulina clawed at the ground, trying to get up, but the man was on her before she was able to even pull herself to a kneel.

"Come on, stupid bitch," he said as he dragged her to his idling car, her screams ringing out across the empty fields and pastures. She prayed for someone to drive by, but the road was empty as far as she could see. The man shoved her into the backseat, then forced his way in next to her, pulling the door closed behind them. He pinned her down, kneeling over her, his body weight painfully pressing her down into the worn bench seat. She looked into his eyes and saw an anger she'd never witnessed in all her life. It was a burning hatred that seared into her soul, and she wondered, as he put his hands around her neck, how he could hate a stranger so much. The constriction, tighter and tighter around her neck, the man leaning forward so his weight shifted to her neck, was too much for her to take. She passed out quickly, but the man continued until he had stolen any chance of resuscitation.

When he was finished, he panted like a rabid dog, a string of drool falling from his mouth until it connected him and the woman he'd murdered. Was she a person who would be missed? Did it matter?

There was no time for him to dwell on the act. What was done was done. He cleaned her down, removing any traces of his presence he'd spilled across her bare stomach, and shoved her inside a large empty duffel bag that Birdie hadn't noticed. He smiled to think of her unknowingly helping him. She was always trying to help.

He dragged the bag out into the field where the tall grass partially obscured it. From the road, it just looked like garbage, tossed away to be someone else's problem. Cars would drive by for days, not paying it any mind. Who would stop to check some dirty old bag tossed in a field? No one. Even the police didn't notice it when the search began at dusk.

SKELETONIZATION

BODY

There is almost nothing left. Bits of leathery skin clutching my ribcage, ready to be torn away by a strong gust. Some of my hair and scalp clings to the back of my head, down one shoulder blade under my ripped sweater, inside the right shoe that has withstood the ravaging of the earth. Final secret places where the elements and animals haven't reached it yet.

A furry coat of mold, white and gray, has slowly spread in patches in a few parts, and a storm brought a fresh, wet bundle of leaves to blanket my left arm. I wonder if I'll ever be found, and though I try to hold onto hope, I know I am close to fading completely. Each day, the weather is colder, and a tingle in the howling night wind tells me that winter has arrived and soon there will be snow. I don't think I can hold on through a whole winter, buried under ice crystals, waiting to be found. I almost never hear footsteps anymore. Hiking season has ended, and few enjoy camping in near freezing temperatures.

The morning sun has moved across the sky, and though my vision has darkened to mostly shadows, the barren branches let me feel and track the light. Afternoon is approaching. I wonder how many days I have left before I've disappeared. I don't remember anything about being human any longer. The only thing that remains is the need to be found.

Find me. Find me.

Then, a sound I can hardly believe. Boots crunching through leaves. Two, maybe three people approaching. I strain to see past the shadows, but there are only gray tones of shadow and light. One shadow falls over me.

"See that? I thought I saw something over here." A man's voice. Is he talking about me?

"Jesus, you're right. Is that a skull?" Another man. They're standing over me now. Have I been found?

I feel a hand gently swipe the leaves away and a pair of quiet gasps.

"It's a body," the first man says, his voice barely audible over a whistle of wind through the trees.

"Do you think it's that girl they were looking for? Aubrey Blanch?" the second man asks, and for the first time in forever, I remember myself.

I am Aubrey. Yes, that's right. Aubrey Blanch. I was camping when he attacked me. A flood of visions pours over me: my mother, my older sister and little brother, still in middle school. I remember them all. And then a sense of relief, like a deep breath finally released. I ease into the ruins of my body, down into the earth, and settle in for a long-awaited sleep.

I am Aubrey.

I am found.

THE DEPTHS OF WINTER

Birdie

The car's there again, but I'm basically a zombie, dragging myself along after a grueling day at work. I trudge down the road from the bus stop and see it parked a couple driveways over, but don't think much of it. Inside, I shed my jacket and slip off my bra without taking off my shirt, my favorite trick, before plopping onto the couch and start watching trash tv, but I'm more zoning out than watching it. That is until I remember I haven't checked the mail in days, and of course, Russ hasn't either.

With a groan, I force myself back up and outside, the wind whipping my hair around and cutting through my shirt. That's when the car jogs my memory. Hadn't I seen it before? I bite my cheek as images flash in the back of my mind. I've definitely seen this car before. There's two men inside, still just sitting there. One of them looks like he's reading a book. I take the pile of letters, mostly bills, from the mailbox and the driver looks over at me. I shoot him a smile, but he doesn't smile back. Instead, he looks back at his partner and they start talking. Something about it feels off and I shake away a shudder before I head back in.

It's a couple hours later when Russ finally gets home, and I can tell he's on edge and flustered.

"What's wrong honey?" I ask. "Dinner's almost ready, don't worry."

"Birdie," he snaps, his face blanching white as he peeks through the blinds. "Did you see that car out there?"

"Oh, you mean that tan one? Is it still over there? I thought there was something strange about–"

"Don't you get it? That's the fucking cops."

"What? Are you sure? Why would they be out there, just waiting around?" I want to laugh at the absurdity, but I know to stop myself. The way Russ is acting, his jerky, fidgeting movements, even the way he has to keep clearing his throat, tell me that something serious is happening. I hate the question that bubbles up my throat, but I can't prevent it from pouring out. "Did you do something, Russ?"

"No. Why the fuck are you even asking me that? It's that sketch! Remember the one you went on and on about? Somebody must've agreed with you. I mean, one of my buddies joked about it a few weeks ago, so I knew some people must see a resemblance, but who the fuck would call me in for it? I'm obviously not the guy they want. I didn't do anything, so why are they sneaking around here, trying to mess with me?" His voice shifted from loud to soft. I could hardly follow his train of thought.

"Babe, what makes you think—" I pause, frozen as a shadow passes behind the blinds. "Is someone creeping out there?" I whisper, but we don't move. We've become statues, a commercial jingle playing on the television providing a strange levity to our frozen terror.

"Go look and see what it was," I whisper, but Russ shakes his head. As I move toward the window, I hear him scurry down the hallway into the bedroom and roll my eyes. He didn't do anything, so why does he feel like he has to hide? Sure, cops are never good news, but it's best to just get this over with and send them on their way. Then they can focus on finding the real culprit for whatever crime they're trying to solve.

Parting the blinds just enough to peek through, I see the strange car's door shut and within seconds, the engine starts, and it moves smoothly down the street. Part of me feels silly. Are we just paranoid? But beneath the relief and assurances, a primal fear throbs in my chest. Why are the cops staking out our house? How can I protect my Russ from their unfounded suspicions? I force myself to go back to the kitchen, kill the haunting thoughts with the aroma of homemade food and the squelch of the spoon stirring potatoes.

"They're gone," is all I tell him about it when he finally pokes his head out from the hallway. "Potatoes are a little runny, sorry in advance. The whole thing just threw me off."

"That's alright, sweetheart," he says, pulling my hair to the side and kissing the back of my neck. "I don't know what's going on, but I think we maybe need to leave for a while. Just until they find some new sap to pin their crimes on."

"I don't know, maybe," I say. "But where would we go? We don't have money to go anywhere and miss that much work. I just hope they catch the guy from the news so they can leave you alone. Fucking pigs."

I scoop some mashed potatoes onto Russ's plate next to the salisbury steak, but he doesn't answer. Still, I catch him stealing glances at the windows and front door the rest of the night and I wonder why he's so worried. It's sure to blow over soon, and we both know they only singled him out because of his record from years ago. I'll have to be extra sweet to him until things ease up though.

Poor Russ, he can never get a break.

Birdie

It's weeks without a sighting of any strange cars or snooping detectives, so we've let our guard down. They must've somehow known, because that's when they strike.

They come early in the morning, before we are awake, still cuddled together, legs tangled in sheets. It'd been a wonderful night filled with love and attention that reminded me of the early days of our relationship, and yet the heavy banging on the door wakes me with a start and my stomach drops.

"Police. Open the door," calls a harsh husky voice followed by further fervent knocking. I'm groggy, rubbing the crust from my eyelashes as I slip on a robe.

"Fuck," Russ says in a harsh whisper, already up, jeans on and pulling a t-shirt over his head. "Tell 'em I'm not here. Got it?"

"But what if they've got a warrant? They'll come in anyway."

"Shh, don't let them hear you talking," he hushes me, and my mouth snaps shut. I nod, but he's already busy maneuvering around some luggage and storage bins in the closet, only succeeding in halfway hiding behind them. He pulls the accordion-hinged door shut while I leave the room, biting at the loose skin on my chapped lip and fussing with my hair as I reach the door.

"Hello?" I asked, looking as confused and nonplussed as possible, but the officer isn't buying it.

"Ma'am, we have an arrest warrant for Russ Swinbank."

"Well, he's not home right now so—"

"Where is he then?" The officer barks, interrupting me, my shoulders jumping to my ears. "Because that's his truck parked out front."

"Uh, I'm not sure but he's—"

"Ma'am, please move out of the way. We need to search the premises to make sure the suspect isn't inside."

He doesn't wait for me to answer, shouldering past me before I can react.

"Hey! You can't just come in here." I follow him, the two other cops following after us. "I told you, he's not home."

"Sweep the house; he's in here," I hear one of the cops behind me say to the other. My heart slips down my body, settling into my feet and leaving me empty and cold.

"Get out of my house! I need to see your badges and—and—the warrant, um," I stumble over my words then cry out, the fear bubbling over in a sharp screech as one of the officers bursts into the bedroom, going straight for the closet. "You can't just go through my things. This is an invasion of my privacy!"

But it's too late. Russ is revealed, his pathetic hiding spot not camouflaging him at all. He's cowering behind the boxes, shaking and eyes wide with animal fear, and I have to look away. I can't stand to see him like this, to see them handcuff him and parade him out in front of our neighbors. As I storm out of the room, my head buzzing, I hear Russ behind me, whimpering. Pleading. Wailing like a child. How could they reduce him to this?

"How dare you come in here and rummage through my things? Get out!" I'm shouting but the cops take their time leaving. I try not to watch as Russ walks out but catch a glance of him. His head is down, face a mess of tears, snot, maybe even drool. My heart shatters to see him in that state for even a moment.

"Don't worry, Russ! We'll get this all fixed. I promise!" I shout after him, but then a heavy hand on my shoulder draws my attention away. One of the officers has stayed behind.

"Ma'am, I'm going to need you to come down to the station with me. Just for a few questions."

"What?" I ask, my voice just a crackle of air, the power completely stolen from my lungs. I don't resist. It doesn't even occur to me to ask if this is mandatory or if I should get a lawyer. Shock keeps me in a cloud of surreal confusion the whole drive to the police station, looking out the window and trying to piece together how this could have become my reality. Memories flash in my mind, bright and fleeting: the police sketch, the shoddy attempt at makeup, the blood splatter, the scratches. I shake them away. I'm trying to make sense of it, my brain pulling together any possible connections, no matter how threadbare and tentative.

I have to believe in him. I love him.

Birdie

Every inch of skin is goosebumps, every muscle tremors, the terror mounting each second the cops leave me alone in this tiny gray interrogation room. Part of me wants to talk to them, answer all their questions because I know Russ didn't do anything wrong, but he's warned me a thousand times to never talk to cops without a lawyer. But why wouldn't I just talk to them and get it over with if I have nothing to hide? It's a mistake, because of that stupid sketch that doesn't even look like him. Hell, he has a few enemies, I wouldn't be surprised if one of those jackasses saw it and called it in as a fucked-up prank. My heart shoots up my throat as the door suddenly opens and two cops come in.

"Hello Ms. Black, how you holdin' up in here? Sorry it's taking so long." The cop's voice drips with a false sugary glaze that makes me want to gag.

"I didn't do anything. I want to go home." I'm surprised at how meek and childlike the demand comes out when it sounded strong and confident in my head.

"Okay, okay, I hear you, but listen, your beau, Russ, is in a lot of trouble right now. If you talk to us a bit maybe you can clear some of that up. What do you say?" The same cop was the only one talking, smiling a fake grin that made my stomach twist the whole time. The second one who followed him in stayed quiet, sitting down and typing away on his laptop, barely acknowledging me.

"He didn't do anything either."

"Well, if that's true, then you could certainly help him out by answering just a few questions for us. Sound good?"

"What kind of questions?"

The cops look at each other, sharing some secret wordlessly between them, and the talkative one pulls up the chair opposite me, sitting with his knees spread wide and an elbow resting on the table.

"Just a few things to help us out. Like, do you think you could remember where you were on certain dates over the last few months if I asked, and if Russell was there with you?"

"Yeah, probably."

The second cop hands the blabbermouth one a stapled packet and he flips through it while I squirm against the uncomfortable chair. A nauseating electricity pulses through me, telling me to get up and run, but I know I can't. Instead, I tap my foot and recross my legs, hoping the discomfort will pass.

"Can you recall where you were on the evening of July 25th?" the smiling cop asks.

"Um, I was probably home. I'm pretty much always home."

"And do you remember where Russ was that night? Was he with you?"

There's something in the way his voice tenses, the slight lean forward, the attempt at intimidation in his smiling yet stern face, that makes my guts turn to ice. Can I remember where Russ was that night? All the days and nights of the last few years blur together, and I realize I can't even remember which nights he was home over the last couple weeks, let alone months ago.

"Yes, he was with me, but I don't want to answer any more questions. I want to go home."

"Ms. Black, we only need to clarify a few more things. Don't you want to help your boyfriend out if you can?"

"Am I under arrest?"

"What?" the quiet officer asks, the first time he's spoken up, his eyes looking up and into mine, their irises so dark to be almost black. I can't let them weaponize me against Russ.

"I said, am I under arrest?"

"No, technically you're free to go whenever–"

I cut him off. "Then I want to go home now. I'm done talking to you. And I'm getting Russ the best lawyer I can because y'all are not throwing his life away over a mistaken identity."

The two cops stare at me, dumbfounded, and I suddenly feel more powerful than I have in my entire life. They need me. Need to make sure I can't provide an alibi for Russ, but I'm not dumb. They've already decided on his guilt, I can tell, and that's not justice. A judge and jury need to come to that conclusion, and since I know Russ couldn't have done whatever they're thinking, I need to be there for him. Somebody needs to stick up for him. Otherwise, he's all alone.

A little voice in my head adds on, with the faintest twinge of guilt, *and so am I.*

Juliana

Birdie rests her head in my lap as I comb my fingers through her hair, gently working out the slight tangles and snags. Her face contorts into a dry sob now and then; for now, she's cried all the tears her body will let her. I hum a lullaby I heard somewhere as a child, its sweetly sad melody coming to me spontaneously in this moment of need.

"I don't understand." Her voice is thick, clogged with phlegm. "He didn't do anything."

"There, there," I shush her, continuously running my hands through the downy hair. "Try to relax. We'll figure this out together. I'm here for you."

"But who's there for Russ? He's sitting in a fucking jail cell, probably terrified. God, I can't bear to think of it." Another round of sobs that devolve into a hacking coughing fit, but I keep trying to comfort her. I can't imagine how she feels and give a secret thanks to the universe for not setting this burden on me.

"Russ will get a lawyer and they'll help him out. No need to beat yourself up about this when there's nothing you can do."

"He didn't do anything! Why does he need a god-damn lawyer? This is all such bullshit."

"I mean, you saw the sketch, you heard the descriptions, and even saw those cops nosing around your neighborhood. I get it sucks, but you can't be that surprised."

She sits up, eyes gone cold and every muscle pulled tight.

"Of course I'm surprised. He didn't fucking do anything. Doesn't matter what that sketch looks like. It's not Russ."

"But how do you know for sure? He was gone an awful lot 'round those times they're saying, and it's not like he doesn't have a temper." I shrug a little but keep compassion in my eyes. I just want her to hear me, really hear me, but I know it's futile. "If he's innocent, they'll let him go. They don't lock somebody up for murder with no evidence."

"How can you say that? I thought you were my friend." I'm surprised as fresh tears squeeze their way from the corners of her eyes in fat droplets. How can she cry for him, even now? "He might have a temper, but he's not a killer."

"I'm just saying, they must have *something,* beyond his resemblance to that sketch. That's all." But I know that's not all. Birdie's lip is quaking, and I can tell she's restraining a contemptuous sneer. It boggles my mind that she's still so protective of that freak when he's under arrest for something so horrific and under investigation for worse. I think of those murdered girls and shudder.

She lays back down, head on my lap and we sit in silence for a few minutes, the coughing and heavy sigh of the radiator springing to life the only noise echoing through my house. I scratch her scalp a little, smooth the hair away from her face and behind her ear. Her breathing softens and I wonder if she's fallen asleep, letting my mind wander away from the drama. Had I paid the electric bill? Shit, I need to double check that. And that pile of laundry isn't going to put itself away. Need to get that done before work tomorrow.

"Do you really think he did…that?" Birdie asks, her voice sending me hurtling back to the present.

"I mean, I don't know. Maybe." The words taste like ash on my tongue, the burnt remains of hope and love, and I immediately feel guilty for uttering them. Birdie doesn't react.

My mind fills with the sound of static, like a finger drawn across the foam of a speaker. I want to tell her the secret I have hidden under my dress, in the depths of my body, not big enough to tell on itself yet. So small, I've yet to feel the quickening, but test after test has proven it's there. Would she be happy for me or devastated? Something warns me, stills my hand when I long to caress the slightest bump and spill over with the waiting joy that bubbles under the surface.

Not now. She can't handle it now. I'll just hold her, combing her hair until she falls asleep so I can slip away, tuck her in with a blanket and let her sleep through the shock on my couch. Even Sean won't dare to complain about her spending the night when he finds out about the arrest. He'll know I feel obligated to stay with her, after I called in that anonymous tip.

Birdie

"You've gotta get me a good lawyer. I can't take those court appointed ones, they're complete bozos. They'd just fuck it up." Russ is tapping his fingers so hard, I can hear their rhythm through the plastic jail phone. I can tell he wants to pace. He always paces when he's thinking, and I wonder how much walking he's done in his tiny cell all those hours by himself. "And I can't believe they won't let you bail me out. Did you try asking your Mom for help?"

"You know she'd never do that," I say, rolling my eyes. "I've tried everything I could think of; they just set it too high. We don't have the assets to cover it. And well…"

"Well what?" He snaps the words and I bristle.

"You heard the judge same as I did. He thinks you're a flight risk."

"But that's bullshit!"

"I know, but I can't do anything about that, can I?" I say, pulling my hands through my hair, tempted to pull chunks of it out, I'm so exasperated. "Sorry. I'm sorry, hon. I'm just as frustrated as you."

"Heh, sure," he laughs snidely, throwing his head back. "You're not stuck in here with all these assholes."

"Okay, maybe not quite as much, but I'm on your side. Russ, I'm really trying. I'm sorry."

I put a hand to the plastic partition and after a grunt, he presses his palm up to mine.

"I know, I know. I'm sorry too, babe. I'm just freaking out in here. I didn't do anything."

"I believe you. You know I do," I say, wiping at the tears flowing down my cheeks. "At least the prosecution said they're moving your court date up as soon as possible. I know you'll be out of there when they realize they don't have any kind of case against you except a dumb sketch and some hearsay from who-knows-who." I force myself to smile, for his sake. "You've gotta stay positive. Stay tough. We'll get through this."

"Easy for you to say," he shoots the words, and like bullets, they pierce through my softest places, tearing me apart. "You better not be fucking around on me out there."

"What? I'd never do that!" I cry out, standing up, but a guard yells at me to calm down, so I force myself back in my seat, hands shaking as I try to compose myself. "I visit as much as I'm able."

"But you didn't pick up when I called yesterday."

"I was at my new job!" I scoff, flabbergasted at the accusation.

"I'm just saying, it's suspicious. That's all."

His eyes have turned stone-gray and just as cold. I cower under their fury.

"I had to get that second job to afford the lawyer you want. It's all I could do—"

"Okay, whatever, I believe you." He tosses the words out, but I'm not sure he means them. Instead, it feels more like he's rushing me away. "Just make sure I get that lawyer. That's the only way I'm getting out of here. You know the cops fucking hate me. They're out to get me, for sure. Fuck, they've probably planted something to frame me for all I know."

"I'm doing my best, hon. Just stay strong," I say, my weak smile faltering as he hangs up the phone and turns to the guard.

Birdie

The months without Russ had dragged by, and yet, sitting on the wooden bench and listening to testimonies felt surreal and sudden. I wriggle and tap my foot, unable to get comfortable. Long hours of sitting and listening, trying to take notes that might help Russ and his lawyer, were already getting to me on only the second day of the trial. The next witness finishes being sworn in and prepares herself.

The medical examiner is stern—her lips drawn in a tight line, back rigid with perfect posture, hair tied back in an immaculate bun. I want to hate her because I know she is on the opposite side of Russ, and thus me, but there's something about her I can't help but admire. The prosecutor paces as he asks her question after question, and I try to focus my attention on their faces and not the autopsy photos blown up and displayed on poster boards or the presentation projected on the wall for the jury to gawk at.

"And were you able to determine the cause of death?"

"Usually, by this point of extreme decomposition, it's very difficult to determine the cause of death, but in this case, there was the telltale damage to the hyoid bone indicating strangulation." The doctor speaks with the confidence of an expert, and I'm sure she's right, but it couldn't have been at the hands of my Russ.

"Are there other causes of death that could result in this type of injury?"

"In theory, possibly, but in my professional opinion, this injury points specifically to death via strangulation."

"And was any DNA recovered from the victim's body?"

"Once again we were very lucky because, by the time a body is skeletonized, usually any DNA evidence would be destroyed, however in this case, the victim retained a few areas of skin and hair, and we were able to recover some skin cells from beneath her fingernails that contained another person's DNA."

"Whose DNA was it?"

Without hesitation, the doctor looks right at Russ.

"Mr. Russell Swinbank's."

The prosecutor asks a few more questions, flipping through more vile photographs, close-ups of the poor decomposed woman's injuries, but I focus on the jurors' faces. They are all gray and sickened, and that tells me everything I need to know.

When he moves on to the other cases with their similar injuries and the used condom found tossed in the sewer drain outside one of their houses, I have to step out and get some air. The photos of their freshly slaughtered bodies are too much to bear. Even if Russ hadn't killed them, somebody had. They had all been someone's loved one. Someone's daughter. It's hard to keep my emotions at bay, but I finally compose myself enough to return. As I take my seat, the prosecutor is finishing with the expert witness.

"I want you all to really think about what these women went through. We've just heard all the grisly details, but I want you to remember that most of these women were just at home, winding down after work, thinking they were safe. Then someone appeared, invading their home and privacy, ripping away any shred of safety, and murdering them in cold blood. Nothing is scarier than a home invasion and these women, all of them, died paralyzed with fear. According to the DNA evidence, that someone was Russell Swinbank."

Russ's lawyer is up and tries his best to raise some doubt in the form of possible contamination or transference of the DNA from somewhere else, even the slightest hint of a framing, but it doesn't seem to have much effect on the sullen faces of the twelve jurors and two alternates who hold Russ's life in their hands.

The next witness called by the prosecution is a wisp of a woman with a bare face and swimming in a floral dress several sizes too large. She's identified as Jody Prescott, the receptionist at the business where one of the victims had worked, Ava DeMille. After being sworn in, Jody sits, and I can tell she's actively avoiding looking at Russ. *Could this be guilt over the lie she's about to tell?* I want to shout, point it out to everyone in the room, saying, "Look, she's lying. Can't you see?" but I know it'd just end in me being banned from the courthouse and my words stricken from the record. Still, part of me wonders if it would be worth it for the sliver of doubt I might sew.

"Tell us about the interaction you had with Ava De-Mille on August 28th."

"Well, a man I'd never seen before came in and brought a box of chocolates for Ava. I thought it was really sweet, and he seemed really nice. Very talkative, a real extrovert charmer type, you know?" Her hands fumbled together in her lap, nervously folding over themselves. "I honestly thought he was just a delivery guy at first, but it was strange that he wasn't wearing a uniform. But when I brought them to her, she was horrified. I'll never forget the way the color ran out of her face." Jody stumbles on her last words, choking up with tears in a sound like a hiccup.

"Did Ava say anything about the man?"

"Not right then, but I asked her about it the next day because I just couldn't get that look out of my mind, and I'd noticed she'd thrown the chocolates in the trash right after. I can be a bit nosey, and I guess I was wondering if it was an ex-boyfriend or something, but she told me she thought that guy had been following her. She tried to laugh it off as ridiculous after she said it, but it really freaked me out. And then, when she was…killed, I right away thought of that man with the chocolates and wondered if it was related." Jody is crying hard by the time she's finished, and the judge has to give her a moment to pull herself together.

"Ms. Prescott, do you see the man who delivered the chocolates in the courtroom today?" the prosecutor asked, and I watched as the frail woman's hand raised, her finger pointing straight at Russ.

"He's right there. I'm sure it's him."

"Thank you, Mrs. Prescott. That's all."

Again, Russ's lawyer tries to do damage control, calling her memory into question, but there isn't much to be said and he's soon dismissed the shaking, crying woman from the bench.

The next expert, and last for the day, is a blood spatter expert and I realize I can't sit through any more meticulous details about violence and gore. I need to go home. I give the slightest wave to Russ when I'm sure I catch his eye, enough to let him know I'm leaving without being admonished by the judge, and he nods, the faraway blankness on his face unchanging.

At home, I turn off the engine and just sit. I don't want to go inside. There's nothing for me there but an empty house and my own demons, waiting to pry into my mind and bring up all the doubt, fear, and sorrow they could gather from every memory of my life. I don't want to go anywhere else either. Juliana has pulled away, taking days to text or call me back, and even the girls from work who had always been moderately friendly are short with me now. I sit in my car for hours, finding the slightest respite in this liminal space between coming and going. A space just big enough for me to catch my breath.

Birdie

My hands are trembling, clutching at one another, and the harder I try to control them, the worse it gets. I'm sure Russ thinks it makes me look guilty or like I'm hiding something. I can tell by the hard way he's staring at me, compelling me to look more natural. He must know I can't help it, plus maybe the jury will see it for the truth of what it is, extreme nervousness.

I've never been one to speak in front of a crowd or perform in any way. I loathe being in the spotlight, but of course, I need to do this for Russ. It's more than just a way to help his case, which I doubt he needs because he's innocent. It's another way to show that I'm not giving up on him, unlike everyone else.

The prosecutor sneers at me like I'm an insect, and I feel like one, with my restless hands and big, terrified eyes. I'm sworn in, and take a deep breath to try to steady myself as she approaches to begin the questioning.

"Ms. Bernadette Black, how long have you known the defendant?"

"Almost four years. Uh, it'll be three in April."

"And how would you describe your relationship with Mr. Swinbank?"

"I'd say we were boyfriend and girlfriend. We have a serious relationship. We live together."

"So, would it be fair to say that you feel confident in his usual routines and habits?"

"Yes," I answer, squirming a little against the hard bench seat.

"Do you recall any nights over the last year where Mr. Swinbank diverged from his usual routines, maybe stayed out much later than normal or left without saying where he was going?"

"Uh, I don't think so." I bite my lip but realize and pull it out again, looking away.

"Remember, you're under oath, Ms. Black. There's never been a night like that over the past year? This man," she points at Russ, his eyes down on a paper he's scribbling away on, "Was home all night with you every night? You never wondered where he was?"

"I mean, sometimes he'd go out with his friends. I don't think that's a big deal though. Everyone does that."

She hums, tapping her pen against the papers in her hand. "And were there ever times he went out at night that wasn't a planned meetup with friends?"

"Sure, that happens sometimes. Doesn't everyone?" I notice I've crossed my arms in front of my chest and quickly correct it. She's getting to me already.

"Can you recall any of the dates of those nights?"

"No. I don't usually keep track of things like that."

"Well." The prosecutor steps closer so her cloud of strong perfume reaches me, and I stifle a gag. "Was there ever a night over the last year where you and Mr. Swinbank had a disagreement and he stormed off for most of the night?"

I swallow to quell the tickle in my throat. I try not to look at Russ, but I can feel his power and judgment radiating from across the room.

"Maybe that happened a couple times. But couples fight. It's normal. He just needs some space sometimes. That's actually a healthy way to deal with conflict." I cringe at how the words come out, sounding more like I'm trying to convince myself than exuding the confidence I thought they would.

"Your neighbors say it happens quite often. At least once a week."

"No, that's not true."

"Then how often would you say conflicts like this happen?"

"Not very often. Maybe once a month."

"Was he ever violent with you? Laid his hands on you?"

"Never."

"Okay, and when Mr. Swinbank would leave after these altercations, do you know where he would go?"

"I don't know for sure, but I always assumed he went to one of the bars he liked."

"But you don't know."

"No, I guess not."

"He never told you when he got back where he'd been for all those hours?"

I can't help myself. I look to Russ for guidance, but he still doesn't look up. I sigh.

"Maybe he did. I don't remember."

She smirks to herself as she looks down at her heels. I fight the feeling of defeat rising up my throat. *I'm trying my best, Russ. Please understand.*

"Did you ever notice anything strange about the defendant when he'd return after these mysterious absences?"

"Objection," the defense shouted. "Leading the witness."

"I'll allow it," the sleepy-eyed judge answered, before telling Birdie to answer the question.

"No. I mean, except that he'd cooled off from our fight. That's all it was. He was just cooling off."

She nods knowingly to the jury, meeting several of their eyes, and I shrink into myself. I'm not holding up as well as I wanted to for Russ. If only I could just speak to them, tell them about him, they'd know this is all a big mistake.

"Ms. Black, did you and the defendant go on a camping trip on November twelfth?"

"Yes."

"And during said camping trip, did you and the defendant have a disagreement?"

"Um." I look to Russ, hoping to catch his eye, to get some hint of reassurance. He still doesn't look up.

"Please answer the question, Ms. Black."

"Yeah, we had a fight. I don't even remember what it was about. Something stupid."

My gut twists in painful knots and all I want is to be back home, curled in bed, the covers over my head. I need to hide away.

"And did Mr. Swinbank leave for an extended period of time after this argument?"

I hesitate.

"Ms. Black, did he leave the campsite after your fight?"

The one-word answer leaves my lips, a soft and quiet "yes."

I realize in this moment that maybe the truth mixed with a couple white lies isn't enough. Maybe real lies were necessary to make sure they didn't pin these murders on an innocent man. Regret floods me, filling me up until I'm fighting to keep it from spilling out as tears.

"How long would you say Mr. Swinbank was gone?"

"I don't remember."

"And do you know where he went while he was gone from your campsite?"

"Just for a walk."

The prosecutor turns to the jury, that smug smile growing at the corners of her lips, and gives them a knowing look.

"Did you know Ms. Aubrey Blanch was camping in the same park as you and Mr. Swinbank that weekend?"

"No."

"And that her remains were found just off the hiking path near both of your campsites?"

"I've heard that. It was all over the news." My face is aflame with shame and rage, but I swallow it down.

"Ms. Black, does the defendant have a temper?"

"No."

The prosecutor's eyes steel over. "I want to remind you that you're under oath."

I calm myself before repeating, "No."

"Has the defendant ever hit you?"

"No." I squirm in my seat at the lie. The jury's eyes are on me, probing behind my words. I have to protect him.

"Have you ever hit him?"

"No!"

"But you admit you fought often."

"I told you already, every couple fights sometimes—"

"But not every couple fights with the man yelling so loudly that the neighbors call the police because they think someone might be in danger, wouldn't you agree?"

My face burns red, and I glower at her.

"I suppose that's true."

She can't help herself, her sick little smile creeping across her face again. I've never hated someone so much in my whole life.

"Do you know why your friend Juliana Perez testified that you told her about a physical altercation between you and the defendant?"

I swallow hard.

"I'd say she's lying." The words feel dirty on my tongue, and I want nothing more than to go wash out my mouth, but I have to do whatever it takes for Russ.

"Let's go back a little. Help me understand. So on the night of November twelfth, you were camping with the defendant, correct?"

"Yes. We were at the campsite and the nearby hiking paths all day."

"And did you two spend the *entire* night at your campsite?"

"Yes."

"Except for the walk you mentioned?"

"That was only for fifteen, twenty minutes." Again, my face burns red.

"And this was after the fight you two had, that's been corroborated by campers at two nearby campsites?"

"He left to cool off, but it was only for a few minutes. Just a quick walk around."

"Ah, I see. So, he left the campsite and you're not sure what he was doing during that period of time."

"But it wasn't—"

240

"And are you aware of the defendant's whereabouts on the night of April 21st?"

"I mean, that was a long time ago, but I'm sure he was home with me."

"You're sure?"

"Yes."

"Then his friends who place him at the Rug Burn, a nearby bar, that night are lying?"

"Oh, well, maybe I'm misremembering." I glance at Russ for guidance but he's looking down. "If they say he was with them, then he probably was."

"What if I told you that they never actually said that?"

"What?" I feel the sweat beading at my temples and upper lip, wiping at it with the edge of my sleeve. "Then maybe he *was* home with me…"

"It seems to me, Ms. Black, that you have no idea where the defendant was most nights."

"No, that's not true. You're just mixing me up on purpose."

"What I think is that you are lying, under oath, for your boyfriend, Mr. Swinbank, and that you have no problem doing so. Do you often find yourself bending the truth?"

"No!" I try to yell, but it only comes out as a breathy gasp.

"Ms. Black, when you called the emergency services after your son was hit by a car, did you tell them the truth?"

I hear Russ's lawyer call out for an objection, but it's overruled again.

My voice shakes, disembodied before me, as I hear myself say, "I told the truth."

"The truth or your own version of the truth? A version where you had been watching your son dutifully, but the driver had targeted him, run him down on purpose? Do you remember telling the dispatcher that story?"

"Yes, but I was just confused. My son had just..." I can't bring myself to say it, even now.

"Or was the truth that you were in fact not watching your son and let him run free and unattended while you texted with a man you were having an extramarital affair with?"

"Please, stop," I beg, no longer able to make eye contact with the lawyer, and it's not until I see the circles of dampness appearing on my lap that I realize I'm crying.

"It seems to me that you aren't always truthful when it's in your best interest to bend the truth. Would you say that's a fair characterization of how you react to difficult situations?"

But I can't answer the question. My throat, full of nettles, chokes any words I try to form. The judge dismisses us for a short recess to allow me to collect myself before Russ's lawyer can question me. I somehow pull myself together, not because I want to, but because Russ needs me. I have to prove I'm a better witness than that. I have to save him.

The sleazeball lawyer Russ picked out of a phonebook approaches and I feel nearly as anxious as I did with the prosecutor. *Not a good sign,* I think, swallowing hard.

"Ms. Black, how would you characterize your partner of nearly four years, Russell Swinbank? A good man? An honest man?"

"Definitely. He's always working hard to take care of me, treat me like a woman should be treated. He's been a wonderful boyfriend."

"Did you ever have any suspicions he was doing anything illicit when he said he was out with his friends?"

"No, never."

"Did he ever come home with bloody clothing or strange injuries?"

I think of the broken nose and double black eyes but brush it away immediately. That was just a fistfight. He'd told me so.

"No."

"Do you have any reason to believe Russell is a murderer?"

"No, of course not."

"Thank you, Ms. Black. The defense rests."

And just like that, my small part in the trial is over. Now there will be only ages of watching and waiting.

The drive home is lonelier than ever. I go over every question and answer, wondering what I could have said, how I could've helped him more. The faces of the jurors replay on repeat in my mind's eye: gray, sullen, and heartbroken. I feel the verdict in the marrow of my bones and doubt the buffoon of a lawyer could ever change their minds in the time left. Still, I have to hold onto a mote of hope, or else I'll collapse into myself forever.

The sun is setting when I lay down on the couch, golden light strewn across the carpet. I can't bring myself to do anything. Not eat, not sleep. I can hardly move. When I finally pull myself from the couch and stagger to the bedroom, it's late into the night. Under the bed, much too big for only one person, something blue pokes out. I pick it up and break into tears. It's Rover.

I hold the toy dog to my chest and cry the rest of the night and well into the early morning. I weep for Russ, for Noah, for myself. I don't want to live without them. Who am I without them? A nobody; better off dead.

Every part of me wants to die, and my mind rolls over each possible option, feasting on every detail, wallowing in the sorrow and basking in the hope of being done with it all. I find myself walking to the bridge where the highway passes over the sickly creek. I'm covered in mud by the time I find it. Wiping the dirt from the crevices, the gun is lighter in my hand than I remember. It could be so easy to end it, here, where I wouldn't be found for who knows how long, maybe never. Nobody ever goes down here. Who would look for me? Maybe Juliana. Maybe the lawyers if they need me to testify again someday. Maybe no one.

But the stench burns acrid in my nostrils and the lonely shade of the bridge is too much for me. I tuck the gun into my pants and crawl back up the embankment. Back home, I take a long hot shower, wipe the gun clean with a rag, and sit on my bed, dripping, naked, holding the barrel under my chin.

I visualize the blood spray. The chunks of bone and brain matter splattered across the bed, the wall, my nude body. I imagine being with Noah again. Even if there's nothing, we'd be in that nothingness together. My finger grazes the trigger. I only need to pull it and it can all be over, but my hand is shaking, and every part of my body silently screams in anguish.

I take a deep breath then lower the gun, toss it onto the bed next to me. It slips off to the carpet with a thud. I kick it under the bed, then tuck myself into a tight ball on top of the comforter and weep.

But no matter how much I want it, I can't. Not yet. Russ needs me. Whether he's in prison or eventually freed, he'll need me to take care of him. There is still enough purpose to be wrung from my pathetic life to continue on. So I do. I force myself to keep going for Noah and for Russ. I hide the precious blue toy away in the corner of my closet, push a few shoe boxes under the bed to hide the temptation from even an accidental glance, and command my exhausted body to get ready for work.

Birdie

The girl that takes the stand is nothing like I expected. She's petite, her gaunt face and thin frame lined with wiry muscle immediately telling the story of rapid, unintentional weight loss. Her hair is thin, a bald patch showing through the strands she'd obviously carefully arranged to hide it. My heart sinks as I watch her whole form tremble; her eyes search the room with the pain of a hunted animal. They find Russ and lock on him, growing hard, a hidden strength revealing itself behind the building tears.

My eyes switch between them, but Russ refuses to meet her gaze. Part of me begs him to look, as if I could tell the truth from their silent exchange, but another part of me understands why he doesn't. This woman is damaged and out for blood. She's sure it was my Russ who caused this trauma, and nothing could convince her otherwise. I want to submerge myself in her story, meet her pain with sympathy, but then who would be left for

Russ? No one seems to believe him except me. No matter how I feel for her, I must stay strong for him.

I watch them swear her in, the way her hands smooth over her long dress again and again, notice how every inch of skin from her neck to her toes is covered. Protected. This poor woman. What she must have gone through. The real monster must be caught before he harms anyone else. I shudder at the thought that he's still out there, probably stalking someone and biding his time before he strikes again.

"Ms. Fairchild, is the man who assaulted you in the courtroom today?" the prosecutor asks, addressing the jury as much as the woman. I scan their faces, some drowsy-eyed, others leaning forward, fist to chin, with rapt attention. Their mouths are all straight lines of anticipation, unreadable.

"Yes."

"Can you please point to identify that man for us?"

"Yes." She stretches out her arm, accusing finger locked on Russ. "He's right there."

"Let the record show that she pointed out the defendant, Russel Swinbank."

The stenographer taps his name in her shorthand onto the tape, and my stomach lurches so hard, I nearly vomit on my own lap.

"Please, Ms. Fairchild, can you tell us, in your own words, what happened on the night of July 25th?"

I watch the fragile woman take a deep breath, and as the air fills her, it seems every bone in her body jangles and rattles in a terrible shiver. I recognize that feeling of going back in time, to a horrible scene you wish you could forget but that haunts you. A lump forms in my throat as she begins, and I find I can't swallow it down.

"It was a hot night. I remember the AC was on and it made me feel uneasy to not be able to hear past it. See, I'd suspected that I'd had an intruder in my house not long before, even though they didn't take anything, and I'd been hearing weird noises, keeping myself on edge all the time. I knew there was some madman on the loose because of the news, but it was so hard to believe it could happen to me. There'd been a weird sound outside my window that night, and that's what made me decide to give up on the work I was doing and try to go to bed. Then—"

I know before she can recount any more of her ordeal that I can't handle hearing the details. Even knowing it wasn't Russ who did this to her, I can't bear her trauma on top of my own. The edges of my sanity fray with each day the trial drags on, slowly pulling apart and unraveling and I don't want to see what remains beneath.

Russ doesn't turn when I stand and leave. I wonder if he knows I left. If he thinks I no longer believe him. In the crisp air outside the courtyard, I count through my breaths and try to calm down. I need to stay strong for him. Yes, this poor woman's been through hell, but being wrongly accused of such a crime must be worse. I imagine Russ in his small, white cell, waiting for each day to pass, hoping that a future outside that room still awaits him.

Russ

My lovely Birdie,

I finally got your letter, and while I agree that things could've gone better, I'm still really proud of you. You gave it your best shot. You did a good job standing up to that bully of a prosecutor for me and I appreciate it. I appreciate you. You're my everything. My whole world. My galaxy and all my stars. The beginning and end of my happiness and all that matters to me. We're soulmates, baby, and there's no keeping us apart. You just watch. I'm getting out of here and we'll be together again.

I don't think the jury is buying this far-fetched shit the state's trying to pull, so we won't have to wait that long, though I'd be lying if I didn't admit that every week in here is like an eternity in hell. So many assholes trying to prove how much of a man they are, it's exhausting. I keep to myself, but sometimes that pisses them off more.

Don't worry, I'm not letting them get to me. I'm staying the same Russ you've always known.

And about the thing with the pictures, I mean, come on, you've known me long enough I think to know I'm not the type to pass something like that around or tape them up on my wall or anything. I miss that gorgeous body of yours so much, it would be the best gift I can imagine to be able to look at it again whenever I want. It's up to you, but just consider it, and I'll be really looking forward to my next letter.

There's one other thing that could make a world of difference in here, and that's your old prescription for anxiety. Remember those? I was thinking about them because I think I've got some kind of anxiety disorder now. I wish I could see a doctor and get some of those. I know a lot of the other guys around here also have really bad nerves and they'd do anything to get their hands on some pills too. Maybe they'd get off my back if they had something for their anxiety. It's too bad they won't let me see a doctor and there's no other way to get something like that. Maybe you could talk to your old doctor and see what she thinks I should do. I don't know, just shooting off some ideas. Sorry about the rambling.

Please, come visit again as soon as you can. I miss you so much every day.

Love,

Russ

Birdie

My feet drag as I make my way to the counter with the white plastic phone and video screen. I want to touch him, run my fingers through his hair, hold him and tell him it'll all be okay, but this is all they'll let me have. I pick up the receiver and watch the screen flicker to life. Dark bags rim his eyes, giving them a slightly sunken, uncanny appearance of a living skull. The irises, still cornflower blue, beam out like a light in the darkness.

"How are you holding up out there?" he asks, a smile pulling up one corner of his mouth, and my heart instantly shatters. The tears pour out and I look at this stunned face through the waterfall blur. "Oh god, Birdie, what's wrong?"

"I can't handle seeing you like this. It's not fair." I somehow stammer the words out through my sobs. "But–but how did they get all this evidence? I don't understand."

Russ sighs, shakes his head then leans over, hiding his face in his hands. I need to see his face. Is he crying?

Angry? Ashamed? My mind runs wild with all the things he's hiding away in that moment. I beg him with my eyes, *please, just tell me what to believe. I want to believe you.*

"I honestly... I can't... shit, fuck me," he trips through his words, and raises his eyes to meet mine. My body relaxes the second I see they're red and filled with tears, though a part of me is shaken by my doubt. How could I betray him like that?

"Listen to me." His voice lowers to a growling plea. "I didn't do this. Any of it. I have no idea where they got that so-called evidence from, but it wasn't me. The only thing I can think of is that someone is framing me, but who and why? It doesn't make any fucking sense."

"Framing you?" My voice quavers as I roll the words over my tongue. Looking at his ashen, tired face in the monitor, I pinch my thigh between my fingernails to make sure I'm not dreaming. The situation feels so surreal.

"I know how that sounds, but it's the only explanation. They say they have my DNA at two of the crime scenes, but how could it be there unless someone planted it?"

"What? But why?"

"I don't know. That's got me fucking stumped." He runs his hand through his greasy hair, some of it unintentionally spiking up where his hand has been. "Maybe I'm just a rando chosen to take the fall for some cop or politician or something. Blue collar guy nobody'll miss. Bit of a temper. History of angry exes. Seems like an easy person to pin this on. Fuck me."

"Do you really think..." My question fades off before I finish it, and I find myself lost in conjured images of police officers planting evidence, scrubbing clean the real perpetrator's fingerprints. "But they said they found not just DNA but your blood at those scenes. How would they do that? They can't lift blood off a thrown away soda cup like they can DNA. I'm just not sure how they could get your blood without you knowing."

"Who fucking knows? Maybe they grabbed it from my last checkup. Remember I told you they took three vials? That was weird. Why'd they need so much? Who all's in on this setup?" He's waving his arms, eyes wild and twitching with rage. Then he slows, looks at me through the screen. No, not at me. Into me. His gaze rummages through my every micro gesture, as if he was trying to read my thoughts. "Unless you're trying to say there's another reason why my blood would be at those goddamn crime scenes."

"No, don't say that. You *know* I believe you. It's just all really overwhelming, that's all."

His gaze softens and I melt beneath it, wiping at the tears that keep running down my cheeks no matter how I try to stop them.

"Okay. I'm sorry, you're right. I'm just losing it in here. God, I need to get out, back in the real world. It's fucking hell in here." The rage broils in his eyes again, but he's not looking at me but behind me, at the world that's decided his guilt and abandoned him before his trial's even finished.

"I'm doing everything I can. Working extra shifts to cover the bare minimum of that fancy lawyer's payment plan. Visiting whenever I can. Maneuvering my schedule around the trial so I can be there for you, even if it means barely sleeping. I'm trying my very best to support you through this, Russ." I sniffle back a sob, choke on it. "What else can I do?"

His eyes go cold again, reptilian, and it unsettles something fragile in my very core. I want him to stop looking at me, but even when I look away, his eyes pierce through me.

"Why'd you walk out today?"

"You saw that?" I ask, but he doesn't answer, only stares with the same intensity as before. "I don't know. I couldn't handle it. That poor woman, she looked terrible. Even though it wasn't you, someone did something horrible to her and I didn't want to hear it. Not from her own lips like that. It's so different when the prosecutor spells it out all matter-of-factly. But when she started talking, the fear in her voice… it was too much."

Russ still stares, his mouth moving just perceptibly as he chews on the inside of his lip, a tell I recognize after so many years together: he's anxious.

"I know it's terrible in there, and you're feeling all alone in the world, but you're not. I'm still here for you. I always will be." I reach out, touch his face on the screen and wish I could feel the bristle of his unshaven face beneath my fingertips. "I know you're innocent and I'm going to do whatever I can to get you out."

He shifts in his chair, eyes darting away. He's holding something back.

"I have an idea, but I need more time to figure everything out."

"What do you mean?"

"Please, just stick around. Keep loving me. Keep being the goddamn wonderful woman you are that I never deserved." His lip trembles and I know his words are true. My heart is putty in his calloused hands. "I'll let you know as soon as I've got it all worked out."

Birdie

I sit cross-legged on the fluffy duvet, leaves of paper spread around me, encircling me like a wreath. His messy scrawl clambers across every page, some long scrolls of yellow legal pad, some small scraps holding only a few sentences, some pristine white copy paper typed in the prison library, still others dingy and stained with graphite fingerprints and dried spots of fallen tears. Nearly all the letters start the same: *My lovely Birdie*. I hate how much it means to me that he starts each one with the same syrupy declaration, but it's everything. It keeps me going, even when the hours drag by, and the workload toils my body to the distorted curl of a burnt-out match.

I run my fingers over the letters and pretend I can feel his warmth through them. Every day without him, the bad times fade, and the good memories shine brighter, polished by my constant visits. I take one of his earliest letters, savor the soft, worn quality of the paper, the way it folds on itself in quilted fourths. Having read it hundreds of times, I glide over the words, more from memory than reading.

My lovely Birdie,

How can I tell you how much I miss you? There's no way to make you understand how much being in here has made me realize what a fucking paradise life was with you. Every morning, I wake up thinking of you. How much I miss your warm body next to mine and the way your morning kisses taste like coffee. I miss your Sunday pancakes and Thursday night meatloaf with leftovers for lunch on Fridays. All the other guys at work were always jealous of those meatloaf lunches. It's those little, dumb things that I miss the most.

When I get out of here, I'm going to make it up to you for all the bullshit I put you through. It makes me almost cry to think I could've lost the most amazing woman in the whole world over my stupid anger issues. Please believe me, I won't be like that ever again. This whole experience has changed me, and as soon as I'm out, you'll see. I'm gonna sweep you off your feet, baby. Gonna work hard to give you that little house you've always wanted. Gonna put a big old diamond on your finger. Gonna never take you for granted again. I've just gotta get out of here and show you.

Please write me back when you get a chance. I know you're working extra hours and you've gotta be tired all the time, but your letters are all that keep me going right now. Maybe some pictures? I promise I won't show anyone else.

All my love,
Russ

I set down the sheet of paper, sliding it back in its place among the semi-circle of love letters. My fingers skate over the leaves, skipping over a few before choosing another.

My lovely Birdie,

Thank you for always being there in court. I know it's not easy for you to get the time, but it really means the world to me. You have no idea how much comfort and hope it brings me to see you over there. Sometimes it feels like you're the only one in my corner. Even my fucking lawyer seems out to get me. I'll never forgive him for asking me to plead guilty. Can you believe that?! Plead guilty for something I didn't fucking do? For MURDER-ING these women! All because he's sure they're going to give me the fucking death penalty. I can't stand him. He tried to walk it all back, say he believes me and all that shit, but I don't trust him anymore.

He hasn't even brought up how these victims are all over the place, different ages, weapons, and locations, after I brought it up with him and everything. He tried to say it didn't matter, but fuck, I know a thing or two about true crime from tv and they just don't make sense as one person. Why isn't he fighting harder for me? There's no way he believes I'm not the sick fuck who did all this, but at this point, I don't know if any lawyer would. Everyone hates me and I didn't do anything to deserve it.

You're the only one I trust anymore. God, I've gotta get outta here. I can't imagine spending the rest of my life in here. To be away from you forever like that? I'd rather die.

Love you sweetheart,
Russ

I slide that one back in its place and choose another, tears gathering on my lashes, gluing them together with each blink until I wipe them clear. I pick up the most well-worn of the collection, a thin sheet of lined paper with doodles of hearts and confetti stars bordering the words.

My lovely Birdie,

I need to get out, not only to hold you in my arms again and cover you with kisses, but to show you the kind of love you really deserve. It took me going to jail to see how bad I'd treated you, and I don't know how you've forgiven me so many times, or why you stuck with me, but if I can just get out, I'll give you everything you deserve. I'll work my ass off and you'll finally be able to travel the world like you've always wanted. And that big wedding I know you're always dreaming about, that's gonna be yours. I promise. All I need is to get out of here.

> *Forever yours,*
> *Russ*

A weak smile crawls across my lips, but I can't make it stay. Not when I see the letter next to my beloved one. A letter I've been tempted to throw out, but for some reason, can't bring myself to do it. Maybe because I want to remember there's a monstrous side to Russ, counterbalancing the cotton candy romance fluff.

Birdie,

I can't believe you think you're so much better than me now. Just because I'm trapped in this living hell doesn't mean things don't get back to me. How come you didn't tell me about your new job? You even applied to that fucking community college again without telling me? What, you thought I wouldn't be happy for the love of my fucking life? I only ever stopped you before because I could see it was too much on your plate, and now you're even busier than before. But I understand now. You were just using me. Now when things get hard, you throw me away. I disgust you.

When you're wearing your slutty little nurse outfit and giving pity blowjobs to bums that "needed your help," I want you to remember how low you were when I picked you up off the ground and dusted you off, put you back together from the shattered piece of shit mess you were. I want you to remember how you begged me to let you kill yourself on that first anniversary. You wanted nothing more than to be worm food in the ground with the kid you basically murdered, but I stopped you. Maybe I should've let you do it. Maybe that's where I went wrong. Think that over. Let it seep into your every thought. Sit with it a long time, then get back to me. Or don't.

Russ

This time, I can't help myself. I wad up the letter and toss it across the room. Angry tears roll down my cheeks, salty hot against my flushed face. Most of me hated him when I first read those words, but a sliver of my saddest depths whispered in agreement.

There's been so many times I've considered ending it all since I lost Noah. I've made many plans, written and thrown away goodbye letters and makeshift wills for my few possessions. And then there'd been the attempts. Four times I tried in earnest to leave the pain behind and pass on to whatever awaited me in the next plane, heaven or hell or nothingness. In those desperate moments, I felt anything would be better than the inescapable torture I had to constantly endure. It didn't matter that everyone said the grief would lessen with time, that I'd grow stronger and learn to live without him. On those four days that I tried to die, there was nothing that could save me. And yet, I didn't die.

The cable snapped, unable to bear my weight. The pills were vomited up, my stomach turning itself inside out until every drop of it was emptied against my will. The belt had stayed but someone had suspected and when the EMS workers busted in, I'd just about lost consciousness. The bruise collared my neck for over a month, a tender, temporary stain to remind me every time I glanced at a mirror of yet another failure.

They let me go after only a couple days, staggering around in a medicated haze. I covered my neck with sleeveless turtleneck sweaters, but even that got strange looks and whispers about me when the summer temperatures soared. Things were okay for a little while. Well, maybe not okay, but numbed to a mindless droll by the regime of drugs they'd prescribed, but even as I dutifully took my various pills each morning and night, the depression crept back in.

I knew it was bad again when I couldn't sleep anywhere but Noah's bed. It didn't matter that much since Charlie didn't want to be near me and moved out soon after. I never changed a thing in his room those first few months. The sheets slowly transformed from his sweaty, childish smell to my own funk of emptiness and endless exhaustion. Even when I knew the pillow didn't smell of him anymore, I still buried my face in it and pretended it did. It was the only way I could manage even a couple hours of sleep. Always dreamless. My only reprieve.

The day I went through the attic, taking down the boxes that Charlie had forgotten when he swept the house clear of his belongings, was when I found the revolver. I hadn't known he'd had one, and he'd apparently forgotten as well, but there it was in a small, dusty box tucked away in the corner. There were bullets too. I'd never held a gun before that day. It was heavier than I'd expected. I just sat, hunched over, holding it in the suffocating heat of the crawl space attic for a long time.

When I brought it downstairs, I was drunk with the possibility of this all finally being over. Fate had delivered this to me, urging me to end my life with this gift. I sat on Noah's bed and looked at his quilt beneath my legs; the gray rockets careening through the navy background, avoiding purple ringed planets and yellow stars. I talked to myself, but I don't remember what I said. Little things to comfort me, talk myself through it. I loaded one bullet into the chamber and spun. I thought, might as well make a game of it, right? Russian roulette for one.

I was two stupidly lucky empty chambers in when I broke down, set the gun on the bed next to me, and called for an ambulance. They kept me a little longer this time. Charlie even came back for a while to help me sell the house and set up a tiny one-bedroom apartment. I never put up any pictures there. Kept it as cold and sterile and free of any memories or emotions as possible. All of Noah's things were packed away in storage tubs in the closet. I got a job. I met Russ. I thought things were better.

I lay back on the bed and stare at a crack that's been slowly growing across the ceiling ever since I moved in. *What do I want? What is my life anymore? Who am I anyway?*

I read the love letter again. Trace the doodled hearts with my fingernail. I feel like such a fool. I hate him. I love him. I miss him with my whole being.

Birdie

The world's a funny place. Full of contradictions and confusion. I lay on the couch, the television muted, flickering colors in my periphery, but I'm staring at the ceiling, tracing the shadows of the outdated popcorn, thinking through and dissecting everything I've heard over the last few weeks and everything I thought I knew about my life.

Three years. It'll be three years since I met Russ in April, and yet do I know him at all? The number three glows in my mind, burning into me like a hot iron. So many years without Noah too. Tears crowd my lashes as I think back to the jumble of memories between losing my sweet Noah and meeting Russ. Only four months between them, but also an eternity.

The whirlwind of planning a funeral, the tiny robin's egg blue coffin and how I had to be pried off and restrained, then the fighting, the desperate resuscitation of

Charlie and my marriage, the speedy divorce, losing the house I'd spent so much time making a home, living in a motel off the money Charlie was kind enough to give me each month until I got back on my feet. He couldn't forgive me, but he pitied me and maybe even loved me still, just a glimmer. I drank it away, keeping myself in a stupor so I didn't have to feel. Even met up with George a couple times, but he just reminded me of that day, so I cut him off too. I wanted to be alone, wallowing in the bed I made of filth and sick, until Russ saved me. No matter what they say about him, he saved me that night at the bar.

I was starting to dip my toes into the warmth of my nightly drunken stupor when he came over and sat next to me. It was lucky timing or else I wouldn't have been worth his time, just some sloppy drunk girl at a dive bar. But he happened upon me freshly showered, just a little tipsy, and in a rare, talkative mood, so when he started asking questions, I opened up enough to let him into my life.

"You don't seem like the kind of girl who hangs out at a bar like this. Why're you here, anyway?" he asked, and when I turned to him, I noticed his stunning sapphire eyes right away. Handsome and fit, he looked like some redneck angel come to my rescue, and in a way, he was. I just didn't know it yet.

"I don't got any reason left to live, so I'm dying here, nice and slow," I said and winked at him, thinking that would frighten him off, but it didn't. Instead, he bought me another round, and soon I was diluting my glass of beer with a steady stream of tears as I told him all about Noah, the affair, the accident. He sat there, listening, his hand on my shoulder. I remember seeing his eyes soft and wet, like he was going to start crying himself.

"You don't see it, do you? You're so fucking strong, girl. You just need someone to help you with the burden for a little while."

"Heh, and let me guess, you're here to sweep me off my feet and take care of me? Fix all my shit? *Poor little broken thing, let me help.* I wasn't born yesterday, okay? I'm no fool and I don't feel like fucking tonight, so you might as well go try your lines on some other girl."

But then, the way he looked at me, it shook me to my core. There was something deep there. Something I hadn't expected. He wasn't just trying for an easy lay. For some unknown reason, this man actually cared about me—some strange, dirty girl at a dive bar. It broke something inside me, and I felt myself cave in, hollowed out and exposed.

Things took off from there. I poured my heart out to him, and he took me out on dates. Nice dates. Not shitty little diners, but real restaurants. It reminded me of when Charlie and I were first in love and he'd doted on me. I ate it up. Little presents, flowers, surprise visits at work that made me glow like a star, everyone else seething with envy. I loved it. Every bit of it. He was too intense, too in love, like a puppy-dog-eyed teenager, but I didn't care. It made me feel important and special again. It gave me a reason to keep going. It brought me back to life.

Somehow, we had everything in common. All the same favorite movies, books, hobbies. We went on long walks on nature trails, and he pointed out different bird calls, his whistle warbling through the trees, calling them closer, and laughing at me when I tried to replicate them too. We spent so many nights talking about life and death and God and grief. He'd lost his mother young, just like I'd lost Daddy. He'd had a nephew drown in a pool who was only just a couple years older than Noah, and they'd been close, so he almost understood. I didn't feel like a pariah with him.

Russ called me his "twin flame" and I ate that up too, hungry for more. Call me your soul mate. Call me the love of your fucking life. I didn't think about Noah every second of the day anymore, sometimes I even forgot him for a moment, and that made me both ashamed and relieved. I'm a monster, and I didn't deserve it, but I was happy again.

It was my fault when the cracks began to show. It was my faulty foundation that left him needing more than I could give, so it made sense when jealousy crept in. Juliana called him controlling, but he was just trying to cope with the shit I put him through. We'd fight, scream until our throats burned, sometimes throw something against the wall just to make a point, and then later we'd apologize, reaffirm our eternal love, have amazing makeup sex. He never hit me during any of those fights. Usually, he'd just leave to cool off.

A bolt of doubt, like an icicle down my spine, freezes my thoughts and brings the sour taste of bile up into my mouth. Had those nights away been enough time for him to do the horrible things they accused him of? Had I driven him to hurt someone else? I shake the thought away, but the goosebumps stay raised across my skin, forcing the possibility to linger like a foul smell, only slowly dissipating back into calm.

It's not possible. Sure, there'd been other women now and then. I'd found enough evidence to know all about it, but that's different. That's just something men do. And yet, the evidence the prosecutor had paraded before me unsettled me to the point I couldn't get comfortable, couldn't explain it away. The many times Russ had exploded with rage rushed through my memories, a red river of hate and anguish. The way he chose his words so carefully, an artist of inflicting pain, with each intricate detail selected for optimum hurt. I couldn't deny the dark side of him I'd seen so many times. He was a master manipulator of feelings, that was true, but I couldn't believe he'd wrapped his hands around those women's necks and squeezed the life from them. Not Russ. He'd never take it that far. Not *my* Russ.

I sit up and look at the coffee table in front of me, the pile of his prison letters stacked neatly in the center. He'd said so much and yet so little during this year away. It must be hard for him. My heart breaks to imagine his life behind bars, and my resolve hardens.

I love him and I believe him. He loves me, saved me, and will save me again. Every possible path of our future burns through me in a tributary of orange magma, so many promising the happiness we deserve. There might be struggle, there might be wealth, there might be a child clutching our hands as he begs to be lifted, and I can't lie down and die without fighting for those chances. *Whatever it takes*, I promise myself then and there. *Whatever it takes.*

BURIAL

BODY

The body was treated with as much somber respect as possible by the medical examiner as she took careful note of every sliver of shriveled organ, leathery skin with dehydrated sinews lurking beneath, dirt-encrusted ridges of exposed bone, the last remaining tatter of scalp and the delicate strands of hair that clung to it. Even after more than a dozen years, she never lost the compulsion to treat the dead as gently and with as much reverence as possible. This had been a living human being not long ago, a girl around her daughter's age. When initial tests and dental records confirmed the Jane Doe was indeed the missing Aubrey Blanch, she promised himself to only think of her as such. Not merely a severely decomposed corpse, but the remains of a young woman who had been so dearly loved by her friends and family.

Aubrey wasn't there anymore, but her body showed its appreciation for the courtesy by divulging the secrets it'd kept hidden away from bacteria and predators. Scraps of skin, torn from her attacker, still nestled under her dirt-rimmed fingernails on the hand that hadn't been scavenged away. She held her breath as she packed it away for processing, hoping there would be enough DNA left to analyze.

Other secrets were not so hopeful, revealing tragedy and pain so great, it cut through the examiner's stoic demeanor and misted her eyes. A fractured skull from blunt trauma, the bone splitting in branching cracks like an eggshell, but that was not the cause of death. Even with the flesh mostly missing, a broken hyoid bone told the story of strangulation, slow and painful. She'd been assaulted in other heinous ways as she died, and the doctor had to swallow the lump of disgust and horror that formed in her throat as she imagined the hopeless torture the girl had faced in her last living moments.

After the autopsy, Aubrey was constructed again, a human puzzle of parts carefully returned to their proper place before she was sent to the funeral home. The mortician informed the family that a closed casket was the only option. There wasn't enough left of Aubrey to embalm, and he'd never let the family see her in her current state. They accepted with enraged silence, pressing hands to the polished wood of the coffin, never getting the closure of seeing her one final time before she was taken by the earth.

Her mother wailed, held up by relatives when she found herself unable to stand on her own. Her loyal boyfriend, Tyler, pulled at his hair with clawed fingers, ripping out chunks as he watched his beloved lowered into the ground. They dropped flowers down on her and left with swollen, bloated faces in solemn silence. When the last loved one had left, the dirt was piled on top of her until only a fresh mahogany pound of dirt and a stone marker remained to be seen.

A YEAR GONE BY

Russ

Birdie, my love,

Where have you been? I've noticed the way your visits have dropped off. You can say it's because of your work all you want, but I'm not dumb. I could smell it on you last time you were here, even from across the table. I know it's not another man. Not yet at least. But don't try to deny that you're thinking of abandoning me. You're afraid. You stink of it. You sweat fear, let it drip down your hair like grease. After all I've done for you, you're getting ready to leave me. To let me rot in this hellhole of a prison. When did you become this kind of monster?

Or have I been wrong this whole time? Maybe this is the true you and I've just been too blind to see it. When I met you, you told me you were broken. Losing Noah tore you to pieces. Pieces I had put back together until you were a person again. But you were never a person at all. It was all a facade, wasn't it?

When you told me you were to blame for Noah's death, I thought it was survivor's guilt. A mother's guilt for not giving every second of your attention to his safety, and then the tragedy that unfolded when you dared to take a moment for yourself. But over the years, you've shown me I was wrong.

When you confessed you were flirting when he died, trying to set up a rendezvous with some stranger on the internet who gave your over-filtered pictures a couple cheap compliments, I kept my mouth shut, but I started to see the real you.

When you began trying to improve yourself, taking those stupid classes, saving up your pennies and hiding them away from me so you wouldn't have to help with our day-to-day expenses, even going to that grief meeting and wailing about your lost son that we both know you didn't really give a fuck about, I saw how it was all a ruse. A long game to get me to care for you, protect you, fucking *fall in love with you*, all for you to use me up for what I'm worth and drop me as soon as it's convenient. And it's awfully convenient now that I'm stuck here in prison, isn't it?

If you want to argue that I'm wrong, I'm going to need more than words. I'm going to need action.

If you're going to prove to me that you care about me the way you say you do, not only do I need to see you on a regular basis, but I need you to get me out. My lawyer is useless. I've done some studying and I have a plan, but I'm going to need your complete trust and commitment. Right now, I'm not even sure if I can trust you enough to tell you, so to prove you're in this forever, ride or die, you need to do two things.

First, send me some nudes. You have no idea how hard it is to live in this shit-pen without any woman in sight. You need to trust me that I won't show them off or pass them around or whatever it is that you're so skittish about. They're just for me, but if you can be that vulnerable with me, that's a big step.

Second, I can't be too specific in case they read these letters, but there's something I would really love to have that I used to take sometimes, something that would mean the world to me if you could somehow get it in here. The thing I used to have around. The thing you didn't like but knew I needed now and then. I know you'll figure out what I mean and find a way.

Please, I want to believe in you. In us. You're the Bonnie to my Clyde, just us against the world, like it used to be. I still love you, Birdie. Just as much as ever. Now you need to show me your love. Prove to me that you've meant all the promises over the years we've been together. I need to know you're there for me, no matter what.

All my love, if you're still mine,

Russ

Birdie

The plastic bag sticks to my chest, warmed to body temperature against my skin, and I hate myself more and more with each step. I've never been much of a rebel, and the thought of how many rules—no not rules—*laws* I'm breaking over a few stupid pills has me screaming internally. It's for love. *For love. For love.* I breathe the words in and out with every step. I'm not sure if I seem suspicious or if it's my paranoia, but the guards seem harsher than usual and their eyes shiftier, more discerning. Sweat collects on my upper lip, seeping past the foundation on the tip of my nose and gathering in dewy drops. I pat at my face and wish I had time to freshen up before Russ sees me. Despite my deodorant, I can smell the stench of fear-tinged sweat on me, and my nicest blouse is sticking wet to my underarms. *For love. For love. For love.*

There's Russ, sitting at the farthest table against the wall. Fluorescent lights hum over me as I walk past the other prisoners with their families and lovers seated across from them, not allowed to touch. I always want to touch him so badly. The way he's waiting for me ,with more excitement on his face than ever before, it is simultaneously endearing and pathetic.

It takes all my willpower not to roll my eyes, but I try to be understanding. I have no idea what he's been going through every day in here. Even with everything he tells me, I'm sure he's holding back the worst. It's worth the risk to bring him a little happiness and prove my loyalty to him. *For love. For love. For love.*

"God, it's good to see your pretty little face again," he says the second I sit down. He's tapping his foot and his knee hits the table just enough to send a vibration through it. So antsy. *Come on now, Birdie.*

"I missed you," I say. "I wish I could come see you more often, but we're still short-staffed and Janine has been a real bitch about scheduling. I just had a huge thing with her earlier today trying to get my shift switched so I wouldn't miss my shift at the gas station. It's honestly ridiculous she, of all people, got promoted to manager." As I drone on about work, which is more cathartic than I'd expected, I notice the nearby guard's eyes beginning to glaze over and Russ catches on. Soon, I'm three work stories deep and I'm sure the guard isn't paying attention to us anymore, especially when a curvy girl in a tight dress walks in and catches his eye.

"How am I supposed to give it to you?" I ask. Russ shoots me a look, one brow slightly raised.

"Well, depends. How'd you package them?" His voice is low, reminding me of the tone he'd take on during sex, something like faraway thunder. He's virtually purring with anticipation. Again, I swallow down the resentment. I wish he'd be that happy to see me, even if I didn't come bearing gifts. Maybe he would, I tell myself. I'm just being insecure.

"I mean, they're just in a ziploc. Was I supposed to do something different?" I half-whisper as I rub my sweaty palms against my jeans. Immediately, the look on his face tells me I've made a mistake.

"I hope it's a small one at least." He clicks his tongue and exhales loudly through his nose. "Okay, let's get this over with. Where do you have it?"

"In my bra." I hate the way my voice sounds, like a chided child. He nods, looking around the room, and I see the anger bubbling inside him.

"Okay, listen, you're going to keep talking about work for a few minutes, then you'll reach down, scratch at your chest, and grab it. Once you've got it in your hand, give me a little wink. Got it?" I nod. "Good. Now the hard part is how you're going to get it over to me. Since we can't touch, it's extra tricky, but we'll try our best. And hey, look at me." He catches me looking down, demands I meet his eyes. There's love waiting for me there. I relax a little. "I love you so much, babe."

"I love you, too."

"By the way, I got your letter with the pictures. Thank you. Don't worry, they're for my eyes only, but god, I needed those. You're seriously the best." His eyes twinkle like a goddamn cartoon and I find myself swooning as always. It's like he casts a spell on me.

"I'm glad you like them," I say and try to dive back into a work story, remembering how Chanelle and I spent over an hour restocking the formula in the display only to be told they were taking that display down.

Russ looks like he's listening, but I know he's merely pretending. I can read in his face that all he wants is for this transfer to go smoothly. He probably can't wait for the visit to be done so he can be alone with his precious fucking pills.

No, I'm wrong. There's definitely love in his eyes. Love for me. He's just never been one for my long-winded bitch fests about work. I can be such a bore. That's all.

When the time is right, I follow his instructions, palming the plastic bag, clasping it in my hand under the table. I smile meekly and give Russ a wink before I find my place back in my personal drama and continue talking. I don't want to talk about anything with the contraband in my hand, Russ anxiously waiting for the next step, but it's an important part of the plan. I need to stay as natural as possible. Don't give them any reason to look over here and maybe this exchange will work out.

After a few minutes, Russ brings his hands up and slowly pushes them towards me, until they've crossed the middle of the small table. I know we can't touch, but I follow his eyes and see he wants me to do the same. I try to keep my chit chat going but it devolves into nonsense as I bring my shaking hands up, both clenched in fists, the right one hiding the hot wad of plastic in its sweaty core.

Russ taps his right hand quietly up and down, show-ing me my final goal. If I can just get the bag to him, it'll all work out. My hair slips from behind my ears and sticks to my clammy temples as I prepare to toss the bag the short distance into his waiting hand.

I slide the bag across the table, but it stops, sticking to the table halfway before reaching his hand. In horror, we both look at the bag with a dozen chalky pills between us. I snatch it up, bending over and tucking it down into my sock, the first place out of sight that comes to mind, but the damage is done.

The way we'd gone completely silent and pale has set the guards on edge. The one nearby moves back closer, listening to our conversation with renewed interest, and it's harder than ever for me to fake small talk so I just ramble about absolutely nothing. Russ's eyelids are pulled back in shock, a rim of white showing all around, but when he notices the guard staring at us, he works to compose himself again.

I can tell by his body language he's not mad, but hugely disappointed. They're onto us and it won't be easy to get an opportunity like this again. I messed it up, and now he won't have the pills he needs for his anxious nights and as potential currency to protect himself from the wrath of the other inmates. It seems I fuck everything up no matter how hard I try. The shame bubbles in my stomach, quickly boiling to a rage. When the guard moves away toward another table, I can't help but lash out.

"I've had enough of all your guessing games and bullshit, Russ. Are you going to ask me for this mysterious favor or not?" I don't mean to be so curt with him, but the stress from the failed passing of the pills has drained the last of my patience.

"Okay, fine." He sets his hands, still shackled together, on the table between us, and laces the fingers into one another. His tone is much calmer than I'd expected, and I can't help but lean in closely as he speaks. "But you know the guards are always trying to listen, so we've got to keep it as vague as possible." His eyes dart to the two guards in the room and mine follow.

They seem preoccupied with the other prisoners and visitors, but he's made his point. There'd inevitably still be a little bit of a game quality to the conversation, with half-revelations and guessing. It's the only way. I nod to show him I understand.

"Listen and try your best to understand what I'm saying," he begins, then takes a long deep breath, locking his icy blue eyes with mine.

"I'm ready. Go on."

"You sat through the trial, heard all the same bullshit evidence from the prosecutor as I have, and the only thing they really have going for them was the partial DNA profile. I don't think the jury could have ever found me guilty beyond doubt without it, and honestly, I have no idea how it's even possible, but I know it's not mine."

"Yeah, I don't understand the science of it, but I believe you."

"So, I've been really thinking this over. Reading all kinds of stuff, researching for my appeal as much as I can, especially since I don't trust that fucking lawyer at all. The DNA is only a partial profile, right? So, what if they found out that the real killer was still out there? What if they found DNA evidence that proved it couldn't possibly be me?"

The slight nervous timbre in his voice, along with the way he can't stop wiping his hands down his clothing, either due to sweat or a new anxious habit, unsettles me. My brows knit together, my stomach squirms with painful twinges, and I realize I've leaned far back into my chair, no longer pressing my body toward him but instead away. Some subconscious part of me tells me to leave and not even hear any more of this plan, but I fight it. I need to hear him out, no matter how outrageous.

"What do you mean? I really don't understand what you're hinting at."

"Shh," he shushes me, his finger darting to his lips and eyes narrowing. "Keep it down."

"Okay, but I still don't get it. How would we get the DNA when we don't know who the real killer is? And even if we did, where would you have me put it? I don't have access to the evidence, and you know there's no way I could ever sneak in there, so I couldn't just smear it on some important item."

"I don't want you going anywhere near the cops or any of that shit. What I need you to do is to plan a visit, take what I give you, and then put it at the next crime scene of the *real* killer."

"But that doesn't make sense. How would I possibly know where the next crime scene is?"

"Think about it, Birdie. It's the only way I'm getting out of here."

My mind races, tracing his words over and over as I lick my lips and try to make sense of it. Then it clicks. The blood runs down my body into my feet, leaving me pale, cold, and shaking. That can't be what he means. I must be misunderstanding. There's no way he could ask that of me.

"No." My own whisper echoes in my head. I expect him to stop me with a laugh and explain my misunderstanding, but he just looks at me with expectant, nervous hope. A guard walks by and eyes us, so I pull myself together. Stay calm. Act normal.

"It's the only way."

"But– but– if you didn't do it, then the real killer will strike again, and they'll find the full DNA profile there. If he just strikes again at all, with the same MO and same patterns that that prosecutor crammed down everyone's throats the whole trial, it'll exonerate you even without that evidence. We just need to wait for the next victim."

"And what if that never happens, huh? What if he realizes I'm in here paying for his crimes and he decides to stay low for years, or forever? Hell, maybe he moves to another country and fucking starts killing girls over there and they never even connect the dots. There's no way I'm just waiting around for this psycho to make a mistake. I can't live my whole life in here waiting."

"Are you seriously asking me to…"

His steely gaze intensifies, sending an electric bolt down my spine. "Yes."

"You can't mean that…" The words form on my tongue and lips, but I can't get out even a whisper, merely mouthing them silently. I don't believe him. This can't be.

"It's the only surefire way to get me out of here. I'd have a solid alibi that nobody could ever question. They'd have to focus on the investigation again, and I bet then they'd find the real fucking killer."

"But… how? I mean, like dig up a—"

"No, it can't be like that. You know that. You're smart, Birdie. My dear, sweet, lovely Birdie." He starts to reach out to take my hand, the chain between his cuffed hands clacking against the table, but when a guard turns his head, he retreats. It's absolutely not the time to get attention drawn to us.

He lowers his voice to the rumbling whisper I used to love to feel hum through my chest when he'd lay his head on me in bed and talk about anything. "I know it's too much to ask. An impossible thing to expect from another person, but it's the only option we've got left if we want to spend our lives together, hold each other, kiss again. Please, don't give me an answer yet. Just think it over. Please. Give it one night before you turn me down."

I rub at my stinging eyes, surely smearing the carefully applied eyeliner, but right now, it doesn't matter what I look like. A roaring wind tunnel fills my head, and the fluorescent lights above burn into my corneas, even when I shut my eyes. I grab my mouth, trying to stifle back the scream and sobs and vicious nausea rushing through me.

And then I nod. I didn't mean to, and yet there was my body, agreeing to give this horrific proposal, a night of rumination. I want to hate him, but I can't. The way he relaxes when I nod, the smile that flickers tentatively across his lips, not wanting to give in to hope, it breathes life into me and for the first time in months, I don't feel hollow and dead inside.

"Say I agree to this, how would—"

"No, shhh, hush hush," he interrupts me, but gently, with a glazed-eye lovebird look. "We can talk about details and logistics later, if it comes to that. Now, I just want to enjoy our time together." He glances at the clock. "There's only fifteen minutes left in our visit, and I want to savor every second with you."

I laugh a tiny snort through my nose, try to relax and smile back, but I'm still reeling from before.

"Listen, I love you. More than anything. I want to sit here across from you and stare into your eyes, bat my eyelashes and hike up my skirt, all that usual stuff, but I can't right now. I think I'm going to be sick actually. I'm sorry, babe. I have to go."

I stand to leave, and Russ gives that toothless, biting smile of sympathy, lips pulled thin, almost like he's embarrassed. He gets it, and I know he won't hold it against me. When I turn to leave, the guard is waiting for me.

"Ma'am, I'm sorry, but I'm going to need to pat you down before you leave. I have reason to believe you might've been trying to smuggle something to that inmate back there."

"What? How dare you imply that?" I ask, narrowing my eyes, and even I'm impressed at how realistic my indignation comes across when I'm usually so bad at lying, especially as my stomach is still twisted into acidic knots.

He hesitates, and for a second, I think he's going to let me leave, but instead, he only softens his gruffness slightly and escorts me to the hallway outside the visiting room.

"Hands against the wall, legs spread apart. I'm just gonna do a quick search."

"Aren't you supposed to ask if I want a female guard?" I ask, already feeling violated and on the verge of tears. The little bag of pills sticks against my ankle bone. The guard doesn't answer, only repeats his instructions, so I follow. There's no other option.

He's rough, not patting but dragging his hands over my body, and he lingers too long in places he shouldn't. I know it's purposeful, an intimidation tactic but one that'd be impossible to prove, and it works. I feel humiliated. He finishes the pat down and I realize he didn't bend low enough to touch my ankles. A wave of relief cascades over me. He missed the baggie.

But it's not over. He gets very close to my ear, the sour stench of his unbrushed teeth hot on my cheek, and says, "Clean this time I guess, but give me another reason to suspect something and it'll be a strip search next time." He licks his lips. "Maybe a cavity search, just to be sure."

It takes all my willpower not to either slap him, vomit on his shoes, or both. When he finally moves away, I make a break for it and he lets me. It's not until I'm out in the fresh air again that I break down.

Birdie

I can hardly breathe as I step out of the prison into the blinding sun. My lungs feel like they've collapsed and I'm wheezing to get even the smallest bit of oxygen in. How could he ask this of me? I take three steps out into the parking lot before I'm brought to my knees with light-headedness. A guard is racing to my side, talking on a walkie talkie for help.

"What's wrong, ma'am?"

"Can't. Breathe. Help," is all I can press through my constricted throat before the world goes black and nausea encapsulates me. I remember the same feeling from the first time I gave blood. I'm passing out. My head hits the pavement, and the world slips away from me.

I wake up what must be moments later, since I haven't been moved, and that same guard is standing over me with terrified, wide eyes and a shocked, dropped jaw.

"Just stay there. No, don't try to get up. I'm gonna call an ambulance," he says, trying to push me back to the ground as I prop myself up on my elbows. I'm sure he means well, but I can't handle this level of stupidity right now.

"Get your hands off me. I'm fine." I scoot out of his reach and bring myself to my knees, then unsteadily to my feet, my heart racing as my mind jumps back to the other guard touching me. His concern grows across his wrinkled brow as he sees me wobble. I sigh. My lungs are working again, though they burn like I've inhaled a handful of live cinders.

"Ma'am, I think it'd be best if you just waited for some help." His face roves my features, begging for some sort of compromise to assuage his growing guilt. "At least let me call the prison nurse. I don't feel like you should be driving after losing consciousness like that."

"I appreciate the concern, but I'll be fine. Please, I just want to go home."

He nods and backs up a little, his body language spelling out that he was only reluctantly relenting and letting this crazy woman leave without medical clearance. Whatever. This rent-a-cop could never understand the billions of questions buzzing through my mind like a hoard of mosquitos, my every thought, every movement aching from the barrage of questions.

How could Russ have asked this of me? That's the core question that fights its way to the surface every time I get close to any sort of clear thought. He claims he loves me. Claims he's innocent. And yet, he wants to put me through this incalculably risky, psychologically damaging, unethical, immoral, horrendous ordeal to ensure his release. And would it even ensure his release? Something nags at my brainstem, screaming he's wrong. Wrong on every single aspect of his plan.

I should toss the plan aside as preposterous. Leave him to rot in prison.

Or go crawling back to him, confess I could never carry out such an unbearable favor and beg his forgiveness. Maybe we can stay together through the thick and thin of prison and appeals until he finally gains his freedom rightfully. Perhaps the real killer will even be brought to justice and Russ ultimately awarded some monetary compensation for the years he toiled for something he didn't do. Or more likely, we'll stay together over the years, either adjusting to this new, not ideal kind of relationship, or drift apart until we end things painlessly, our relationship long dead. Those were the practical outcomes of groveling at his feet and admitting I could never do what he's asking of me.

So why is there a part of me that's still considering it?

I need to talk to someone. I need some kind of support. There's only Juliana.

Her phone seems to ring a hundred times before she picks up. My heart leaps into my throat the second I hear her voice. "What's up, girl?"

"Are you busy? I really need to see you."

"Oh my god, Birdie, are you alright? You sound... I don't know, off, I guess."

"Yeah, I'm fine. I just really need to see you."

"Come on over, girlie. I'm just chillin' around the house anyway. Or do you want to meet up somewhere? I haven't had lunch yet and—"

"No. I'd rather come to your place. I'll be there soon."

"Okay. But drive careful, okay? You sound sick or something."

I see the guard eyeing me as I get into my car, but he stays at his post. Probably sees all kinds of breakdowns, though he does have a point that I shouldn't drive, but right now, there's no other option. I need to get to Juliana. She'll know what to do.

By the time I pull into her driveway, I've gone from blind panic into a dissociated state; floating above the body that no longer feels mine. It doesn't feel like such a thing could have happened. I pinch myself, bite the inside of my cheek, trying to get myself to wake up from what is surely a dream, but I don't wake up. Did I hallucinate him asking me? Am I fucking losing it? It seems like reality is slipping farther from my fingertips with each passing second.

Juliana notices me parked, sitting in my car, and she comes out to get me. She doesn't ask questions or pry or laugh in that awkward icebreaking way people do. She helps me out of the car, props me up with a strong, gentle arm, and walks me inside to her couch. I try to snap myself out of it when she leaves the room and I hear the tap, but I'm trapped inside my own head. She comes back with a glass of water and a couple cookies on a small plate, sits next to me, her hand caressing my arm while she waits patiently for me to be ready to speak.

"Sorry, but we have to be quiet," she whispers with a finger to her lips. "Luna is napping. Just got her down."

The mention of Luna sends a wave of nausea down my throat, coating my stomach. I've only met the baby a handful of times, refusing to hold her every time. I know it hurt Juliana, but she must understand. And in this moment of need, I'm thankful she's not out, gurgling and giggling with the happy infant sounds that never fail to rend my heart to shreds.

"I saw Russ today." The words stick against my tongue. I stop, breathe deeply, and take a sip of water. "I'm not sure what's going on with him, but it's not good."

"Birdie, listen. He's in prison. Fucking federal prison. Of course things aren't good. He's been convicted of murder. When are you going to understand that?" She sighs, slapping her thighs and gritting her teeth. "I keep waiting for you to get it, to see things are over, no matter how much you think you love him. To get that he's never going to change and that you need to move on, but you just keep hanging on. You need to stop visiting him. Burn his letters." She softens, sets a hand on mine, woven together in my lap. "I'll help you. We can move past this together."

"No, how can you say that? You don't understand. He's just… different. Things are different now."

"Different how?" Juliana leans closer, her warm breath against the hair on my arms. I want to tell her everything. Pour it all out in a slimy puddle between us, to poke and prod until I understand the jumbled emotions cartwheeling through my brain. I crave her lecture that he's crazy and terrible for asking such a thing of me, but if I tell her the specifics, she'll get him in trouble. She hates him, and I can't betray him like that. I believe that he's innocent. He's just not thinking straight.

"I feel like he's losing it in there. Saying weird stuff. His letters are all over the place, and then when I see him in person, he's so intense. I'm worried." I hesitate but her eyes and the way she holds her hands open beg me to continue. "He asked me to do him a favor."

"A favor? No, no, nope. Hell no. I don't even need to hear what it is to know that you're not doing it." Juliana hung her head. "Fine. Tell me. He's asking for drugs, isn't he?" She looks up at me, her expression changed to something hard and discerning. "You didn't smuggle drugs in there, did you?"

"No, of course not," I shoot back, but the reality of all I've done crashes over me. I quickly try to mask my guilt, but something must've shown through for a split second, because Juliana latches onto it right away.

"You did! I can't believe you. You know you'll end up there yourself if you get caught. I couldn't fucking stand to see you go to prison for him."

"I didn't do anything like that."

"Then what the hell did he want?"

"I don't even really know. He wasn't making a lot of sense, like I said. He's losing it."

"Don't lie to me. That man asked you for drugs. I can read it all over your face. And you're gonna do it. Even after the way he treated you. All those nights you had no idea where he was, we both know he was screwing around. There's no other explanation." Her eyes dart to me, green and catlike. "Unless…"

"Don't say it."

"I know you love him, but you can't deny there's a lot of evidence saying he raped and murdered these women. I watch all those true crime shows, and you have no idea how many times friends, neighbors, even wives of serial killers didn't suspect a thing. They always say they were the nicest people, but then it comes out, all the messed-up shit they were pulling when nobody was looking. And Russ isn't a nice guy at all. Is it really that big of a leap for you to imagine that those women who testified were right?"

"Don't you dare say that about Russ." I can barely get the word out through my clenched teeth. "He's a good man. He might've made a lot of mistakes, but he's no murderer." My fingernails dig into my palms as I ball my fists as tight as possible to keep the anger inside. It's not Juliana's fault. She just doesn't get it.

"What do you want from me?" Her voice rises up and she quickly quiets it again, looking to the hallway with anticipation, but Luna stays asleep. "You call me having a breakdown, then come over and won't give any details, only sing the praises of a man found guilty of murder. A man that you and I both know is exactly where he deserves to be. I know, I can't make your choices for you, but it's too much to watch you fall apart, working two jobs, for that piece of shit."

Her eyes meet mine and suddenly I realize there's heartbreak there. Every muscle in my body sags. I pull my feet up onto the couch and tuck them under me. Tears gather, linger in my eyes, but they don't fall.

"I don't know what to do anymore." The words fall from my lips, sinking heavily in the air between us. "Please, just be with me. I'm always alone. I don't want to be alone right now."

When I feel her arms wrap around me, holding me while she hums softly into my hair, I let myself meld with her. We are one entity for this moment, and it gives me enough relief to set down the burden of thoughts and decisions I've been carrying ever since seeing Russ. I can just be me in the arms of my best friend, loved. Not alone.

If only that moment lasted forever. Instead, she pulls away, her eyes bleary with tears as they lock with mine, pressing her forehead to my own, and I know this is it.

"I can't do this anymore, Birdie. I can't watch you fall apart over that man. We both know that if you don't leave him, then you're going to end up killing yourself or wasting your whole life waiting for him to get out. He *murdered* those women. It's the truth. You have to accept it and move on. There's no future for you with that bastard and—"

"No." The single word stops her, and I watch her lips snap shut. I plead with my eyes, *please, understand how much I love him. How much I need him.* But she has no room left in her heart for my burden. I understand that my choice means I must bear it alone.

"Then that's it. I can't have you come around here anymore if you're choosing him. I won't let Luna grow up seeing this bullshit. I've done everything to help you. Everything!" She shouts the last word, her breath and eyes wild, a deep agony weighing down each word. A cry rattles through the hallway. Luna is awake, but Juliana's eyes don't leave mine. "How can you be so stupid? Maybe you deserve each other."

I get up to leave, but she pulls me back to the couch, even after I fight to free my arm.

"No, I'm sorry. I didn't mean it. But I just can't. Don't you understand? I can't anymore." She's crying. Luna's wailing, each howl louder and higher pitched, but Juliana doesn't tend to her. Instead, she wraps her arms around me one more time. We sit in the wet sound of her sniffles and Luna's shrieks.

"I have to go get her," she finally says. We stand together. Before she leaves the room, she kisses my cheek, tears in her eyes, and I know this is the end. As the screen door flaps closed behind me, I hear her humming a lullaby in the nursery, Luna's cries deescalated to bubbly coos. I've never felt so alone since I lost Noah, and I hold myself with a tight one-armed hug the whole drive home. It's the only way I keep myself from shattering into a thousand irreparable pieces.

Back home, alone in my bedroom, I think about calling Mom, thumb hovering over the contact, but decide against it. Instead, I scroll up and down the few numbers

I've bothered saving, working up the courage to dial Charlie's number. I need to talk to someone who understands me, someone who maybe loved me at one point. When I finally hit call, a robotic female voice tells me the number is no longer in service. He's done it. Changed his number. Just like he's threatened to do so many times.

I can't bring myself to cry, yell, or feel anything at all. A husk of a person, I take a handful of Nyquil and slurp ramen noodles in the dark, not even bothering to switch on the TV. I take a long, scalding shower, but the guard's breath seems to linger in my hair. Then, I stare at the wall for hours, fighting insomnia until sleep finally takes me.

Birdie

Noah sits on his bed, facing the wall. All of his toys are just as they were that day. The scattered Legos I wouldn't pick up for weeks; wouldn't even let Charlie in the room for fear he'd tidy something. It made no sense but I had to preserve it. It took so long before I allowed myself to realize it didn't matter anymore. But there he is. Everything exactly the same. The same little boy I'd loved with all my heart, arms crossed and faced away from me, waiting.

I approach in painstaking slow motion, the world decaying around me with every step. By the time I've made it halfway, the spaceship wallpaper has yellowed and peeled away, the shelves have fallen, the bedroom door unhinged itself, white paint cracked in spidered fissures. The carpet grows filthy beneath my toes, gathering dirt and mold until it squelches with every step. When my hand rests upon the astronaut quilt, it tears like tissue beneath my fingers, a cloud of moths fluttering away.

Noah hasn't changed, still holding himself, eyes on the wall. I feel my own body ache with the pains and exhaustion of old age. Looking down, the backs of my hands have grown knotted and spattered with sunspots. They look just how I remember my grandmother's hands the last time I saw her.

Pulling my failing body closer, I have finally made it to my son. My tremoring hand takes his small one and my voice echoes out distorted, as if we were underwater.

"Noah?"

He turns to me, tears in his eyes, and shakes his head. Then he crumbles into dust, his hand still in mine as it disintegrates.

I wake to a high-pitched, fevered screaming. For a few panicked seconds, I think it's my Noah and not my own voice ringing in my ears.

Birdie

Russ's smile is stretched across his face, skull-like, when I enter the visitor room and it pulls a shudder down my back. He's lost so much weight since they locked him up, skin pulled taut like a mask over his face, his arms still large and muscular but visibly withered compared to before. Veins bulge from him everywhere, ropey worms sliding under skin too pale from not enough sun. Lines feather out from the corners of his eyes, and I realize just how much he's aged since he left. He looks nothing like the man I fell in love with, but I know he's still somewhere hidden under the harsh visage.

"Babe, I've missed you." His face genuinely lights up as I take my seat across the metal table from him. "It's been a long month without you."

"Yeah. It's been hard for me too." I sniffle, push the tears back into my eyes as best I can with frantic blinking.

"So, you've thought about it?" He tiptoes through the question, fingers tapping quietly at the table, splayed like he's preparing to pounce on a butterfly, cup it gently in his hands, hold it captive. I wince at the way his fingers dance.

"Yes."

"And?" His eyes nearly bulge with anticipation, and I notice for the first time that they are slightly yellowed. Could he be sick? Of course they're not taking care of him in here. Nobody cares about prisoners.

I chew my lip, scrutinizing his skin to see if it is jaundiced as well, worry circling me like buzzards. All the apprehension I'd had, the defiance in my gut that urged me to refuse him, cut him from my life, melts away like wax under the flame of worry. And below, there is only love.

"I'll do it. Or I'll try my best." I lower my voice to a whisper, but the guards aren't listening. Their glazed eyes tell me they're busy in their own fantasies. "I don't know if I can do it."

"I know you can." He licks at his cracked lips, his tongue lizard-like, a new tick he's developed since they took him away. I hate the animal he's becoming, transforming under the beatings, hypervigilance, and isolation. I need to get him out of there, no matter what.

"I can only try my best, Russ."

He nods. "And you understand exactly what you need to do?"

"Yes."

"You've done your research on any... equipment you'll need?" His sunken eyes dart around, always wary, but no one is listening.

"Yeah. I'll keep everything as clean as I can and tidy up after." I can scarcely believe the words that pour from my throat into reality. Am I really signing up for this?

"You have to be extra sure not to leave anything because you're linked to me. They have your visitor files, they're sure to check you out. Everything has to be air-tight for this to work."

"I know," I say. He clicks his tongue, pale eyes searing into me, searching every part of me. I wonder if he even trusts me. Does he think I'm wearing a wire? Does he think I don't believe him?

"Tell me again."

"Tell you what?" he snaps back, his brows furrowing, but when he sees the tears brimming my lashes, he softens again.

"You know what."

"It wasn't me. It really wasn't, Birdie. I swear to God. I swear on my own mom's grave."

"Then why do we have to do this? Won't the real guy fuck up soon enough? Then none of this will matter." I sniff back the sobs, swallowing them down and trying not to draw attention to us.

The corner of Russ's mouth quivers but stills after a slow inhale and long blink. I can feel he wants to lecture me, but there's no time or privacy for that.

"We don't know when he'll strike again, or if he even will. Maybe he's moved somewhere else, knowing it's too hot here, and they'll never connect those crimes. Or some of the guys here have said there's no way he'd be so careless again to leave any DNA. I could be in here for the rest of my life if you don't do this. It's the only way."

"Okay. I'll try." I sniffle again, pushing my hair behind my ears and trying to steel myself. My throat rumbles with my whisper. "Do you have it?"

Russ nods and I watch as he pretends to scratch his ankle. His arm moves quickly, and under the table, a rubber glob lands in my lap. My hands fall to my lap, and I feel the tied end and the congealed fluid inside. I almost laugh as my fingers dance along what is definitely ribs. "Ribbed for my pleasure," I suppose. Also pretending to scratch an itch, I slip the tiny, precious package into my bra. It quickly warms against my skin to body temperature. The first of many hurdles is almost over.

"I love you, sweetheart. See you soon," he says as the guard approaches, our visit coming to an end.

"I love you too. With all my heart."

I keep catching myself holding my breath as the guard walks me out. The fresh air mixes with the rancid, recycled atmosphere of the prison as we near the doors. Then the guard stops me, his hands suddenly darting into my sweater pockets, fingers searching.

My heart stops. My mouth goes dry and I could choke on my tongue which is suddenly too large and sandpaper rough.

"Huh, I thought I saw something. Never mind, sorry ma'am," the guard says, backing away from me with a sheepish look in his eyes and the hint of a blush dappling his cheeks.

"Jesus, I hate this place," I say, more to myself than to him, but his blush grows a deep radish red and I'm glad he heard me.

I walk through the doors, get in my car, and drive home. I wait until I'm all the way back in my bedroom to slip the condom out of my bra and examine it. I hold it to my cheek, the white-gray semen a tiny bit of Russ I freed, and the key to freeing the rest.

Russ

He lies on the cot with his eyes closed, staring at the red backs of his eyelids illuminated by those incessant cell lights. The fluorescent brightness so unnatural, he's sure it was dreamed up as yet another covert punishment for men like him, locked up and forgotten by everyone. Except for Birdie.

A dry, crackling cough comes out when he tries to laugh. Thank God for Birdie. And who knows, maybe she'll prove herself useful for once in her life and get that gunk spread over some fresh kill to get him outta here. Wouldn't that be just the kind of fucked up miracle he'd always prayed for? How would they ever get him for taking one out again? No way in hell could they use that DNA bullshit after a mix-up like that. No, no, the bad publicity would have them on edge, and the people would be on his side. Out for blood. Demanding they catch the real killer, still out there, still raping and strangling women, leaving them to rot all alone.

He smiles when he remembers the women he'd lovingly wrapped his hands around and squeezed every last breath out of, or penetrated with a blade, spilling their hot blood over his hands, releasing their life into the void. Oh, how he misses it. An aching throb shoots through him as the memory of their frantic eyes, their last breaths, the warmth of their necks under the pressure of his fingers returned to him, the fear in their eyes, their tremoring hands clinging to him or clawing at him, begging him. He could be out there again, and if he doesn't make another stupid mistake, he could keep on taking their lives for as long as his strength permitted.

His eyes flutter open, and he scowls when he remembers everything that would need to go exactly as planned for him to ever see the outside again, and all of it in Birdie's little, incompetent hands. He licks his lips and lets the fantasy overtake him as he rides out the details he'd been over thousands of times, the only kill he could never bring to fruition because they were too close. He'd have been caught right away, but damn, did she deserve it.

All these years, even after seeing him dragged through the mud, she looks at him with those wide, doe eyes like she believes he's innocent. Oh Birdie. There was no way she'd have agreed to his plan otherwise. It was ridiculous, and no matter how smooth he tried to be, Russ knew that persuasion could only go so far. She *wants* to be seduced by him. She wants to believe, but deep down, she must know.

She wants to be a victim. Wants to be a punching bag, a dumb whore, a sack of meat to be fucked and discarded.

And a little part of her must want to feel the other side, a sliver of the power he always possessed. The thought of her fucked-up duality brings a trace of a smile across his lips.

He unties the drawstring of his pants, fumbling with himself as a wave of heat crashes through him. There was more to it than that. She'd always chased after danger and shame. A closeted masochist, even to herself. She liked it. There was nothing she craved more than for him to take the reins and berate her, hurt her. A groan rumbles at the back of his throat. She wanted him to grab that delicate neck and wring it like a wet rag until there was nothing left. He should've given her what she wanted all these years.

The way she'd have looked at him like a baby fawn, calling him "hon" or "sweetheart," and begging him to back up. Their manufactured dialogue echoed through him like a memory.

"Now, come on there, hon. What's got you in such a mood? Let me fix you something to eat and we'll be right back–"

"Shut up or I'll shut you up."

The way her mouth would've snapped shut like a turtle, eyes gone dumb and scared. It was beyond tantalizing. He could see her hair pinned up in one of those tangled messes with a brown claw clip and pictured himself yanking it straight out. Her face contorts in shock, pain, and betrayal, sending a pleasurable shiver through his every nerve.

"Kneel." The vision so vivid that he mouths the command with his lips. The word is honey and lavender against his teeth. She kneels, eyes saucer-big and wet but not crying. Birdie would know better. Always trying to be so fucking perfect, as if she wasn't broken beyond repair.

302

She'd open her little rosebud mouth, always careful with the teeth, thinking that's all he wants, but he'd surprise her with a smack so hard she nearly falls over. Maybe there's a little blood. Bloody nose, no, a split lip. He salivates at the mental image of her mouth spilling open like a pomegranate, her trembling fingers dabbing at the wetness and confirming her fears. Then raise those pretty eyes back up to his, oh yeah, it's almost too much.

A sound in the cell startles him from his fantasy, and Russ props himself up on an elbow, half sitting, listening. Silence. A thick void of silence holding his breath for him. Then finally a phlegmy snore followed by the steady breathing of his cellmate's sleep again. He must've just repositioned himself on his cot. Russ settles himself back into bed, finds his bookmarked place in the well-worn fantasy.

"Please, you don't have to do this, Russ." The throbbing passion takes him back to the edge of relief immediately as he watches her try to stay strong, try to stay human, but it's no use. He won't let her.

One last scream of his name that she only half gets out before he's pinned her down, his hands tight around that thin, pale neck of hers. Squeezing so hard that he can feel the blood stop at his fingers, thumping against him as her body desperately tries to stay alive. He has all the control she'd never give him before.

Her lips move with words like "please" and "no" and "stop" but he ignores her, pressing harder, his body against hers, pushing her down into the carpet as she wriggles like the pathetic worm she is. Her eyes lock with his and it's the betrayal that he loves most of all with her. It's what makes her unique from all the others. She trusted him. Took care of him. Loved him. And now she's dying for him. For his viewing pleasure. And she knows it.

Every ounce of pride, trust, kindness, even humanity bleeds out of her, leaving her nothing but the sniveling, cowardly animal she is, and that they all reduce to. In a burst of excitement, he slips over the edge, submerged in dark ecstasy.

In his fantasy, he smiles at her as the last shimmer of life goes out in her eyes. It's the one creative license he'll take, because the strangulation takes too much energy for him to ever remember to give that final smile. He's always too concentrated on the task at hand. But maybe it could be different with Birdie. Maybe it could be better than all the others.

She always thought she was so much better than him. It would've been the sweetest thing to prove her wrong once and for all. But there would have been no denying who took her out. They were interconnected in every conceivable way. It had always been the forbidden fruit. Too close to home to get away with.

He turns over, the slimy wetness oozing down his hip to pool against the bed. It wasn't that there was no hint of affection there. She'd taken care of him in many ways, and she was out there once more trying to do right by her man. Sometimes he'd even loved her. There were days he'd looked into that sweet face and wanted to change. It stung to see how deeply she cared for a bastard like him. He'd nearly taken himself out from the guilt her pretty little smile gave him.

She was the closest thing to the way a woman should be, and yet, despite those moments of endearment, the overwhelming feeling he harbored for her was hate. He couldn't shake the truth he was sure of that all women were trash, no matter how much they tried to paint and polish themselves into something different. At the end of the day. Birdie was just like any other. And if he could get out there again, he was sure he'd wrap his hands around a few more throats. They didn't deserve anything better.

Birdie

I wake up before the sun and take such a long shower that the hot water runs out and leaves me shivering in the cold. Despite the discomfort, I stay in for another half hour, thinking. Maybe torturing myself as a sort of penance, I don't know. I don't know anything anymore. My mind is a jumble of white-hot electricity, and I can't hear anything beyond the rumbling static.

I pull on a fitted sweater and short skirt, patterned tights, high heeled boots. It's hard to control the eyeliner with my shaking hands as I paint my face. It's not makeup today but camouflage. Warpaint even. Despite the way my gut trembles and spasms in revolt, I'm going on the hunt today. I must. For Russ.

I've taken every precaution. The rental car. A blonde wig, real human hair, not synthetic, so it looks as natural as possible. The kit is in my purse of everything I knew I'd need based on what I'd learned from the trial. The gun waits at the bottom of my purse, in case of emergency. I force myself to swallow an English muffin and a cup of coffee before I head out. Something to steady my stomach.

It's a long drive to the college town I've decided on. I had to make sure it was far enough away from me, but still close enough to be connected to the others. On the drive, I lose myself and a blank version of me takes the wheel, steering me to my destiny. I let her. Anyone but me. *Don't make me do it.*

I'm a little early for check-in when I pull into town, so I sit at a cafe by the river and sip at a tea. The day is warming up, so I change into the slinky dress in the bathroom. It's cooler and I feel eyes on me as soon as I come out. Just sexy enough to catch attention but nothing too unique to be memorable. Just another woman on the prowl for love. That's what I hope they'll think at least.

Once I'm in the hotel room, I touch up my makeup and wait for night. It'll be easiest to find someone at night, after the bars open and the libations loosen up their patrons. When darkness has fully settled over the town, I walk down to the neon-lighted strip and find a bar that's busy but not packed.

With a gin and tonic in hand, I sit at a table in the corner and scope out the crowd. There are several couples, some already in their cups and getting handsy, others holding private conversations, enthralled with each other. *To be young and in love again.* I sip my drink and remember, trying to stave off the thoughts of the inevitable that's to come.

My gaze flits between each single girl as they order and nervously preen their hair, or pick at their nails, or take shot after shot. A few ooze confidence, but they're quickly snatched up by the most attractive men, who've sniffed them out among the pack of the love-hungry and inexperienced.

One girl in particular catches my eye. She's tall, with dark features and long waves of hair down her back and curving over her shoulders. She's beautiful but not in the striking way some women stun onlookers. Her beauty is the kind that you don't notice right away, but the longer you look, the deeper it worms its way into your thoughts. She looks quite young, barely legal to drink, or maybe with a fake ID. Her clothes are fashionable but worn thin in places, and I recognize them as thrifted. I know her because she was me a few years ago. She's perfect.

When she looks my way, I smile and gesture with a little nod to the side to approach. Her eyes dart around, and she bites her lip, but she finally comes over to my table.

"I'm sorry, do I know you? Are you in one of my classes?" she asks, her voice a soft, breathy one, still half-child. I hate myself for finding her, but I must.

"I don't think so, but you do look familiar," I say, but before she can ask any prying questions that I don't have answers for, I add, "I'm just feeling a bit lonely and you looked lonely too, so I thought, hey, why not make a new friend? Isn't that what college is for?" I flash my best smile and she relaxes. She thinks I'm just like her. I've convinced her I don't want a thing from her but her company. I'm no threat. She sits down, her sugar-rimmed drink slipping in its own condensation on the table.

"Kind of quiet out for a Saturday, huh," she says, sipping at the pink syrupy cocktail and I nod.

"I'm Lindy by the way," I say, the fake name bitter on my lips.

"Oh, sorry, I'm Bernadette," the girl says, flipping her hair over her shoulder, and I gag on the alcohol in my mouth.

Bernadette. A name all too familiar to me. The name my mother and father had given me, but that I'd hated because it sounded like an old woman's, so I'd adopted a nickname and never looked back. She's *just* like me, I think, coughing and finally swallowing the liquid trapped by shock. Could this be a sign? I shake away the thought as soon as it surfaces. If anything, it makes it feel even more wrong than before.

"Oh my god, are you okay?"

"Yeah, went down the wrong pipe," I say, taking another long sip of my drink and clearing my throat.

"So, you go here?" Bernadette asks, her eyes running over my face. I'm sure she's noticing the beginning of crow's feet at the corners of my eyes.

"Yeah. School's a bitch, heh," I laugh. "I don't usually even have time to go out, so this is a nice break."

This seems to satisfy her, and she starts talking about her own course load, how many papers she still needs to write this weekend, and how she can't imagine how much harder graduate school would be. I try to listen, but my nerves are getting the better of me. I jump at every song change, take too long to laugh at jokes. I can tell I'm making her uneasy and try to snap myself out of the haze of anxiety.

The night wears on, and as our bloodstreams marinate in drink after drink, her stories begin to blend into each other. It's not until she slurs a nonsensical sentence that I finally decipher as a suggestion to keep drinking at another bar nearby that I realize I've drunk too much to go through with anything tonight. When she heads to bar to grab two more shots, I curse at myself under my breath. I've fucked it up like I fuck up everything. Stumbling through the crowd, I'm gone before she comes back.

In my hotel room, I take a long hot shower, curled up in the corner of the tub while the water plasters my skull, wet strands stuck against my cheeks. When I pull myself out of the steaming room, I flop onto the bed, facedown into my pillow. I scream until my voice cracks and stumbles into a whisper no louder than television snow and my body collapses into exhaustion, every inch of skin slick with cold sweat. Pulling my face away from the soaked pillowcase, wiping at my mouth, wet with saliva and perspiration, I take a breath and slowly let it shudder out.

Who am I? What have I become? I think of all those photos of women's bodies from the trial. The victims and witnesses who took the stand with trembling lips and tightly clasped hands. My entire world was destroyed when my son's life was taken. I look at my wrinkled palms, the lines a fortune teller once told me were strong and full of prosperity. Are these hands that can ruin another mother's life by snuffing out the light in her daughter's eyes?

Noah's body, crumpled and broken, bent in unnatural ways, flashes in my mind's eye. I force the image back down into the black abyss I try to contain it, but nevertheless, it reminded me that I am already a murderer. It's my fault I don't have my sweet boy anymore, and it'll be my fault that an innocent man spends his life behind bars if I can't make myself do this one terrible deed.

Russ. His smile, the way he kisses my neck, the bouquet of white lilies he brought home for our first anniversary. I can nearly smell them. Smiling, I let myself daydream about what we could have if only I can do this, but then the smile fades and other memories emerge from the depths. A twitch of his lips in a slight sneer when Tallulah took the stand. His hands around my throat, tightening. Could he be guilty? No, not my Russ. But could there be another way? Does it have to be *this*?

I take deep breath after breath, calming the flickering sparks of adrenaline chasing through my veins. It's funny. I can't remember what it was to live without him. Even these months when he's been physically away, he's still with me in a way. My hands wring together, making nervous circles, and then I grab my phone.

Seconds tick by as the harsh ringing cycles once, twice, three times before my mother picks up.

"Hello?" Her voice is textured, rough through the fragile connection. She waits only a moment before the rage builds behind the question. "Hello? Is there anyone there? Hello?"

Somehow, I can't bring myself to say a word. When I try, nothing but a squeak emerges.

"I can hear you breathing, you fucking pervert! Don't call here again."

A loud click followed by the drone of the dial tone. I sigh.

This number only rings twice before a voice, gentle and clear, answers.

"Hello?" Juliana's voice floats out, and before I realize what's happening, I've burst into tears. "Birdie? Is that you?"

I can't bring myself to answer her, ending the call in a panic. Falling face first into the pillow, the phone buzzes next to me. She only calls back once. She doesn't really care what I have to say, she just feels sorry for me. I wish I could call Russ, but he told me to wait until after it's done. Somehow that will seem less suspicious in his mind. Taking deep gulps of my own hot breath, I feel myself spinning into sleep. *Please, let me dream of Noah. I need him.*

The girl from earlier's face is the last thing I think of as darkness consumes me. I'll have to try again tomorrow, but not here. Someone might remember me here.

Birdie

My night was dreamless, and I wake with the throbbing band of the pain of a hangover. Chugging glass after glass of water from the probably filthy glass by the sink, I try to get back to normal as quickly as possible. The decrepit mattress sinks under my weight as I sit on the edge, head in my hands. Noah fills my thoughts, suffocating and sublime.

Please, I find myself praying directly to him, tell me I'm not a monster like the man who did all these things. Tell me I'm not the same. Salt fills my mouth and runs out of my nose. *Forgive me. Just tell me you forgive me.*

Sitting up straight, I pull myself together. Change clothes, reapply my makeup, try to look approachable. I ball my fist and strike it against my thigh again and again until it aches with the deep throb of a fresh bruise forming beneath the skin. Get it together, fucking idiot. There's no going back. I've gone this far; I need to trust

Russ. Time to burrow inwards, turn on the autopilot, and get this over with. It's the only way.

My mind wanders as I drive. It's like I'm a balloon pulled along by the car, tossing in the wind as I float, tenuously attached to the body inside and threatening to cut the string and disappear at any moment. I flit through memories and fantasies, compelling myself to stay positive as my hands guide the wheel and eyes scan the road, seeing yet not. Soon, I've made it to another satellite town, well within the hunting ranges of the depraved killer, but not a place I'll be recognized.

This motel is older and more rundown in some ways than the other, but at least it's cleaner. I toss my bag on the bed and force down the burger I picked up on the way. It settles my stomach a little and will be good for soaking up the drinks I'll inevitably be downing later. I kill the hours little by little, reading news articles and celebrity gossip on my phone, scrolling social media, staring at the ceiling and pretending this is all a terrible dream.

The bar I decide on is a little honky-tonk shithole. It's busy enough but not crowded. Men's eyes scan my body as soon as I enter, but I pay them no attention. I find my mark easy enough. There are only a few women there who are seemingly alone, and the one I zero in on immediately is a petite, slender young thing with a blonde ponytail that bounces with each thrown dart. I find myself more confident in this fake persona of "Lindy" and slide into her game and comfortable conversation effortlessly.

"Long day?" she asks, and I laugh, tossing my hair over my shoulder.

"Oh yeah, and you?"

Her face lights up as she meanders through the trials of her day job, the rude customers she dealt with, her dumbass boyfriend who she thinks is seeing somebody on the side. She needs someone to listen to her ramble on and on, even if they don't really care. I know that feeling well, and my heart swells for her, but I can't concentrate.

Instead, questions flutter and flit through me with the erratic flight of a thousand moths. Is this the right thing to do? Panic fills my mouth with a battery sour taste. Obviously, it isn't the "right" thing to do, but is it worth it? I'm already irredeemably terrible, aren't I? A mother who cared more about a fling than her own son. I've already lost my right to humanity.

And Russ? He might not be perfect, but he's innocent of these crimes. I'm sure of it. I promised I'd do anything for him. That I would never leave him. What else can I do? My soul seems a fair trade to free him, give him back the life the corrupt justice system has taken from him. But this girl is so young and naive, her whole life ahead of her. She shouldn't suffer for the burden I've taken on for him. I'm sure he's never done anything to deserve this.

I harden myself. The world is an evil place and sometimes sacrifices must be made. Russ loved me even when I was unlovable. He saved me from myself. I owe him everything I can give. There's still a chance we can have a life together. Some semblance of happiness. I feel this girl, so much like me just a few years before, falling under my spell, and I can't turn back. I swallow the shame and tears and fear and self-loathing. There's nothing to do but continue forward.

"I'm sorry. I'm just chatting away. Why don't you tell me something about yourself?"

"Oh, I don't mind, sweetheart. My life's not so interesting, so it's nice to hear all about yours." My lips barely obey when I command the muscles to pull upwards in a smile. "Go on. Tell me more. I'm all ears."

Birdie

It was too easy to get here. A few cheap, overly sweet cocktails and PBRs, and here I am, having a beer with Mandy at her grungy efficiency apartment. Women trust women too easily, I think as I watch her girl shuffle over to the fridge and grab another silver can, the foam bubbling over her hands as she cracks it open. We're wary of men, but women can be just as sinister.

Mandy is the perfect victim. Fits the killer's type exactly. She's conventionally attractive, with beachy waved hair like out of a shampoo commercial tumbling over her deeply tanned shoulders. When she smiles, her eyes curve up into cute little half-moons, and I hate how hard she's making this for me already. As Mandy bounces back over, eyes hazy from the alcohol, I focus on burrowing my feelings away, becoming as detached as possible so I can build the courage to do what I came here for.

"It's so incredibly nice to finally have someone to connect with, you know? Most other girls," she gestures broadly and clicks her tongue, "they don't get it. They think they do, but they don't really get it. You know?"

I raise my eyebrows and nod before taking another sip from my beer.

"Yeah, I know you get it. I've always been told I am an old soul. Do you think that? That's why I always fit in better with older kids and grownups when I was little. I knew what was up; how all this," she gestures a circle, spilling some of her drink on the discolored linoleum floor, "was going to work and I wasn't going to act like some dumb little kid about it. No, I was on my way, and look at me now!" She gestures again, more of the beer splashing out of the can and down her wrist and forearm. "Dammit. Ugh, fuck! I'll get a paper towel."

Despite her perfect hair and wasp waist, there's something depressing about the whole situation that makes me sigh and long to get up to leave. I remember being just like her. It feels like a lifetime since I was young and happy. Was it so long ago? While she mops at the mess with a fistful of paper towels, swaying as if she might collapse headfirst at any moment, I get up and try to make my way out, quietly pushing in the folding chair at the cheap kitchen card table and toward the door.

"No! Lindy, don't go! I'm cleaning it up, don't worry."

Hearing the fake name stops me in my tracks. Russ's smile flashes in my mind, and I cringe. I turn back to see the girl smiling but tears are streaming down her cheeks. I know she's probably only crying because she's trashed, yet something delicate shatters inside me when I look into her face. My mind reels, asking over and over, "How can you even think about doing this?" yet still my purse hangs heavy at my left side, open and waiting for my dominant hand to pull out what waits patiently coiled at the bottom.

Pursing my lips, I look at the woman, really more of an overgrown child, and feel the weight at my side. I don't want to do this. Mandy is someone's daughter. Even without knowing her, I'm sure her life has meaning and someone loves her. That's more than can be said about me. Shivers travel down my limbs like fluttering rows of insect legs.

I think of Russ, all the letters, all the years, how everything in my whole life was wrapped up, tangled around this man. How I wish I could be the martyr for him, but there's no way I could make it convincing enough. I walk back to the table and sit down, picking up the beer can and drinking the last few drops. With each breath, I force myself into a hidden corner of my mind, a place I can stay safe and separated from the act. I have to do this. He's all I have left in the world. There's no real choice.

Mandy turns back to her role as the bubbling drunkard, still wiping at the spill, spreading the sticky liquid around rather than actually cleaning anything. There are names and places and brands all dropped into ceaseless winding narratives, but they're just words that float in and out of my consciousness. All I can think about are the next few steps, visualizing them over and over until I feel the rehearsal so complete, so rote, there's no room for error. That's when I simultaneously stand up and grab the taser from my purse, sending the electric probes shooting across the distance between us, to attach to the girl.

She screams, the sound so startling and loud, I almost flee. No, I can't do that to Russ. Not now. Not after coming this far. Working fast, I kneel on the incapacitated girl, stretching the duct tape across her mouth to silence the shriek. Mandy's eyes widen and she shakes with fear, the acrid smell of urine permeating the air. She begins to fling her head back and forth, clearly saying a muffled "no" through the tape.

Riding the adrenaline high and trying not to think about the reality of my actions, I reach again into my purse and produce the rope. Bringing it over the woman's head, I wrap it around her neck and pull it taut. The life fades from her eyes so much quicker than I'd expected. I hate myself for how easy it is, and yet I'm relieved. I don't think to check her pulse, instead retrieving the condom and carefully untying it, dribbling the cold semen over the girl's body, but just as I finish, a loud sputter startles me. I fall backward, shaking with fear. Mandy wheezes against the tape, breathing through her nose as she struggles to stay awake. I stagger backwards, bile rising into my mouth. The blood drains from my face as my whole body breaks into a cold sweat.

"No. No. No. No. No." I can hear myself say it, but it doesn't feel like I'm the one speaking. It must be someone else doing this terrible thing. Not me. *Not me!*

Mandy's cries begin to intensify, and I have to slap my hands over my mouth as a wail threatens to break free. As I scuttle backward in blind panic, my spine hits the wall and I bleat before sinking to the floor, my hair and then hands covering my face.

A thousand thoughts flit around my mind, each like a dust mote, visible and real and yet, when I reach for them, intangible. I know I must decide, and quickly, but I've lost so much of myself, I'm not sure I can come back. I'm so confused. Nothing in this goddamn world makes any sense anymore. My hand reaches back into my purse, fingers curling around the cold metal of the gun. Do I end it now? I imagine my skull exploding and then the sweet nothingness that follows. A moment of pain and it's over. No more guilt. No more confusion. No more anything. Then my eyes focus on something across the room, taking my breath away as my fingers drop the gun back into the depths of my purse.

I can't believe what I'm seeing.

Above Mandy's bed, on a small shelf secured to the wall, something peeks out from behind a picture frame. A blue toy dog, well-worn with scratched black bead eyes, is looking at me. It is exactly like the one Noah loved so much.

I swear I feel Noah's sweet baby breath against my skin, through my clothing, blanketing me with his presence. First I gag, then retch, and finally wails pour out in a steady stream from my throat. My fingers claw at my mouth, but there's no stopping this release.

"Help!" Mandy is yelling, having ripped the tape from her mouth, her voice far away. "Somebody help me!"

The deluge of emotion rushes forth. This has to be the sign I've been waiting for. He's finally come to me. He stopped me before I ruined another life. He still loves me. Forgives me.

My Noah forgives me. I can feel the relief tingle in every bone, sparkling and bright.

I can let go of Russ, let go of my guilt, move on. Be myself again.

It doesn't matter what happens next. It will be okay.

I am forgiven.

AN EMPTY CLEARING

The last remains of tattered leaves scatter across the small clearing between trees, not far from the hiking path. Sunlight filters through branches tipped with the green buds of leaves starting to develop. It is a quiet place now. If one listens closely, there's a scratching of a beetle foraging under the thawed rot from winter, the tapping of water droplets collecting in some unseen puddle as the morning frost melts away, and a faraway songbird announcing the gradual return of the migrating flocks. Mostly, it is quiet.

The dark patch near an edge where the foliage grows thicker, a bush growing outwards and partially obscuring the humanoid shape, was where a person became a body, and a body became earth again. She was taken by the sterile men with gloved hands, photographed extensively before being laid in careful, somber decorum in a body bag. Her family grieved, buried them in some pristine plot with a headstone and a vase to put fresh flowers every week, then every month, then to match each season, until those who knew and remembered her join her in death.

But even though her bones are buried there, her body returned to the earth in this clearing, with these families of insects and passing carrion hunters. Her flesh was scraped, torn, dissolved, and eaten by the nature that resides here. Her organs festered, burst, ripened, and shriveled in this patch of earth stained with her existence. She is in the soil, grass, tree roots, and stomachs of the forest, and though that is a terrifying thought at first, it shouldn't be. She was found. She was avenged. And she is at peace, part of the world that birthed her and welcomed her back into its warm, eternal embrace.

Acknowledgments

So many people helped this novel blossom into what you hold in your hands, and I am so grateful for all their help. First, my husband Martin, who has supported me in every way as I worked to make my dreams of being an author come true. He has shown me what real love is and is always there for me. My love for him, Mason, Dylan, and Vera is never ending.

My incredible agent, Clara Chuiton, not only helped me find a home for this novel, but also worked tirelessly with me to polish it so it could shine as brightly as possible. Thank you, Clara, for always being there for me and sticking with me. May our careers continue to flourish together.

And of course, a huge thank you to my fabulous critique partners including Evelyn Freeling, Steve Neal, Brett Mitchell Kent, Chelsea Pumpkins, and my ever-supportive sister Hannah Murray-Carmack. All of you have been there for me through the eureka moments as well as the depths of writer's block. I am so thankful for all the advice, support, and critiques you gave to help make this book what it is today.

Next, I need to thank Ben DeVos and Apocalypse Party from the bottom of my heart for giving both this novel and *Crushing Snails* the perfect publisher as well as making sure it was skillfully edited and ready for readers. Also, thank you to Matthew Revert for the beautiful cover art for this novel, and Mike Corrao for formatting it.

Last, I want to reach out to every person struggling with an abusive partner. You do not have to live like this. You deserve a better life. I know it's hard, but I believe in you. I will be donating a portion of proceeds from the sale of this book to charities that help victims of domestic violence for as long as it is in print.

www.ingramcontent.com/pod-product-compliance
Lightning Source LLC
Chambersburg PA
CBHW061630190726
48289CB00006B/1550